50 DRAGONS

ROD MARSDEN

Night to Dawn Magazine & Books LLC
P. O. Box 643
Abington, PA 19001

www.bloodredshadow.com

Copyright © 2020 by Rod Marsden
Paperback ISBN: 978-1-937769-62-8
Ebook ISBN: 978-1-937769-63-5

Cover Artist: Sandy DeLuca
Editor: Barbara Custer
Published in the United States of America

To the Marsden mob who may see this writer claim a better future. I must have more faith in you and leave the past behind.

Also, to Lyn McConchie my New Zealander friend who is one hell of a novelist.

****

Fifty Dragons was inspired by Steve Carter and Antoinette Ryder who are the best Australian artists of their generation.

Fifty Dragons was also inspired by Stan Lee, Jack Kirby, Bill Everett, Gene Colan, Steve Ditko, Marie Severin and the rest of the Marvel Bullpen of the 1960s and 1970s that have always been there for me.

CHAPTER ONE

It was a hot, sunny day in early May, mid-23rd century, when a life capsule belonging to the late 21st century was discovered in the outskirts of the ruined city. Radiation levels had dropped enough for archaeologists to dig among the piles of loose bricks. No one had much hope for the person found inside the capsule.

"His clothing and whatever else he has on him will tell us something about his time," said Jens, the lead archaeologist, sweat trickling down the front of her dust jacket. She was a small, wiry woman with her blonde hair always in a bun. Those around her noted that her drive more than made up for her lack of height. Some called her the rock spider because of the way she could crawl in and out of tight spots.

"Are you thinking mid-21st century or late 21st century?" Megan asked through her specs. She was second in charge. She wore glasses because her eyes were allergic to contact lenses. This made her unique because very few people wore them for eye correction. People suggested she get robot eye replacements. They didn't have to be red like the ones the robots had but of a more human colouring. Even so, faulty though they were, she preferred to keep her own eyes.

"Possibly late 21st century," said Jens noncommittally. "Look! It is early days. We need to get a floater in place to lift him onto our flyer."

"Why not just open the capsule here and now?" asked a young man of the maverick class.

"And risk destroying evidence, historical data?" cautioned Jens. "No. We will open the capsule in a more sterile environment back at my lab. In the meantime, Frank, get the floater. The rest of you look around, shift more bricks but be gentle when you do. There may be something here, among the debris that will tell us more about him than what he is wearing."

Jens helped her students dig for more clues. They found an old computer so battered it was useless. Whatever information it might have contained was gone for good. Even so, she had her people load it onto the flyer. There were cups and plates, most of them broken, which were also to be taken away. The university paying for this excursion wanted exhibits they could show off.

As the sun began to set, they put what minor treasures they had found into boxes and laid them beside the capsule aboard the flyer. Then they piled in for their return journey.

The flyer was white, mostly circular, with swept-back wings and a jet engine on either side of its body. It gleamed as if new, even in the twilight. There was a large windscreen to see out of, seating for six plus storage space.

"Do you think he was a maverick?" asked one of Jens' students.

"Hard to say," said Jens. "'Maverick' had a different meaning back then. I don't know if we would consider him a maverick or even a knight if he were alive today."

"Well, he isn't a dragon." Megan fiddled with her glasses. "He doesn't have any scales, and I don't believe he has a tail. Besides, dragons, as we know them, didn't exist back then. He would have called one a mutant if he ever came across such a creature. It was the bad times that came after the 21st century that made our dragons."

"And it was the dragons that gave us use for our knights," said one of Jens' students. "One slays the other, and all is right with the world."

"Yes," agreed Megan. "Nowadays, only those who need to die are killed. Sometimes, I feel sorry for both the knights and the dragons."

"You're too soft-hearted," said Jens.

Megan rubbed the hardened glass portion of the capsule with a rag made damp with some of the contents of her water bottle to clear away the dirt to get a better look at the contents. She noted the occupant was wearing some military uniform.

"You are probably right," agreed Megan. "I can't see the face clearly, but I gather from the clothes we are dealing with a male officer of some sort. For all we know, this was someone who sent thousands of helpless people to their deaths."

At Jens' lab, the capsule was opened, and a burst of frigid air issued forth. It was a good sign that not much decay had taken over the body within.

Jens was surprised to discover the eyes of the subject she was examining reacted to her use of a flashlight. They were still closed, but there was movement as if there was REM sleep happening. She choked back a startled breath to learn, despite the short-cropped hair and military attire, that the occupant was female rather than male. A scan revealed removable brain cancer.

"Two hundred years ago, this would have been a death sentence." Jens held up the cancerous tumour with tweezers, which lay in a silver dish. It was a grey, ugly mass no bigger than a marble.

"No doubt freezing her this way was an attempt to preserve her life for a time when science could deal more effectively with her illness," ventured Megan, adjusting her glasses.

"Our subject's eyelids are beginning to flutter," said Jens. "Quick! Fill a plunger with adrenalin and hand it to me!"

Megan obeyed, and Jens injected adrenalin into what moments before was thought of as a corpse.

The female gasped, and her eyelids fluttered more. Lungs that hadn't operated for a very long time went into service. A heart that hadn't beat for a great many years was once more beating.

"This is a miracle!" cried Megan.

"Someone back then had managed to solve the ice barrier problem."

"The ice barrier?"

"Once ice forms in the freezing or recovery, so much damage is done to nerves and synapses that life cannot return. Time and time again, we have tried to revive people from this state without success. I don't know what was done to this woman so long ago to avoid the disruptive formation of ice, but it worked."

A mouth moved, and archaic English came out. Then eyes snapped open, and more archaic English followed.

"Easy now," said Megan, but her words only confused the newly awakened woman. She screamed and tried to get up.

"Sedate her!" cried Jens. "If she struggles, she might do herself harm. We'll fit her with a language module, so when she next awakes, she will understand what we say to her."

The module was placed on the newly discovered woman's forehead and hummed its message as she resumed her slumber.

The following morning, the eyes that had been closed for so long opened once more. Jens and Megan had returned to her just in time to see this happen. Megan decided to initiate a voice recording with the little black box she carried with her in her pocket.

"How are you feeling?" asked Jens.

"Strange. And what's this thing on my head?"

"You can take that off now. It's just a communication device, but it has already done its job."

"Where am I?"

"Wollongong. Can you tell me who you are?" asked Jens.

"I'm Lieutenant Amelia Warren RAAF. I was in Sydney."

"Yes. That's where we found you."

"I thought the facilities in Sydney would have been more advanced for my reawakening."

"Not anymore. We made you well again."

"That was possible?"

"Yes. There have been a few advances in medicine."

"How long was I gone?"

"What was the year you went under?"

"Twenty forty."

"There were religious wars in France and Germany in twenty thirty-five," put in Megan. "The United Nations was disbanded long before that, and so was the European Union. What we know about what was happening in Australia in the twenty-thirties and twenty forties is still hazy."

"Those days must have been horrific, but what followed was worse," Jens said.

"What did follow?" asked Amelia.

"They were dark days for the world, but all better now," Megan told her.

"All better?" wondered Amelia.

"Yes. Thank the Goddess, we don't go to war at all anymore," said Megan.

"Really?" Amelia was still emotionally numb from being in what Jens told her was her world's distant future. *Is this real?* She wondered, but the bed felt solid enough. Military training dictated that she stay calm and assess her current situation while drawing in more information.

"War is now a distant memory," said Megan.

"Have people changed that much?" Amelia couldn't imagine that being the case.

"In some ways, yes, they have. Can you tell me your name again?" asked Jens.

"Amelia Warren. I was born in Sydney on the 20th of January, 2021. I am a flight lieutenant in the Royal Australian

Air Force. It was because of cancer I was relegated to desk duty before I was selected for the preservation process. I don't have any military secrets worth knowing even though I did sign the Official Secrets Act."

"The questions we are likely to have are cultural rather than military," said Megan, removing her glasses and then putting them back on again.

"Can you get off the bed?" asked Jens.

Amelia tried. Her hand had functioned well enough to pull the linguistic gadget from her head and give it to Jens. Otherwise, her arms and legs refused to work though she sensed they would eventually do so. They reminded her of strands of cooked spaghetti that had plenty of give but as yet no take. She strained to get up a few times, but it was no good. It even hurt to try. She felt trapped and frightened but quickly dismissed those emotions as unproductive.

"Steady now," advised Jens. "Your legs are bound to be wobbly after not being used for such an extended period."

"They're all pins and needles."

"Rub them to get the circulation back then try again."

The next day, Megan flew out with a pilot to the site where Amelia was found. She was hoping to find out more about the woman now in her and Jens' care by sifting through the remaining rubble. On this occasion, her search was unsuccessful.

CHAPTER TWO

On the fourth day of Amelia's awakening, she was moved, in the middle of the night, out of the hospital via what one of the medical staff told her was a low gravity chair. The doctor showed her a switch on the chair that made it lighter than it otherwise would be, defying normal gravity. It was, in fact, a comfortable, almost floating-on-air wheelchair without the need for wheels. Then came a ride in an ambulance and from there back to the low gravity chair and into a student cottage adjoining what the driver told her was Wollongong University.

Everything she had seen so far, except for the occasional male in orange, was of a subdued hue. The walls and beds were white, and the women she talked to wore off-white. All this was meant, no doubt, to keep her calm. Having been in the military, she knew something about colour coordination and how it was supposed to work. Uniforms were based on standing out and clothes in the field of battle, the absolute opposite. Jet fighters were better off if they were harder to locate in enemy skies. Outside, she caught a glimpse of green shrubbery and almost laughed with joy that that particular colour still existed.

As the medical staff moved her out, she passed by a ward marked "For Knights Only," which from the smell emanating, Amelia took to be a burn unit. There was the odour of recently burnt flesh plus camphor and other ointments she associated with the healing process. She had known of air force pilots who had returned to base badly scorched and had spent time in such wards. But why was it marked "For Knights Only?"

Amelia also passed a ward exclusively for dragons, but all she could smell coming out of it was the usual industrial-strength antiseptic used to clean floors and walls. She asked to look into the ward to see what the dragons looked like, but the medical staff wouldn't allow it. They said she'd get to meet dragons soon enough but not to rush things. She had a lot to discover, and she should take it slow or be overwhelmed. She felt cheated but let it go for now. Since she wasn't in control of her low gravity chair, she would have to wait to view dragons.

Amelia didn't see much on her short ambulance journey. A glimpse of a house here or what appeared to be an office building there. She expected to see fewer trees. The future, then, was not a nightmare of immense structures blocking out the sky and overflowing with people killing and then stomping on one another for space. It didn't have pollution of every type imaginable, overwhelming the senses and land so overworked it could no longer support life, and so corpse-eating had come back into fashion. Then again, she told herself, she was only getting glimpses, and the area she might be in could well be the garden spot of the entire country, if not the world. For all she knew, people might travel days to visit for a few minutes and imagine how wonderful life would be if the whole planet were as beautiful.

As they settled Amelia in the cottage, she marvelled at how much wood the builder had used on the dwelling. Wood was everywhere, from the creaking floorboards to the walls and ceilings. None of it smelled artificial. It was going to be like living in the centre of a small forest. What's more, there were books and magazines on a coffee table that were made out of paper. The need to conserve resources had been stamped on her conscience from her first days in primary. Waste was a terrible sin. So much wood and paper in one dwelling were at first shocking. The medical staff, when settling her in, told her it was a typical home for students or university professors. She wondered why conservation wasn't still on everyone's mind and in everyone's heart.

"They haven't provided me with a computer," Amelia told a male orderly who was tucking her in bed. He wore orange like the other males she had so far encountered.

"That's right, miss," replied the orderly. "Anything you want to know, ask Jens or her assistant Megan."

"I will." Moments later, Amelia drifted off to sleep.

The next morning, Amelia managed to move, via low gravity chair, from her bed to her bedroom window a hundred feet away. She smiled as she watched a little girl in pigtails, in the park outside her cottage, run, leap, and fly to her mother via the use of a low gravity harness. It was apparent to her that the harness the child was wearing had a similar function to her low gravity seat. The controls on it looked to be the same, only smaller, and it allowed the child to play in ways that were unique to having less gravity. Amelia would have loved to have such a harness at that age. She could have pretended to be a bird. The mother then turned off the low gravity harness; she gave the child a big red ball so that she could play. It was a plastic ball. Then it came to Amelia that both mother and child wore light, multicoloured clothes. *There's nothing dull about what they are wearing,* thought Amelia, who smiled at that revelation.

Moments later, a creature with black, shiny scales and a spiked tail walked by the park not far from the mother and child. It had on a white, short-sleeved shirt and short white pants that made allowances for its tail. Its arm was bandaged; Amelia thought there might be a few scales missing on its neck. It had sandals on its feet and a white, metal collar around its neck. When it came within a few feet of the mother and child, the collar glowed, and the creature winced. In response, it put more distance between itself and the mother and child. The glow stopped, but the hurt in its eyes from the shock continued until it was out of sight. *Could this be a dragon?* Amelia wondered. *It was strange that neither mother nor child paid any attention to it. Are dragons that common?*

The male orderly who came to serve Amelia breakfast was surprised to find her out of bed. He told her so, got her back to bed, and then reported the matter to Jens. It was with delight Jens discovered what the orderly had told her was true. She took Amelia's pulse and looked into her eyes. The pulse was steady, and the eyes clear. After having a doctor further examine Amelia, testing her ability to swallow solid food, she changed the breakfast from all liquid to bacon and eggs with orange juice. Amelia was recovering faster than expected.

"I'll get the orderly to massage your legs," Jens told Amelia, "so you'll get the feeling back into them sooner and will be able to walk."

"Can I ask you some questions?" Amelia moved toward Jens on her chair.

"What's on your mind?" asked Jens.

"Pollution seems to be a thing of the past," Amelia said. "The same can be said for conservation. What happened?"

"Conservation?"

"Yes. What happened to the need to conserve wood and paper?"

Jens took Amelia's temperature and smiled when she saw the results.

"We'll talk about this later. I've got to go," Jens told her. "Megan should be along soon to keep you company."

"Can I have a computer?"

"We'll see."

Megan had no idea how to put Amelia's mind at ease. Eventually, they got around to discussing the world population. For this, Megan started the little black box she was carrying.

When it came out that, due to the plagues which had struck humanity repeatedly since Amelia's time, the human population throughout had been reduced to less than a third and had retained this reduction level for a very long time, something clicked in the woman from the past's mind which made sense in her present. Conservation was still being enacted, but now it had more to do with keeping numbers of human offspring down rather than husbanding natural resources and avoiding waste. For instance, because there were fewer people than in her time, those who wanted to enjoy newspapers, magazines, and novels made out of paper products could do so. She was yet to learn, however, how this reduced level was maintained.

Upon leaving Amelia, Megan went to her study in an adjacent cottage, where she laid her black box recording device amidst the piles of stuff already on her desk and went to lunch. While she was gone, a janitor entered her study, took the recording within Megan's black device, and made a copy onto his device, then left.

This janitor, who was a knight, occasionally got paid by the media for sensational stories. He was told by one of Jens' team that something unusual was happening and that he might get the details off of Megan. He knew, however, that Megan wouldn't divulge anything worth knowing to someone in his lowly position, but he suspected her study would reveal something. He was right. He was also dismissed from his post when it became apparent who was responsible for the resultant trickle of what management deemed sensitive information.

CHAPTER THREE

Dean Judy Renate burst into Jens's office without any fanfare, her strawberry-blonde hair all over her face, and cried, "We've got a leak!"

Jens looked up at the dean, who was out of breath from running. Before the interruption, she had been studying an ancient text on bioengineering found in the same area of Sydney Amelia was located. She thought the 20th century had strange notions on the subject. No doubt, the 21st century saw improved knowledge in that field.

"What do you mean?" Jens put the book down and turned toward her distraught boss. Dean Renate, always in a smart, chequered suit and tie with her hair tied back by a plain black ribbon, was usually the epitome of dignity. Seeing her flushed with her hair so untidy made Jens not only feel concern for the woman but also for the great institution in her charge.

The dean sat down on one of Jens's rickety, old stools and pulled a paper clipping from her top right coat pocket. The headline read: "A Living Treasure from the Past?" She passed it to Jens.

"Does it give much detail?" asked Jens.

"Not much," confessed Dean Renate, "but it is still worrying. We wanted to keep a tight lid on your discovery until we understood more about how others will react. We could pretend it is a hoax, but that would mean it would be difficult, if not impossible, to reveal the truth later on, if that is what we should do."

"How did this happen?" asked Jens soberly.

"It doesn't matter. The person responsible won't do it again, but the damage has been done. That's what counts. What do we do now? The media are after an official statement. They want to know if it's true. They want to speak to her, and I don't know if that is a good idea or not."

"We were going to present her to the public sooner or later." Jens shrugged.

Dean Renate grimaced. "You don't understand what the ramifications might be."

"Unfortunately, we can only go forward on this," Jens told her. "You may be panicking over nothing. All indications are Amelia likes the present. She thinks that where she is couldn't be better."

"I don't know." The dean shook her head. "She might change her mind. I have board members, financiers, and lecturers to consider as well as researchers, technicians, students, and parents. The board doesn't like things thrust up in front of them like this. They thrive on order. There are a lot of mavericks on the board as well as priestesses."

Wollongong's High Priestess had already been notified of Amelia's existence but had been assured by Dean Renate that it would remain hush-hush for the foreseeable future. Researching the past, via someone who had been there, was permitted; but any information gotten was not to leave campus. Amelia Warren and her ideas, whatever they might be, were to remain safe from the general public. Not until they were thoroughly examined were they to go to general consumption. Now Dean Renate was afraid the High Priestess would question her competency to run a learning facility and so arrange for her dismissal from a post she'd worked all her life to obtain.

"How long before we need to introduce her to the public?" Jens grabbed a pen from her pen holder and began playing with it.

"I don't know." Dean Renate shrugged. "I've never been

in this position before."

"Give me two weeks." Jens clicked her pen off and on. "We'll have her ready."

"How?"

"Megan knows the 20th and 21st centuries better than anyone else I know. If anyone can bring Amelia up to speed on present-day matters, so she doesn't embarrass herself or anyone else, it'll be Megan. Besides, there's a lot we still don't know about the 21st century and what happened to her civilization. She'll be able to fill in some of the gaps."

"Two weeks then." Dean Renate stood up and straightened her clothes and hair. "Please don't let our university and me down."

As Dean Renate left, Jens punched the intercom and called Megan to her office.

CHAPTER FOUR

On the fifth day of Amelia's awakening, she hobbled to the window and looked outside. A bright, blue Volkswagen Beetle with a sticker on its bumper bar flew past. The sticker read "Volkswagens for Reliability." The lettering was in bold red on a sharp white background. She wasn't surprised that, by now, Beetles could fly. No one in her squadron would have been astounded she was able to read that sticker though she suspected the locals here and now might have been. It was a large bumper bar, more prominent than what you would have found on a 21st century Beetle and her eyesight was still that of a military pilot. She let the words flash into her mind first and then collected them so they'd make sense to her. It was a technique she had mastered and could now do on a semi-conscious level. In the last article she read before she went into hibernation, the writer hinted that flight would eventually occur when it came to certain automobiles. *Are Beetles still made in Germany?* She wondered. *Is there still a Germany?*

The rays of the mid-afternoon sun warmed her skin and made her feel sleepy in a gentle sort of way. The window was open to let in fresh air. The smell of newly cut grass rose from the cottage's front lawn. A Willie Wagtail was dancing near a bed of chrysanthemums, and a student nurse in a white starched uniform had stopped for a moment to watch the little black and white bird hop around. When she noticed Amelia observing her, she went about her business, once more caught up in her duties of delivering herself to a distant lecture hall.

15

A knock at the door took Amelia's gaze away from the outside world. The door opened, and in walked Jens and Megan. Jens looked flustered. Her cheeks reddened as if she had been running.

"You're on your feet," said Jens. "Good!"

"Care for a stroll around the grounds?" offered Megan.

"My legs are still sore," confessed Amelia, rubbing her left thigh, "but I could manage that, and it would be nice to have a proper look around."

They walked for a while. There was a light breeze. With every step, little by little, the pain left Amelia's joints, and she felt her legs gain strength. Before she knew it, she stopped hobbling and was keeping pace with her companions. They walked past a rose garden to a bench where she had observed, from her cottage kitchen window, students sitting to read and talk about what they were studying. The students were no longer there, and she suspected it was because of her presence. They had no doubt been moved, Amelia reasoned, to prevent them from communicating with her. As if to confirm her suspicions about being kept from the general public, she caught sight of two men in shining armour carrying swords. Later on, she was to learn they were not guarding or spying upon her. They had simply been there. *Just when will I be allowed to socialise properly?* She wondered.

They sat, and Megan brought out her little black box from under the folds of her lab coat.

"More questions?" Amelia sighed. Her eyes narrowed, and then, for a moment, she shifted her gaze from Jens to a nearby flower bed before coming back to her.

"Only if you want to answer them," said Jens, realising Amelia was getting a bit miffed with all the questioning she had already had.

"I have more questions of my own," Amelia put forward. "And I want detailed answers."

"We'll do our best," replied Megan, tweaking her glasses.

"First up, are you both maidens?" asked Amelia. "I have heard the term a few times since I have been here. Not sure it means the same in my time as in the now."

"If you're asking if we are no longer children, then the answer's yes," fielded Megan.

"Then, I'm a maiden," said Amelia.

"Fundamentally, yes, you are correct," said Megan, "though you haven't had the training."

"Do you each have a knight of your own?" asked Amelia. "From what I have overheard, maidens are supposed to have knights. For what purpose, I can't, as yet, fathom."

"No," said Megan shyly. "I suppose I should have a knight as a companion, but I've been rather busy for that sort of thing. Jens used to have one, but he died, and she has been too preoccupied of late to put in for another one."

"Should I have one?" Amelia shrugged her shoulders and smiled. She was still vague on what a present-day knight did and why a maiden would accompany one.

"When you are ready." Megan smiled.

"I'll give you a book on the subject," said Jens.

"Tell me more about mavericks," Amelia went on. "Are they like knights?"

"Heavens, no!" Megan blushed. "We'll talk about them later."

This made Amelia think about the concept of the good afterlife. Apparently, there were still people who believed in Heaven. How close their Heaven came to the one she was introduced to in Sunday school when she was a kid, however, she couldn't know until she learned more about this society. She knew from doctors and interns that, instead of an almighty God, there was an almighty Goddess. She wondered how that would alter things, not only in the afterlife but in the present as well.

"Knights and mavericks will be in the book I give you," said Jens.

A bee buzzed past Amelia, heading for the roses.

"Now about a computer," began Amelia.

"I'll have to get permission to have one installed in your room," said Jens.

This is not the age of mobiles then, thought Amelia.

"You'll need to be taught how to use it," said Megan.

"I'm sure I can learn," Amelia told them.

"We'll see." Jens sighed; her concern for Amelia was thus apparent to Megan if not to Amelia. Both were aware that if Amelia learned too much too soon, it might be detrimental to her mental health.

That night Amelia, via a popular book for girls given to her by Jens, began to unravel the mysteries of her new home. According to the book, knights killed dragons to please their maidens, and a maiden should morally support her knight in such endeavours. That is, moral support only. A maiden must never interfere in any way in the slaying process.

The book went on to say that a maiden should be displeased with her knight if he attacks a dragon with a gun or a rifle of any kind. What's more, it was unlawful for him to do so and carried a death sentence for the knight. Any maiden who thought her knight had done wrong was obliged to report him to the nearest authorities. Likewise, dragons were forbidden from using firearms of any sort.

She turned to mavericks. Apparently, maidens dated mavericks and married them. Presumably, they could have sex with mavericks but not with either the knights or the dragons. Unlike knights and dragons, a maverick was made perfect. A lot of medical and psychological research had gone into making them so, and scientists were always on the lookout for ways to improve them. The mavericks shown to Amelia in the book she thought were handsome enough but also rather wooden.

There was a chapter on priestesses who were also called Marthas after Mother Mary. This Goddess-worshiping religion they belonged to was worldwide and had replaced every other religion. When the public was permitted to see her, Amelia figured she would be asked to attend temple prayers. Temple services occurred every Sunday and had little if anything to do with Christianity or any other of the mainstream religions that existed before she went into the deep freeze. Amelia wondered what the temple was going to be like. There was no mention at all of male priests or monks. *Maybe they're not required in a Goddess-based religion.*

It took Amelia half an hour to get to the last page. She found that the book created as many questions as it gave answers. Some illustrations didn't make sense. There was one of a black dragon bowing before the shinning image of the Great Goddess with tears running down its scaly face. The caption read: "I was born. I have thus sinned greatly. Please forgive me." *What was there to forgive? Was being born a crime?*

There was also one of a knight slaying a dragon with a sword. Here the caption read: "One down and forty-nine to go." *What could that possibly mean?* Someone else might have thrown the book across the room in disgust, but that was not her style. Her military training came to the fore. If she could fly a jet fighter, she had a brain that could figure out the information here without resorting to anger-fuelled frustration. She took out a pen and some paper she'd been given and wrote down what she didn't understand so that either Jens or Megan could explain it to her later.

****

The following morning, Jens and Megan offered to take Amelia to a bout between a young dragon and an equally young knight. Even with all the talk in the book and elsewhere of killing, she thought it would have something to do with harmless boxing or jousting. After all, she was told that this civilization had managed to eliminate war. Why then the need for full-on bloodshed?

CHAPTER FIVE

Jens and Megan took Amelia to what appeared on the outside to be a nearby theatre. There were old movie posters at the entrance, some featuring films going back to when she was a kid. Overhead was a sign in red on a white background that blazoned: *Knights and Dragons Today.* She was thus expecting a movie or a live-action play. When she went inside, she was open-mouthed, shocked by what she saw. A hundred people were seated overlooking a small stage where sawdust covered the floor, and a steel cage encapsulated much of the space. There was only one entrance into and out of this cage. If animal cruelty of any sort was involved, Amelia didn't want to stick around.

"I know there was nothing like this in your day," said Megan as she took a seat a few rows up from the stage. She sat down, and Jens and Amelia joined her. The seats were comfortable. They had the cushioning effect Amelia liked, but not so plush she sank into one and had to be rescued. What's more, there was a man Amelia thought might be a knight because he was shabbily dressed, selling popcorn and soft drinks. His clothes were clean but threadbare, and he had patches on the knees of his pants. Jens threw some coins his way and got a bucket of popcorn to share plus three bottles of soft drink.

"There was nothing like this at all," agreed Amelia, wondering if her worst fears would be confirmed. The sawdust worried her. *You don't need sawdust for a pretend fight.* That's what she was thinking. Sawdust was sometimes used to soak up blood.

"Shhh!" Jens made the quiet sign with her finger. "It's about to begin."

The overhead lights dimmed as two figures stepped into the cage. One was a knight dressed in plate armour, and the other was a dragon clothed in leather, his black scales shining in the dim light. Then the lights came back to full strength. An announcer on the speaker system assured the audience that, though the knight and dragon were young, both had been properly trained and were eager for action. The audience responded by clapping and cheering.

The announcer waited for quiet, and then he said, "In this corner, we have an axe-wielding knight, and over there to the left, a sword-carrying dragon. Their twin destinies will be settled here and now, on this field of battle. They await the sound of the bell to begin."

"This is exciting." Megan quickly polished her glasses with a tissue, so she didn't miss anything. "The season has just begun. This is the weeding out of both knight and dragon. Is your seat okay, Amelia?"

"Yes, I'm just not used to this. Are they really going to...?"

"Just watch and you'll find out," Jens told her.

Megan put her glasses back on and leaning forward, looked expectantly at the combatants.

The bell rang, and they squared off; the dragon moved his sword about in his hands, getting the feel of it. Amelia thought such a weapon belonged to the Middle Ages, as did the knight's axe. The sword blade was flat, heavy, and not very sharp looking. The knight likewise tested his weapon. It would stick to an enemy's ribs but, since he had only one opponent this day, that didn't matter. He could take his time retrieving it after the kill if he was successful in that endeavour. Amelia felt sick, her mouth dry and stomach queasy. She could still convince herself this was an advanced pretend, and no one was going to get hurt.

A second bell sounded, and the overhead cameras on both knight and dragon came on. Amelia understood from the book she had read that the fight would be recorded so there would be no doubt as to the legitimacy of the victor's victory. The book, however, didn't state the seriousness of these battles. She was still clinging to the notion that it was a contest but that no harm would come to anyone, not even the dragon.

"If the knight wins," said Megan, "he will have forty-nine kills left before he can move up in class and, of course, in society." Amelia then remembered the illustration in the book she'd read. One down and forty-nine to go now made sense.

"Has that ever been done?" asked Amelia. "I mean fifty kills?" The very idea of kills brought home to her just how this event was going to go.

"Not in my lifetime," said Megan, "but the World Council agreed on fifty, so it is fifty."

"And what does the dragon get out of this?" asked Amelia. There was nothing in the book about any reward.

"The notoriety of beating a knight plus his life," said Megan.

"That doesn't seem much," murmured Amelia.

"It is more than enough for a dragon." Jens shrugged.

Amelia noted that neither Megan nor Jens had much compassion for either knight or dragon. The upcoming fight was merely entertainment for them. They were happy to eat popcorn, drink soft drinks, and watch.

"I gave the knight my handkerchief for good luck," said Megan. "If he survives, I may take him on as the one I look after between battles. He should be good for at least a year."

"What then?" Amelia asked.

"My dear maiden, knights and dragons are not meant to last," said Jens. "If he remains in good shape for the next five years, he will be doing well."

"So every year, he will be risking his life?" Amelia asked.

"Every six months," replied Jens. "There are two seasons. But I do believe this young knight has what it takes to last at least a year. He looks fit enough."

"Yes," agreed Megan.

"Oops!" cried Jens. "I was wrong! The knight is down, and the dragon victorious!"

It took the dragon some effort, but he managed to sever the knight's head and hold it up to the onlookers. Some cheered; others were silent. Then he drank blood from the head and tossed it aside. More cheers, more silence. Amelia was stunned, all emotion drained from her because what she was taking in was, for the moment, too difficult to mentally process. Jens and Megan, however, were enjoying the spectacle. Their faces were lit up as if they were at a circus and had just witnessed a successful highwire act. Amelia, quickly getting over her shock, found the attitudes of her companions revolting.

"Lack of proper training if you ask me!" cried a spectator. He was a maverick. His loud clothes gave him away.

"Not so!" yelled a maiden. "The dragon was just too good for him."

"He may live till he is thirty, that dragon," said Megan.

"He has made a good start," said Jens.

Covered in blood and still wielding his sword, the young dragon was escorted by other dragons out of the cage. It was then Amelia realized he had been fighting without a pain collar around his neck. That device was put back on him by two of his fellow dragons soon after he was out of the cage, but still on stage. Later, Amelia learned that if they didn't do so, a robot close by would have shot all three to the delight of the crowd of maiden and maverick onlookers.

"So what do you think?" asked Megan of Amelia.

It took Amelia a while to answer. She was trying not to vomit. She took a swig of her soft drink to settle her stomach. It didn't help much. She wasn't at all used to death being so upfront and personal. She may have once destroyed countless lives from the air, but she didn't get, back then, to see anyone die, except perhaps one enemy pilot, just patterns of country-side in flame and swirling debris when she was using non-nukes. When that one time she unleashed a nuke, she saw nothing but an artificial cloud, was buffeted by high winds, and felt the heat from the blast.

Here she could see the blood shooting forth from the headless corpse. *This is so wrong,* she thought. But, looking sheepishly for a moment at those she was with, she concluded that was something she no longer felt comfortable telling Megan, especially in front of Jens. Acceptance, even delight, in this sort of horror was too ingrained in both her companions. She figured that this violence was part of the reality of the world she was now living in. But she knew she had to keep both Jens and Megan friendly even if they lacked somewhat in the humanity department.

"So what do you think?" asked Megan once more.

"Remarkable," said Amelia.

"Oh, that was nothing compared to two veteran fighters in the cage," enthused Megan, "Nothing at all."

Later that day, Jens was called into Dean Renate's office. The dean wanted to know how things were going with Amelia.

"I think she will be fine," said Jens. "She'll be no trouble at all. I honestly don't know what the fuss is about. She's only one maiden."

"The first High Priestess was only one woman," reminded Dean Renate. "She was alone when she found the Goddess in pain from what men had done to our world, and together, they were able to remedy the situation. The Goddess granted her wisdom and called her Martha after Mother Mary, and so began our way of life."

"True," agreed Jens.

"Everything is in balance," Dean Renate told her. "We do not want that balance disturbed. The university board members won't stand for it, and neither will I."

CHAPTER SIX

The night after the visit to what she thought would be theatrical style entertainment, Amelia slept poorly, pushing her blankets and pillows every which way with her hands and feet. In a dream, she recalled her last mission for the Australian government. She went on that mission in the late twenty-first century. At the time, she was stationed at a secret location in the Northern Territory. Later, when the doctors wanted to put her in that life-preserving capsule, she was sent to Sydney, where, in the twenty-third century, Jens had found her among the ruins.

At the Northern Territory secret location so long ago now, she remembered being strapped into her cockpit and then given the nod for takeoff by a ground crew member. She taxied to position and waited for word from the tower to come over her intercom. When it came, she revved her jets, and then, like a tight rubber band released, she shot forth. Within moments, the ground melted away, and she was airborne. She glanced back at her airfield and saw a black rectangle with white lines.

With not much effort, she climbed to fifty thousand feet. At sixty thousand, she levelled off and proceeded toward Indonesia. Then, after passing East Timor, she moved away to the right to Papua New Guinea. Before long, Port Moresby came in sight. A dense jungle surrounded the city. *I'd hate to go down there*, she thought. From that location, she turned left toward the greenery of Borneo and then dropped down to Jakarta, her target.

Amelia didn't have to look out her cockpit window. She had pre-programmed her flight, and her onboard computer would take her to her destination, provided there weren't any glitches. She could sit back and watch the dashboard screen. It informed her of where she was and how she was going to get to her intended destination. The computer could also make flight corrections on its own if unforeseen circumstances occurred.

A short distance out from Port Moresby, an albatross came in sight. Amelia was about to change course to avoid the bird when the computer did it for her, then got back on course. *I'm a passenger*, she thought.

One thing she wanted to do was to avoid any contact with Bali. Even though the Balinese were technically part of Indonesia, they were not the enemy. They had been friendly toward the Western powers for generations. They had been picked on by other Indonesians for their friendliness.

One of Amelia's ancestors had been killed in the Bali bombing that had taken place at Kuta in the early 21st century. It was a surfing trip that had gone wrong because a religious fanatic wanted to kill westerners as well as Balinese. Both the people of New South Wales, Australia, and the local Balinese had suffered for reasons as hard to fathom then as now.

No Australian wanted to harm the people of Bali for what other Indonesians had done or were doing. They still registered on the minds of many Australians as good people forced to be a part of a corrupt regime. Hence, if Amelia had anything to do with it, they would be spared.

Avoiding Bali was fuel-consuming, but Amelia and her superiors felt it was worthwhile. Besides, coming at Jakarta from an unexpected direction would likely help what she needed to do rather than hinder. If sudden, it might take the Indonesians too long to scramble fighters to intercept her. Ground missiles might still be launched, but she was confident her countermeasures could blow them out of the sky before they could come into contact with her craft.

This is it, she thought as she approached Jakarta air space. *No backing out now.*

She came in hard and fast, dropping her load and veering off the way she had been trained. The computer did most of it, but she was there to make sure it didn't mess up.

The cloud coming up from an overpopulated city the way it did was magnificent. Film footage she had seen showed such clouds as black and swirling grey, forming a mushroom shape. Well, the shape was right, but the cloud glowed red and gold with energy at its centre as if putting on a show just for her. Amelia didn't have to think about innocent lives lost. She was too high up. All she saw was patterns below before the cloud happened, not people. There was the screech from the high wind she'd created and the buffeting. The computer went dead, and she was back to being a genuine pilot.

An Indonesian fighter tried to intercept and fire off its missiles at her craft but was too badly knocked about by the wind to get a solid lock on her. Then this enemy plane began to wobble. She thought she saw the shock on this enemy pilot's face when his fighter dropped from the sky, heading for the ground. *First person I know upfront I killed*, thought Amelia.

She didn't see the other aircraft explode. There was too much cloud in the way. Even so, she knew it had occurred. She imagined she would have seen him pull out in time and fly back toward her had he lived.

There had been shantytowns below where people eked out a living as best they could with material thrown down from the high-risers or tossed up by the sea. Wharves with leaky boats, rats, and humans added to the scene. A short distance out, warships headed for Australia sinking fast, their crews doomed.

Still, it was the high-risers and the warships that had contained the enemy. Those who lived on high had kept the majority of their people poor and scrambling for two square meals a day while they lived in luxury and demanded more and more from other governments. She had smiled at the thought of those towers of greed coming down and then going up in pieces, swiftly reduced to carcinogenic powder. The people in those monuments to corruption had played the Australian public for fools once too often and so had to pay the price along with everyone else. *The world will be better off without them,* thought Amelia.

When civil war broke out in Australia and had to be crushed, what was then the Indonesian government should have known their time was up. Once the rebellion in Sydney was traced back to Indonesia and other Muslim-majority countries, something was bound to happen. No one wanted to declare war on Indonesia. When Australian leaders discovered that many of the rebel leaders had come from there, it became impossible for them not to act. Nuking the bastards as well as the innocent was deemed the best way. They had to learn a lesson that the survivors, if there were any, would remember forever. Amelia was one of the teachers.

Amelia had just enough fuel to make it back to base. Of the squadron sent out to nuke, her craft was one of three to return. The others were not so lucky.

She was not greeted as a heroine, but her commanding officer did say he was proud of her. Long-range scanners indicated she had done well.

When did it all go wrong? Amelia wondered in her sleep. By 2026, there were the beginnings of civil strife across Europe. The European Union, blamed by many for creating the havoc through sponsoring mass immigration from Africa and the Middle East, tried to find reconciliation where it could. In too many instances, this was not possible.

The truth was that, economically, nations already suffering from earlier monetary downturns, could not cope with the influx of new people in their millions. What's more, there were religious clashes in cities where that had not occurred for centuries.

Newcomers to Europe expected better food and housing, but those things were not forthcoming. The numbers of people entering what were once much smaller communities overwhelmed local authorities and resources. Even major cities found it difficult to manage. The migrants resented what little they got, and this angered the locals who were now doing it tougher because of them.

What food and how this food is to be prepared became significant issues. Those new to Europe wanted their places of worship and more say in how they were to be governed. Some thought bikinis an abomination, and they also considered dogs as being unclean and therefore having no place in society. For locals with their ideas on food, bikinis, and dogs, such attitudes from the newly arrived became intolerable.

Poles and Hungarians resisted inclusion in accepting migration into their countries. In this, they went against the European Union and the United Nations. They watched on the news riots breaking out in Paris and other major European cities and so held firm. Their faith, culture, and safety of their women and children meant a lot to them since foreigners had previously attacked these things.

The people of Poland remembered being invaded by the Germans during World War II and then taken over by Russia after the war. They recalled their religion under threat from the communists and wiretaps on phones to make sure they behaved the way the communists wanted them to. *Never again will we be subjugated in our land by a foreign power* was what was being said. Angry banners waved in the streets and on television backed this up. Hungarians had been through similar twentieth-century trials and so were also not keen on having a great many foreigners with different belief systems enter their country to stay.

Grooming gangs, that is, criminals grooming young girls into servitude, sexual mistreatment, and slavery to much older men, became infamous in England, sparking violent uprisings of locals who were intent on driving out anyone who might support such gangs. People said on social media that girls had a right to a childhood, and no one, especially these foreign grooming gangs, should take that away from them. People not associated with those gangs but who had come from the same parts of the world the gangs did were not spared the violence, and so they had to fight back.

The European Union and the United Nations had limited muscle but sent in troops where they thought they might do some good. Having created the mess, they discovered they had no way of cleaning it up.

From the European Union and the United Nations flowed the propaganda that Europe, Australia, Canada, and the USA required the influx of new blood because birth numbers in those places were down. The truth was that the numbers were where they should always have been and that elsewhere, they were far too high. It did not take the people of the western countries long to realize they had been duped. Despite the European Union and the United Nations pushing the false information, it became all too obvious to the average working-class person living in Europe, Australia, Canada, and the USA that something was wrong with it. Population replacement shouldn't mean the creation of slums to pack people into, yet that's what was happening.

The financial powers that be wanted people they could more easily manipulate than those that had grown up in the west, and so they supported the European Union and the United Nations in their propaganda efforts. They thought people from the poorer parts of the globe could be better controlled. They were wrong.

In the South Pacific, fuelled by what was happening in Europe and elsewhere, religious extremists carved out kingdoms in Indonesia, where they became the new wealthy elite, and in parts of Malaysia where they could manage the ports against possible communist infiltration. Australia saw the threats to liberty mounting, and the USA gave the okay for nuclear strikes. A decade later, this was where Amelia came in as a fighter pilot.

What happened after that was unclear. Her craft had not been adequately shielded from radiation. Cancer had crept into her head. Jakarta had been destroyed, and so those in power in the Australian Air Force wanted to do what they could for her. Freezing seemed the only possible solution. She was told the doctors were trying out a new technique that might work. It was a slim hope for survival against the growth within her, but she felt she had to take it.

She had no idea she would awaken in a future that at once seemed heavenly compared to what she had left behind and, at the same time, monstrous. Food in the twenty-third century was plentiful, and yet people were dying, and in ways she thought were barbarous.

CHAPTER SEVEN

Amelia watched as the ten-year-old students were seated for their written exam. The school hall it took place in was much like the school halls of her day. The seats were hard, and the doors creaked when the wind blew. She was surprised the students were all male and were issued pens and paper instead of computers. She wondered why Jens and Megan had brought her here the morning after that young knight was beheaded. She suspected a connection, and she wasn't wrong. Outside the hall where the boys were seated, the parents had joined Amelia and Jens in watching from the open doors, some failing to suppress nervous sighs, as their sons were about to do their best with the material given to them by supervising priestesses in white cowls.

Jens informed Amelia that part of the process taking place involved the deciphering of the student's handwriting. "You can tell a lot about one's personality by looking at one's handwriting," Jens told her. "No selection process would be complete without handwritten evidence."

A bell rang, and the boys were all hard at work, scribbling away as if their lives depended upon the results, which were the case. The writing lasted half an hour; then, the bell was rung to stop. Priestesses in white collected the papers. The boys looked frightened.

The interviews came next. This involved three priestesses and a load of questions. Amelia noticed that the boys who showed irritation by chewing their nails or covering their faces with their hands were often selected to become knights. Boys last in line gathered it was best to appear mild-mannered with broad smiles. That did not always save them. Jens told Amelia the parents were allowed to look on, provided they did not speak. Each parent tried to look positively at their child, urging them on with nods and smiles as if they could non-verbally push them to success.

"There is an obstacle course and swimming," said a priest-ess. "We need our mavericks to be fit as well as intelligent."

"What about your knights?" Amelia asked.

"It doesn't matter. If the boys are unfit, they will not last long in combat against our dragons. Besides, they have until they are fifteen to get into shape."

"But being out of shape now can lose them maverick status?"

"Yes. It is the law."

There were not many fat boys around. Amelia gathered that, from a very early age, they strove to be great at everything. All their hopes and dreams relied upon the results of this one day of performance. Only success in becoming a maverick mattered.

The priestesses smiled at those who were to become knights and also smiled at those who were mavericks in train-ing. Fathers and mothers looked on anxiously, holding hands so as not to show their anxiety, as decisions were made con-cerning their male offspring.

Jens told Amelia that the husbands were all mavericks. They were dressed rather foppishly in suits that would have outraged the military from her earlier time. Their soft, mani-cured hands told her they didn't do much hard work. For Ame-lia, the term *toyboy* came to mind; then, she wondered if she was being fair to them. She didn't know this society well enough to make that judgment.

"The ones selected to be knights will learn how to fight dragons," a priestess, a middle-aged woman in white, told Amelia.

"And the others?"

"They will acquire manners and deportment. They will learn how to make themselves more attractive to our maidens."

To Amelia, this did sound like foppish behaviour.

"And if they don't learn how to please maidens?"

"If they don't have that ability, they should have been weeded out here and now with our tests. Pleasing maidens is mandatory for a maverick as well as being able to learn good business sense. If it turns out they are mentally or physically un-fit to be mavericks, they can always be made over into knights. If we later discover a fault in them that cannot be corrected, then they are to become knights instead of mavericks. This does not happen very often. We strive to be thorough."

"I bet you do."

Amelia couldn't imagine someone wanting to fight for their life time and time again when they had an alternative. *Better to be classed as a maverick and wear silly clothes than a knight likely to die at the hands of a dragon.*

"Do you approve?" asked the priestess. There was no hint of threat in her voice, just curiosity. Even so, Amelia felt it best to be cautious. She didn't know what would happen if she gave a blatantly wrong answer.

"Is it my place to approve?"

"No, but I will have your thoughts. Jens told me I could have your thoughts on the matter."

This sounded like a trap, and Amelia didn't want to step into it.

"I don't know. All this is still very new to me."

"You come from a more savage time in which the slaughter of millions of innocents happened quite often."

As far as Amelia knew, it happened only once and with American approval and only after the other alternatives had been exhausted.

"It wasn't that bad," Amelia replied. She wondered if she had just stepped in it with that answer. She knew honesty wasn't always the best response.

"The scorched earth and devastated cities would tend to contradict you," pointed out the priestess. "Now, all that hostility over this country or that has been eliminated. It is a much better world."

"But not for the knights and the dragons." Amelia knew she had done it again, but she couldn't help herself. *I'm too outspoken when I don't know what the score is*, she thought.

"It is necessary that we have our knights and dragons. You will come to understand this." The priestess nodded knowingly.

Amelia was thinking of that battle she saw between a young knight and an equally young dragon. To her, it had been pointless and awful. To the people around her, she understood it was something else. It was somehow connected to their religion; otherwise, priestesses would not be deciding which males get a good life and which males ended up fighting dragons. The general rule of not messing about with someone else's religious belief system, especially when you didn't fully understand what it was about, she realized, still held true.

"Think on this," offered Megan. "There was always cannon fodder, to use an old-fashioned term. There will always be cannon fodder. Nowadays, the violence is contained. There is less damage."

"Those who would have been sacrificed in war still die." The priestess stated this open-handedly as if presenting a fact a child should know. "Nothing can or should change that."

"But you decide?" Amelia felt out of her depth and struggled not to show it by putting on a blank face. This was indeed a strange conversation.

"Someone always decides," the priestess spoke with a measured voice as if she were talking to a child who didn't quite understand the lesson. "I believe the barely educated in your day became foot soldiers."

"Not always." Amelia remembered people joining the armed services for a better education. She had joined the air force in the hope of learning how to fly since flying lessons would otherwise have been too expensive.

"But much of the time?" The priestess asked, still with a soothing voice. "Here, we acknowledge who is expendable and who is not and act accordingly, and all for the greater good."

Always for the greater good, Amelia thought but kept her mouth shut. She realized she might have said too much already.

She remembered stories about people in Germany in the 1930s, believing Adolf Hitler as the strong leader who would rescue them from poverty. Despite his attitude toward the Jewish people, they could envision that what he was proposing for their nation was all for the greater good. That was why they voted him into power. In the end, thanks to Hitler, the people of Germany ended up worse off than they were before.

Later, in the 21st century, the United Nations pushed for a centralized world government, also for the greater good. The results of this were a string of civil wars that spread across the planet, making the United Nations a bigger failure than the earlier League of Nations.

Amelia still had much to learn about where she had come to live. Even so, she was sceptical about what she had seen so far. Military training kept her from making angry outbursts at Jens or the priestess that would reveal too much about how she felt and would most likely get her into trouble she might not understand or be able to either physically or mentally handle. It wouldn't do to show how she really felt about some of the less than honourable events she'd recently witnessed. How could a world run on the lines of bloodshed and sacrifice be any better than what had been attempted in the century she had come from?

Dean Renate phoned Jens about the day's activities.

"Was it wise to take Amelia to that school?" asked the dean, sounding concerned.

"I believe so," said Jens.

"But you let one of the priestesses know about her?"

"It was necessary. We needed her help in explaining things to Amelia. Everything is fine. Our woman from the past is learning and is adjusting well to her new surroundings."

"I hope you are right." The dean sighed.

"I know I am. Besides, we cannot keep Amelia a secret for much longer; hence we needed to bring that priestess into our confidence. She knows how to talk to young girls who need instruction on knights and dragons. Even though Amelia isn't a young girl, I thought she might ask the kind of questions a young girl might ask, and I was right. The priestess handled her well, and she has taken a vow not to reveal Amelia's past until it has become common knowledge."

"And you believe her?"

"Of course, I do! She is, after all, a priestess."

CHAPTER EIGHT

Amelia visited the dragon barracks not far from where she was staying with Jens and Megan as her guides.

"Don't be afraid of them," Megan said to Amelia. "With their pain collars on, they don't dare make an aggressive move towards us. The collars are only removed when they are to go up against our knights."

The dragon barracks were Spartan. There were bunks in the sleeping quarter with the occasional book, magazine, and chair.

"They have books and magazines?" Amelia asked. *Are they more human than they look?*

"They're taught to read," Jens said, "but college or university is out of the question. Not many of them would live long enough to finish a degree anyway. Even an apprenticeship would be a waste of money, resources, and effort. When they're not fighting, they earn a living through manual labour. Today happens to be their day off. The knights are the same way. No one expects either a dragon or a knight to be around for too long once they are old enough to enter the arena."

You start a book and you don't know if you are ever going to finish it, thought Amelia sadly.

They were visiting during the day, so most of the dragons were in the gym practicing their moves with various weapons or lifting weights.

A dragon that looked to be in his late twenties approached the women. He bowed to show he meant them no harm. The pain collar that was beginning to activate subsided. There was an initial glow that quickly vanished.

"I am the Den Massster," he told them. "Is there something I can do for you?"

Amelia stood open-mouthed, astonished to discover that this dragon could talk. Not only that, but he was speaking the same language as Jens and Megan. The only difference was, he tended to hiss between, in, and around certain words because of his long, red-forked tongue. What's more, he understood that, like his fellow dragons, he was just a "throwaway" person, lower than even the knights he fought. She could see this in his eyes. He had to act subservient because of the collar, and Amelia got the impression he hated that.

"Are all these weapons used in fighting?" Amelia pointed to an array of instruments of death displayed on a nearby wall.

"Yessss," said the dragon.

"Could you tell me more about them?" asked Amelia.

"The first on the left isss a double-headed axe. Good balance. Not too heavy for a newcomer. Here we have a mace, an excellent choice. Not one of the heavier maces, so also good for someone new. This is a broadsword. It is heavy and awkward, requiring a lot of practice. Many have died going into battle with it too soon, but sometimes maidens do insist this should happen, and so it does. One of our own went into combat with it recently. He was so young, and yet he prevailed against a knight just as immature."

The dragon paused for a moment, remembering that confrontation. It was the one Amelia had witnessed. Then he went on, "Next, we have the long sword. It is a more elegant weapon but deemed too good for our use, though that wasn't always the case. Now we come to the morning star. We used to be able to wield it, but now only knights are permitted its use on special occasions, and these occasions haven't arisen for some years now. Maybe their use is also banned for knights now asss well. It is a mace with spikes. It's rather unsporting if you ask me!"

"Nobody would ask you." Jens glared with contempt at the dragon.

"Quite right," said the dragon, "My apologies to you for my transgression."

"You are forgiven." Jens was feeling generous.

The dragon had sounded humble in his reply, but something in his eyes told Amelia how he really felt. He resented not being able to have his say.

"The rest are spears and javelins," the dragon said matter-of-factly. "Anything else I can help you with?"

"Have you seen much combat?" asked Amelia.

"I have sssurvived a dozen bouts," said the dragon. "I have been wounded three times, but they patch me up and send me out again and again. It is what I am here for. My mother, if she lived, would have been so disappointed in me. Cast your eyes in my direction. I have black scales. Look around! Over there, you have white scales, and silvery ones. I once knew a friend with red scales. Regardless of colour, we are all dragons, and we do our duty."

Amelia noticed that some of the dragons had spiked tails, and others had smooth tails. She was told by the dragon answering her questions that the smooth tails were more flexible.

"What happens to female dragons?" asked Amelia.

"There is no such thing. His mother was a maiden much like I am. Some women give birth to these monsters. We don't know why. It just happens." Jens knew there was more to it than that, but she felt she wasn't at liberty to say.

"It can't just happen if male dragons don't have sex with women as it says in that book you gave me," said Amelia.

"We can't," stated the dragon. "And even if we could have sex, we cannot father children. We know thisss to be impossible. That is why we are so expendable."

"Show us the rest of your facilities." Jens was using her authoritative voice. It was the one Amelia suspected she used on subordinates getting out of line.

"Very well." With that, the dragon lumbered off.

There was a kitchen. The bench on which meals were prepared was clean, and nearby, there were two refrigerators. What could be prepared with what was there was plain but good, nothing fancy. There was a rec room that had a dozen chairs and one lone television screen. Amelia imagined the screen was used to show combat films. She stood open-mouthed, surprised to discover this was not entirely so.

"We like comedies," the dragon told them. "We particularly like slapstick. It takes our minds off things we would rather not think about."

The tour ended out back in the garden where not only food was grown but flowers as well. There were roses, chrysanthemums, bottlebrush, old man banksia, and waratah.

"Why the flowers?" asked Amelia.

"Are they not beautiful?" replied the dragon.

"Answer the question," Jens commanded in an icy tone.

"They are for the graves," replied the dragon. "They are for our dead as well as those of the knights we kill. It is what we do."

Amelia's stomach was doing flip-flops. The nightmarish reality of the lives of dragons and knights was at once overwhelmingly grim. Thinking of how she had taken innocent lives as a fighter pilot helped pull her back together. Maybe she had no right to feel the way she did about this society. The flip-flops stopped.

Later that day, Amelia was taken to a small, wooden building with pews, where the local priestess talked about compassion and noble sacrifice. She was a middle-aged woman in a white cowl with a white stone on a necklace around her neck. Jens told Amelia the stone represented purity of spirit.

About two hundred people were listening to her, some leaning forward in their seats, keen to get to grips with their religion.

The priestess explained how noble the knights were and how needed they were to do what they do. She complimented the dragons on how brilliantly they tested the knights to make sure they were worthy of the name.

Seated in one corner close to the priestess were two dozen dragons, and across from them to the left were two dozen knights. Some of the dragons, as well as some of the knights, had recent injuries. For example, one of the silvery dragons had a few scales nicked off the left side of his face, revealing reddened white flesh.

The dragons were all wearing pain collars that no doubt guaranteed their good behaviour. The knights did not require that sort of incentive to behave appropriately in mixed company. Both lots wore plain clothes which included jeans, T-shirts, and overalls. In Amelia's past, they wore working-class togs.

Then there were the maidens and the mavericks, some with young children. They sat further back from the priestess. They came dressed as if they were attending church service. Amelia's last church service, she recalled, was at an air force base. There, everyone, including herself, was in their very best military uniforms. Not a button missing, not a thread out of place. Here, the maidens had on silks as did their female offspring. The mavericks and male offspring too young to be tested wore suits less colourful than they would typically wear. It was a case of black stripes on grey rather than an explosion of reds, yellows, greens, and pinks. Amelia was seated with the unmarried maidens. Some of the unmarried mavericks, seated close by, no doubt, wondered who she was.

Amelia could smell burning incense, and there were lit candles all around what looked like an altar. She could tell that many of the dragons, knights, maidens, and mavericks were listening intently to the priestess as if they were buying every word she said.

This is a farce, thought Amelia, but chose to say nothing during the gathering. There was nothing she could say to make any of this right in her mind.

She imagined dragons and knights having to have faith because their lives had been made so short by violence. Death came swiftly for them, and she could see that this was their way of preparing themselves for the great beyond.

Amelia gathered that maidens went along with this belief system because it excused their delight in what was their spectator sport. She could not fully fathom the bloodlust among what were otherwise decent people. Then she thought of the ancient Romans and what they had been like.

The mavericks no doubt continued to thank the Goddess they were neither dragon nor knight in this strange, twisted world. Going to this place was no doubt one of their ways of not falling from grace and becoming knights.

A maverick reporter noted the presence of a strange maiden in the temple. She moved away before this maverick could get a good photo of her.

The headline the next day read: "Woman from Past Here at Temple?"

Jens wasn't too badly shaken by what was written. Most of it was speculation but, for all that, it wasn't bad. The time was drawing near when Amelia would have to make some kind of statement to the press. At present, however, she had done nothing to embarrass those looking after her. For this, the dean would be grateful.

CHAPTER NINE

Megan took Amelia to an exclusive Wollongong site. Amelia gathered, by the size of it and the seating above an empty space, that it was once a sports stadium. Megan told her that once, in ancient times, the game of soccer was played there. Both where the spectators sat and the players no doubt played were open to the elements. High walls enclosed the area, reaching up to the sky, but without a roof against inclement weather. Megan said the walls were to prevent combatants from reaching seated priestesses, maidens, and mavericks. There were also robot guards stationed in various areas to prevent those able to climb from getting up to mischief.

The robot guards, with arms, legs, and torsos that looked human enough, were made to look alien, inhuman in other ways. They had shiny, silvery faces with red eyes that showed no sign of life. Their mouths were slits without lips. They wore blue uniforms with blue caps and had firearms at the ready.

Amelia was frightened by the sight of these mechanical creations. She did not look directly at any of them for fear her gaze might get their attention. Without examining them, Amelia thought the pistols they had holstered at their sides looked like fifty calibre desert eagles. They were capable of doing a lot of damage with just one bullet. Later on, she learned from Jens that only these robots, under the command of maiden officers, were permitted to carry guns and rifles.

This was the first time Amelia had come across such sophisticated mechanical men. "I am impressed by the guards," said Amelia to Megan, "but why are knights and dragons given menial tasks that these walking, talking technological marvels are more capable of doing?" Amelia would have been happier and less frightened of the guards if they were without firearms and repairing roads or digging ditches.

"We only require our knights and dragons to fight during certain months of the year," Megan told Amelia. "The rest of the time, they have to do something, or they will get bored. Besides, robots are expensive. We can't afford to have too many of them."

Amelia noticed there were movie cameras just above the combat area. Screens were strategically placed in excellent locales where the audience was seated so that the viewers could see choice moments of the action close up. Megan told Amelia that what was shown on the screen was being televised to the locals unable to attend and also sent to other cities for the enjoyment of the people there.

Amelia gathered from the happy murmurings of those seated around her that they eagerly anticipated what was to soon occur.

"This is our main event," said Megan. "Sometimes, some of our knights compete in other cities, but what is happening here today is something many of us do look forward to."

"Do these knights have a choice?" asked Amelia.

"None at all," said Megan. "There is, of course, that remote possibility that one of them might kill enough dragons to rise above his station and then have a choice."

"For most of them, if not all of them, that is not going to happen." Megan added this after a thoughtful pause. "Yet, a portion of them will fight in the hope that it will. Hope is a powerful force, especially when you only have your life to lose."

A loud, reverberating horn sounded overhead.

"They're starting," said Megan.

First, the knights came onto the large, sand-covered platform. There were a hundred of them, all wearing armour. A great cheer went up.

One of the knights, a fellow whose knees were knocking together, making a clanking sound as he walked, stood apart from the others as if he didn't belong.

Megan pointed him out. "There's Jack Faro. He was caught stealing a purse from a young maiden. He wasn't very bright doing what he did. I almost feel sorry for him. He was a maverick. Now he's a knight. At his age, he must be in his forties, there's no chance at all he'll ever become a maverick again."

"They provided him with a Roman-style short sword," Megan added after a short pause. "I doubt if he has had much practice with it or the shield he's carrying. He won't be around much longer. It serves him right, though. He had it made, but he had to get greedy and stupid."

"Are there many such thieves?" asked Amelia.

"We don't have much in the way of crime here," Megan said with pride in her voice. "For mavericks, knights, and even dragons, it's just not worth it."

"What happens to knights and dragons that are caught stealing?" asked Amelia.

"Lined up against a wall and shot by robots if they're lucky." Megan winced. "There's also hanging or being speared to death by knights not in disgrace. Oh! And there's also slow death by having their hands or claws chopped off. Bleeding to death that way isn't very nice. I've seen it happen."

"What about runaways?" Amelia asked.

"We get them on occasion," Megan replied. "Some knight or dragon decides to bolt rather than fight. The thing is there's nowhere to go. You have your cities and towns, and some forested areas are making a comeback, but that's it. You can't survive for long in the places that were once bombed. Even now, I wouldn't spend more than a day in the Sydney ruins. The radiation is going down, but it is still not a hundred percent safe."

"But surely, there are ways for them to at least get away from here." There was concern in Amelia's voice she knew, by the standards of this world, shouldn't be there.

"To get away completely, you need a flyer," replied Megan, "and you have to know how to operate one. Knights and dragons never get instructions on how to do this, never!"

A loud horn sounded and reverberated. Then a hundred dragons trouped onto the platform. They glared up at the audience and then across to their opponents. Some maidens cheered them on. They were all lean with a hungry look about them, forked tongues flashing and lips smacking. All wore pants, and some had on a padded shirt over their chest scales. None had pain collars. They sported various weapons, including swords, maces, and spears. Some, though not all, had shields. They flexed their tails in anticipation of combat.

Twenty of the silvery ones climbed the walls of the enclosure they were in with their claws to spring out at their enemies.

"Those silvery dragons can't fly." Megan pointed them out to Amelia. "But that leathery membrane they have under their arms allows them to glide short distances. Have no fear of them getting at us in the stands, though. If they get too close to us maidens, the robots will shoot them down, but they know not to get too close."

"Why are they climbing then?" asked Amelia.

"It's a way of taking a knight by surprise." Megan was in her element, explaining this to Amelia. "Those silver dragons have smooth tails that they can wrap around an opponent's neck and choke him to death."

"Charming," Amelia said sourly. She was now sure she was not in for what she would call a good time.

"Yes," agreed Megan, not registering Amelia's tone. "There are black-scaled dragons with spiked tails that could stab vital organs. Over there, we have brown dragons with either smooth or barbed tails that could trip or cut an enemy at an opportune moment."

Amelia found she was afraid for the knights and knew

that was wrong; her eyes focused primarily on them and what they could do to stay alive. According to Amelia's sense of values, neither side deserved to be there. The dragons, she knew, had no choice but to defend themselves and, whether they were beasts or not, they could speak and read as she found out when she visited one of their barracks. Of course, according to her sense of right and wrong, intelligence shouldn't be at the core of why someone shouldn't be maimed or worse.

For a third time, a horn sounded. The dragons on the walls leaped from their perches, glided, and attacked. The knights clanged their shields together in a defensive posture against this tactic. Still, a couple of the dragons got through this barrier, and a few knights were either knifed or strangled.

Meanwhile, the knight who was once a maverick was quickly dispatched by a brown dragon with a javelin. It was too easy. He fell, gasping, looking at the blood flowing out of his chest as the dragon retrieved his javelin in time to use it to defend himself against a more experienced knight.

A couple of silvery dragons managed to trip knights with their smooth tails and thus create gaps in the shield wall. They moved in and were taken out by knights wielding swords and battle axes. The guts and blood now on display made horrid patterns in the sand, like an anatomy lesson at an abattoir gone wrong.

"Dragon's blood!" cried Amelia. "It's just as red!"

"Why should that surprise you?" asked Megan.

"It just does." If a dragon's blood was different, more alien, Amelia knew she would somehow feel better about the dead and dying dragons.

Despite the sand, there were now slippery areas that the dragons exploited to bring down more knights. Tails went into play to make the knights lose their footing.

"That big fellow over there," said Megan, "the one with the determined look who won't stay down. He has thirty kills."

"That knight?" Amelia pointed.

"Yes," said Megan. "I don't know how he's done it, but he's still here, and he's still doing it. Thirty kills! Now thirty kills plus! Wow!"

"Thirty kills plus." Amelia rolled that around in her head.

"His name is Dreadnought." Megan sounded proud of knowing this. She beamed at Amelia.

"That's a funny name." Amelia wondered where it came from. Was it something new? "What does it mean?"

"There was once a dreadnought class battleship." Megan was in her element dealing with the past. "Dread means fear. Nought is another way of saying nothing. Put them together, and you have Fear Nothing – Dreadnought, a good description of this knight."

"Very good, indeed." Amelia felt it was best to agree with Megan. She was here, after all, to fit in and find out more about this strange city.

Dreadnought managed to get to his feet and to pull the shield wall back together by putting to the sword two black dragons attempting to widen the gap. Then he lay three more down, and this meant there were enough bodies to make it difficult for the enemy to climb over their dead to get at his men.

More silvery dragons climbed and sprang at the knights. The wall of bodies crumbled, and it then came down to one-on-one fighting. The crowd roared with excitement. At first, the dragons were doing better than the knights; then the knights rallied around Dreadnought, their large leader. At given moments, it seemed that his dragon opponents hesitated a few seconds too long with their maces and swords before striking. This gave him a better than average chance of eliminating them. Amelia wondered if anyone else had also picked up on that odd delay on the part of those slain dragons.

Steaming intestines, stomachs, and hearts piled up on the ground. Maces bashed in skulls showing the grey, wormy looking brains of both dragons and knights slipping out in bits and pieces onto the already wet sand. Amelia gasped and looked around. Every other spectator was having a great time. Encouraging cheers went up when a knight scored a decisive blow. Even the children joined in with delighted cries for their favourite knights to do better against the dragons.

Amelia wanted to leave, but she knew she couldn't without offending Megan.

The smells rising from where the fighting was heaviest were awful. They offended her nose like the dead rat Amelia had once found as a child in the basement of her parent's home back in her other life, only a thousand times worse.

Dragons and knights were pissing on themselves and others as they had metal objects thrust into their bowels and other organs. Spiked maces skewered or popped out eyes, and combatants got their noses sliced off right in front of the eyes of the watchers, thanks to the screens that brought the action up close. It was nothing like what happened in the gladiatorial movies made in the 1960s and '70s. They were made fake; this Amelia understood was real.

An hour and a half into the killing, a horn sounded. The fighters retired to their respective sides of the arena. The dead were left. The wounded that could not walk were carried by their companions. There was applause from the maidens and the mavericks. Amelia clapped so as not to appear the odd person out. The bad odours continued to rise, doing terrible things to her stomach.

A score came up on the screens: Knights 45 dead and Dragons 50 dead.

Another horn blasted, and first, the knights and then the dragons left the arena. Amelia couldn't see the exit tunnels from where she sat, but she knew they were there. The screens then showed the highlights of what had been going on.

There was a dragon that bit the ear off a knight to get him to let go of his sword. The knight refused to do so, and so the dragon was cut deep. Blood sprayed all over the knight's armour. Something pinkish-grey hung out of where the cut was deepest. The dragon collapsed in convulsions to the applause of the audience. "Well done!" cried out a priestess.

The visuals changed to a black dragon using his spiked tail as a whip to flay a knight who had lost his shield. When the knight was down, the dragon used a battle axe to finish him off. This time, no one made any comments or applauded.

The visuals altered again to Dreadnought, the big knight dispatching two dragons with apparently little effort. They just stood there and got slain. The audience clapped loudly at this. Someone shouted, "Cowardly dragons!"

"Every once in a while, pacifists among either the knights or the dragons refuse to fight," said Megan.

"I imagine that happens." Amelia could understand an intelligent creature either not wanting blood on its claws or deciding it was time his life came to an end. She sighed deeply.

"They might as well fight," reasoned Megan. "Otherwise, they die without honour like those two."

The maidens, priestesses, and mavericks left, but Amelia took her time getting up. Her stomach bothered her. The stink was making it do flip-flops in ways it hadn't done before.

"What do you now think of our knights?" Megan asked of Amelia on the way back to Amelia's residence.

"Different," said Amelia.

"Not what you are used to."

"That's right."

"You will have to choose a knight of your own." Megan was serious about this. It was in her eyes. "A maverick can wait. We will also have to get you a job."

"I want to be a pilot." Amelia was thinking about how wonderful it would be to get up high to escape the sort of carnage she had just witnessed. She remembered how clean it was up there. "Can I be trained?"

"We'll see." Megan brightened up toward Amelia. She wanted this woman from the past to think about her future. "I can't imagine why it wouldn't be possible. I doubt Jens would object. I think it is a splendid idea. You were a pilot then, and you'll be a pilot now."

"But here, you won't be killing innocent women and children." Megan added this after a pause then wished she hadn't.

"That's right," Amelia agreed in a sad voice. She looked a little crestfallen. "No more innocent women and children."

****

That night, after getting a report from Megan, Jens phoned up Dean Renate and told her that Amelia was almost ready for that interview with the press.

"It would be good if she had a knight to sponsor," said the dean. "The press and the public, in general, would love that."

"All right then, we'll see if we can find her someone suitable." Jens sighed, wondering if that was such a great idea. "She has shown little interest in our mavericks, but I take it that this has more to do with her upbringing than any sexual abnormality. Megan tells me that Amelia has claimed to have had boyfriends in the past. In time, we will also find her a suitable maverick."

"The knight we call Dreadnought is beginning to worry our Head Priestess." The dean sounded concerned. "Too many kills and he has, generally speaking, lived for far too long."

"He'll never get fifty." Jens was sure of this. Her voice was firm.

"No," the dean agreed. "Not fifty, but his score is high."

"I am certain it won't get much higher," Jens predicted.

"We'll see," replied the dean.

CHAPTER TEN

The following day, Jens and Megan took Amelia to the nearest knights' barracks. It wasn't that far away from where the dragons dwelt, and it was just as Spartan. The gym was similar, and the recreation room had the same lone television screen.

They met Dreadnought, who showed them around. He had his left arm bandaged.

"Are you hurt badly?" asked Amelia.

"No," answered Dreadnought, wondering why he was being asked such a question by a maiden he didn't know. It was apparent his arm was still attached to the rest of his body, and that's what counted.

"Not badly hurt, then?" Amelia thought it was an impressive bandage. It covered much of the arm.

"A blade nicked the skin. The doctor who patched me up said to keep the bandage on for a couple of days to prevent infection." He offered a smile made crooked by a facial scar.

"What about your face?" Amelia felt she had to ask. It was quite a long disfigurement.

"What about my face? Oh, the scar! That takes me back a few years to one of my earlier encounters in the arena. That dragon taught me a lesson, but I got him with the axe I was wielding." Dreadnought touched his face in remembrance. "It's not as if I could forget having it, but few maidens and mavericks mention it nowadays." He once more smiled a crooked smile at the naivety of this maiden. *Such questions!*

"Tell us your role here," Jens said coolly. She glared at Dreadnought. She felt his attitude toward Amelia was bordering on rudeness. He looked into her eyes for a moment, unperturbed.

"I train the young." Dreadnought delivered this in a matter of fact tone. "I try to keep them alive for as long as possible. Most can expect to live two or even three years as knights. More than that is just wishful thinking."

"But you have lived longer than that," said Megan.

"Yes," agreed Dreadnought. "I am an exception; therefore, I am a trainer."

The weapons on display were similar to those the dragons had. Some were now bloodied and required cleaning. Knights with minor injuries were lying on their bunks.

"The seriously wounded are in hospital," said Dreadnought. "A couple may die there. The ones that will recover will not be fighting again this year. They have that golden ticket."

"What's that?" asked Amelia. She remembered the golden ticket in her earlier time was a soldier or airman wounded in such a way they were not expected to go into combat again. It was golden because it got them out of danger.

"The 'golden ticket' is a slang term," said Dreadnought, shrugging as if it didn't matter much. "It refers to a wound that will keep a knight out of the fighting for six months, maybe more. Knights are not happy with taking their chances of going up against dragons like that. Of course, if they're not fighting during any part of May or November, they're not killing dragons. So they're not getting any points that might someday elevate them from knight to maverick. Once they recover, of course, they're expected to fight and pick up points if they can. But for some, the rest in hospital does them good mentally as well as physically. If you ever had to somehow stay alive in a place of death, you'd know what I mean."

"You hate dragons?" asked Amelia.

"Sometimes," said Dreadnought.

"And at other times?" asked Amelia.

"When I can afford it, I pity them," said Dreadnought. "There is no point system that will ever give them liberty from combat. With us, of course, it is only the promise of liberty."

"I think you have said quite enough on that subject." *More impertinence!* Jens thought icily. *Didn't Dreadnought understand his place in society? Were his many kills going to his head?*

"My apologies for my wandering tongue," said Dreadnought. He bowed his head, thus adding to his words. Jens smiled a cold smile. She was not at all convinced he was sincere. His face, except the scar, reddened for a moment. Amelia caught sight of this and understood there was more to Dreadnought than he was supposed to reveal.

"You enjoy the killing?" asked Amelia.

"It is what we do," replied Dreadnought.

"But do you enjoy the killing?" persisted Amelia.

"No," said Dreadnought. He looked at Jens, but she was blank-faced with indifference. What did it matter if he liked it or not?

"But it is what you do," said Amelia, taking in what Dreadnought was telling her and, at the same time, remembering her role as a fighter pilot.

"Yes," agreed Dreadnought. His palms were open as if to say he had little if any choice in doing what he was expected to do.

Dreadnought introduced Amelia to several knights. They were all fit men. She reasoned that if they were not so, they would already be dead.

There was nothing wimpy about the way any of them dressed. Most wore T-shirts and jeans. There was no pretence in mannerisms with them, even with Jens around. In the barracks, there was no need for that sort of thing. They were not going to be community leaders. They would not be asked to help raise children. They were to be sacrificed again and again for the pleasure of others.

"Well, what do you think?" asked Megan.

"About what?" Amelia enquired.

"About choosing a knight," said Jens. "Why do you think we came here?"

Amelia blinked. Her mouth flew open to form an "o," then closed.

"Have you made a choice?" asked Dreadnought.

"If I must choose now," said Amelia, pointing, "I choose you."

"Me?" Dreadnought was taken aback by this as were Jens and Megan.

"Yes, you," said Amelia. "Are you available?"

"Yes," said Dreadnought, "but are you sure you want me?"

"I'm not sure I want anybody," confessed Amelia, "but if I have to have a knight, you'll do."

"Why Dreadnought?" asked Jens.

"He's brave, he's honest, and he knows his way around," said Amelia. She wasn't a hundred percent sure all of that was true, but she had a feeling that it was, and that was at least something to go on.

Amelia had also gathered from Jens' reactions to him that Dreadnought had been a tad too honest with them; that was a tick in his favour. Also, whether Jens accepted the notion or not, Dreadnought was a leader and leaders had to know their stuff. Amelia remembered her flight instructors and how precise they were in every aspect of keeping her alive in the air. If Dreadnought was keeping knights alive longer, he was someone she should get to know better.

"Honest?" inquired Megan; she was taken aback by this. What did Amelia see that she didn't?

"He doesn't like to kill," said Amelia. "He said so, whereas some of the others pretended they love it." Amelia knew she was taking Dreadnought at his word but felt it would be an all right thing to do for now until she was further acquainted with him.

Amelia recalled, in her days as a fighter pilot in training, there were recruits always eager to tell their supervisors what their supervisors wanted to hear. They'd look at the person asking the questions and give what they thought were the appropriate answers. Many of them tried to get by without doing their homework. They thought charm would work every time. She knew the best trainers weeded them out in about a week or two. They were a danger to themselves and to anyone who would fly with them.

Amelia saw the equivalent happening when Jens asked certain knights what they were thinking. They all too obviously wanted to please. Under other circumstances, this might be fine, but having one of them as a companion would not get her any closer to understanding the society in which she had landed.

One of those knights would be like a mirror, reflecting back at her what she already knew. And so, she didn't want anything to do with such pleasing knights, at least not on any personal level. Dreadnought didn't appear to be like that at all. He could get up Jens's nose, which made him a good choice. If Amelia wanted to know from a knight how knights feel about being knights, then Dreadnought would do.

"Maybe there are knights that do like to kill," assured Jens as they continued walking.

"I suppose a few might," agreed Amelia, "but I don't want to be hanging around with them if they are like that."

"No?" Megan was surprised. There was an exaggerated o in her "no," and her eyes widened for a few seconds. After all, the point of a knight was to slay dragons. If they enjoyed slaying dragons, then that was great. Who wants to spend time with a gloomy knight?

"No," confirmed Amelia, "not at all. I don't want to spend time with a knight that does enjoy that sort of thing."

"Oh!" Megan was again surprised. The "o" shot up with her eyebrows, and her eyebrows threatened to knock off her glasses. Maybe Amelia still didn't understand what knights were for. As far as Megan was concerned, it was all about killing.

"A decision has been made." Jens shook her head sadly. She wasn't happy about Amelia's choice but felt she should press on with it. Dean Renate wanted it done. The dean needed Amelia to sponsor a knight. "Do you accept this maiden?"

"Yes," said Dreadnought. His eyes twinkled, and he was smiling that crooked smile of his.

"Then it is settled," said Jens. "Amelia, there's a booklet you must read, but it's all straightforward. I'll get it for you."

"You go to my matches and other fights," Dreadnought told Amelia. "Other than that, we can meet any time you want."

"That's it?" asked Amelia

"Read the booklet, and we'll talk," said Jens.

****

That night, Jens contacted Dean Renate over the phone.

"I've done what you wanted," said Jens warmly. "I've teamed up Amelia with a knight."

"Good," replied the dean. "That will make her more presentable to the public. You've done well."

"I knew you would be pleased," said Jens.

"Who is the knight?" asked the dean.

"Amelia chose Dreadnought."

"She did what?!" cried the dean.

"It'll only be temporary at best," Jens assured her. "Dreadnought can't live for much longer."

"Oh, yes, he can!" the dean shouted. "There are things about him you don't know, and the general public must never know. Now you've shone a bigger spotlight on him. It was big enough already. He will be mentioned to the entire world when we introduce Amelia. That has to happen for the sake of appearance. Thanks to you and Amelia, he'll be harder than ever to dispose of. A mistake was made decades ago when it comes to Dreadnought, and we may all pay dearly for it."

CHAPTER ELEVEN

The flyer skimmed over the Blue Mountains. It manoeuvred beautifully; all that was needed was a light touch on the controls to get the flying machine to cooperate. Even for a beginner like Amelia, this aircraft was the closest thing to her being like a giant seagull or an enormous tern. She found her skills as a former fighter pilot handy in avoiding hawks and other large, predatory birds.

Flocks of wild ducks proved to be more of a challenge, especially when they were flying in the opposite direction. In one instance, turning sideways and climbing allowed her to avoid damaging the flyer and killing a troublesome kestrel.

"You're doing very well," said Malcolm, her instructor. He was a maverick who didn't seem as wimpy as the others she had met because he knew something about aircraft.

"Why, thank you, sir," Amelia replied.

"It's as if you were born with wings."

"It feels that way too. This is truly an amazing machine."

"Does it beat your military jet?"

"It isn't as fast, but it does a tight turn very well."

"I'd love to have gone up in one of those jets." Malcolm sighed. For a moment, he had that faraway look as if visualizing what it would be like to be in a craft with more speed.

Amelia liked Malcolm, but not in any sexy way. She figured he'd make a good friend. He reminded her of Ben Stiller from the movie *Zoolander*. It was an ancient film she saw in a history class. She was amazed at the time at how anyone could act so goofy. She put it down to comedy and the period in which the film was made. *If Malcolm just dropped the pretentious mannerisms, he'd be a lot more manly and human*, thought Amelia. It was the silly hand gestures and head bobbing that got to her. As for the head business, she'd seen male seagulls do that sort of thing when trying to get the attention of female seagulls. The male seagulls, however, were not in outlandish costumes that could have resulted from a sparkly unicorn vomiting on them.

At times, she felt like laughing at the mavericks. She had to hang tight on a smile and, at times, look away. What prevented her from bursting out was the fact that no one alive, here in this new world, could understand what she was laughing at or why she was laughing.

Offending mavericks, especially Malcolm, will get me nowhere, she reasoned. Besides, they were trained to please, and if they didn't do so, she figured, the powers that be could always demote them to knighthood. She noted that Malcolm kept himself in pretty good shape.

The Blue Mountains were the way she remembered them. The Three Sisters formation was still there, as was the town of Katoomba. Some of the homes looked art deco. These simple shapes gave the impression of speed rather than the more complicated in design stately houses she recalled from a much earlier trip. The shops hadn't changed at all. They were still tourist traps, offering all sorts of exotic goodies such as various forms of chutney and hand-made clothing. She set the flyer down on a pad near a health food store. The retro-rockets allowed for a gentle, vertical landing.

"We may get you your pilot's licence by the end of the week," Malcolm told her. "Then you can work for the air ministry or some private firm."

"Are there still artists about?" asked Amelia. She recalled painters and writers hanging out in the coffee shops, all sorts of fantastic art on the walls waiting for a buyer to come along. She remembered the weird and wonderful conversations she had with some of them. All were gone now. She hoped the lot of them had died of old age. In one of the cafes, a portrait of a yellow-tailed black cockatoo in flight had grabbed her attention. She hoped it was now in some museum somewhere.

"Yes," said Malcolm. "There's an artist colony not far from here in Faulconbridge."

"Over there, in that valley, I see smoke," cried Amelia.

"That's not a bushfire," said Malcolm. "That's a knight's training camp. Those still too young to fight are trained there."

"Where they learn to kill dragons?" asked Amelia.

"What else are knights good for?" replied Malcolm. "Once he was selected to become a knight, Dreadnought trained there. He must have learned a lot."

"He must have," agreed Amelia. "And he has been passing on what he knows to others."

"Good for him," said Malcolm.

They got vanilla milkshakes at the store then took the flyer back to base. On the way, Amelia cut across to the coast and followed the coastline home. She flew close to the waves, hoping to see a whale or some dolphins.

At one point, there was a creature that came out of the water to splash them, but it looked more like some ancient aquatic dinosaur than anything Amelia was familiar with. It had a brown whale-like body and an extraordinarily long neck, ending in a dozen rows of glistening teeth.

Later on, Amelia would learn its ancestors had been whales, and thanks to radiation, it was a menace its ancestors hadn't been. Megan told her it was a waleba and that there was no accounting for how the neck got so long or why it had developed so many teeth. Maybe there was also shark and eel DNA in that thing.

"That was close!" cried Malcolm, not caring for his aircraft to be targeted like that by a waleba. "Those creatures can bring down flyers."

"I'll watch out for them next time," said Amelia, "and fly a bit higher."

"Please do!" agreed Malcolm. "We don't want to end the day as a snack for some mutated monster. I didn't think you were going to go that low. I suppose I should have realised you didn't know about them. They have been known to break open flyers and eat the contents. They cannot leap very high out of the water, so it's not that difficult to maintain a safe distance from them. I suppose we were only just a safe distance, a splash being better than sharp teeth grinding away on metal and then getting to us."

"That's good to know," said Amelia. *Malcolm's no daredevil*, she thought. *Then again, why should a maverick be a daredevil?*

There were a dozen landing pads available at Wollongong, but Amelia decided to land the flyer where it had taken off. The Wollongong airport signalled them in. She avoided a flight of seagulls as she brought her craft to a successful landing.

"Very good," said Malcolm, smiling.

CHAPTER TWELVE

Amelia couldn't believe there was still horse riding. Horse racing for profit had been banned, but getting out onto country trails via horseback was something many people continued to enjoy.

Dreadnought suggested a horse ride that would take them into the scrub near Towradgi and from there to a beach.

"That's a great idea," said Amelia. She thought it was about time she learned more about her knight and got some fresh air into the bargain. "What are the horses we'll be riding like?"

"The ones we'll be on have been in jousts, so they're sturdy and don't easily shy away from trouble."

Dreadnought rode a palomino with a white stripe running down its light, brown face. Amelia was on a white brumby with a black mane.

The trail meandered as Amelia expected it to, and there was plenty of wildlife on what was a pleasant, sunny day. A diamond python crossed their path. She expected Dreadnought to leap off his horse and kill it with the sword he carried for protection. He did no such thing, and she was pleased. She smiled at him as if he had done something special, and he wondered why.

"It's harmless," Dreadnought told her as they waited for the snake to move on. Amelia seemed to be friendlier toward him, not so cold. Did she like snakes, or was it to do with his not killing the creature? She was a strange maiden.

There was the harsh laughter of kookaburras and the moaning of ravens in nearby trees. Then, halfway into the trail, the birdsong stopped.

"Danger!" cried Dreadnought.

"Where?" asked Amelia. "I don't hear a thing."

"Exactly!" cried Dreadnought.

In the next instant, three silvery dragons emerged from nearby bushes where they had blended in with the ghost gums. In a surprise attack, they rushed up to Amelia and Dreadnought with claws at the ready. They pulled at both Amelia and Dreadnought's saddles and clothing, attempting to tear them from their mounts.

Amelia, not wanting to be yanked off her horse, kicked the clawing dragon, as hard as she could, in the head. He fell and then received a kick, where his tail met his backside from her horse. He yelped and scurried away. The horse whinnied in triumph.

The dragon trying to dismount Dreadnought was slashed by Dreadnought's sword and fell, bleeding. The wound to the dragon's arm didn't look deep, but he appeared to be in shock and thus was rendered harmless. Dreadnought's horse snorted at the downed dragon and shook its mane.

"You killed my brother!" yelled the third dragon and came at Dreadnought with a mace, a large ball of metal on a metal stick. He threw it, and it bounced off of Dreadnought's chest. For an instant, Amelia thought she saw scales form where his clothing had been torn, but they disappeared to be replaced by the beginnings of a nasty bruise. "My best shirt ruined," grumbled Dreadnought as he leaped from his palomino. He grabbed the offending dragon and slammed him into a nearby tree.

"Are they dead?" asked Amelia. Both dragons now lay still.

"No," said Dreadnought. "Both will recover. Not much blood spilt. I only kill when I must. No doubt, I will meet them again at a more suitable venue. I don't get points this way. They're young, inexperienced. Someone was wrong in putting them up to this. Now we must go back."

"Must we? Yes, I suppose so." Amelia sighed. She had enjoyed the ride up until those dragons interfered.

"I doubt if there will be more of them, but you never know."

"I understand."

"You handle yourself well for a maiden."

Minutes later, a black-scaled dragon leaped at Dreadnought from high up on a tree branch. Dreadnought was knocked off his horse by the weight of the dragon coming down on him from above, but when they hit the ground, he managed to land on top of his new adversary. Dreadnought's horse snorted, shook its mane, and stepped back from the combatants. The dragon, first to recover from the fall, pushed the bulk of Dreadnought's body away from him and then wrapped his spiked tail around Dreadnought's throat, squeezing. Dreadnought gasped loudly, his eyes bulging. Amelia jumped down off her mount, seized the mace where it had earlier landed, and struck the dragon several times in the face. The dragon hissed and loosened his grip on Dreadnought, who then peeled the tail off his bleeding neck. He slammed his fist into the dragon's left eye. A second blow rendered the dragon unconscious. There were now scales missing from the dragon's face and red, swollen flesh exposed. Dreadnought noted that the mace, wielded by Amelia, with its solid metal ball, had done a fair bit more damage than his fist.

Amelia and Dreadnought gathered up the horses that were only a short distance away, got on them, and so made their way back to the stables. At the stall, they gave the horses water and brushed them down before handing them back to their maverick owner, who inquired how the ride had gone.

"Splendidly," answered Amelia. Dreadnought was taken aback by this answer. He shook his head and smiled with amusement.

The maverick didn't ask about the drying blood near Dreadnought's throat. He no doubt considered it to be none of his business provided his horses came safely back to him. Knights got into scraps with fellow knights, and it was best not to delve into that. Also, another animal could bring a horse rider down, something mutated running wild. Megan had earlier asked about liability and was told there was none. All that was guaranteed by the maverick horse owner was the horses were healthy and not too skittish. Apparently, in this age, knights were expected to protect the maidens they were out with, and that was that. Malcolm, who was their pilot for the day, also didn't initially show any signs of curiosity. Blood drying on a knight's throat wasn't that unusual.

Moments later, in the flyer, Amelia asked, "Why were they trying to murder you this way?"

"I got the impression they were trying to do away with both of us," confided Dreadnought. "It is most unusual for dragons to attack a maiden. Did you notice they were not wearing pain collars?"

"Yes," said Amelia. "Someone must have taken the collars off them."

"To my knowledge, only a maiden or a maverick could do that," said Dreadnought.

"But why? Why attack us?"

"It is because of my thirty-nine kills so far that I have come to represent hope to my knightly brothers. Some people want that hope, and others do not. I have fellow knights who are now my food tasters, so I will not be poisoned. They are willing to do this on the off chance that I reach the goal of fifty. I did not know that those opposed to me would come at me when I had a maiden in my care. That was most unethical."

"Am I a danger to someone, too? I can't see why."

"I don't know. They may not have counted on you being with me when they went into action, but I can't be sure. But be on guard. We will not go horse riding together in the future."

"Yes. We might not be so lucky next time."

On the way to Wollongong in the flyer, which was piloted by Malcolm, Dreadnought said to Amelia, "I think I am going to like being your knight."

Malcolm listened in as Amelia and Dreadnought talked more about their recent adventure. He was silent, occasionally grinning as a juicy bit came to his attention. Malcolm wasn't looking at either Amelia or Dreadnought. He was, after all, piloting the flyer. His ears, however, were active.

Amelia later discovered that Malcolm was happy to gossip and was not one to let a good story get in the way of the facts. Amelia was also to learn this was typical maverick behaviour, yet another reason why it was difficult for her to take mavericks seriously.

CHAPTER THIRTEEN

The following day, Amelia and Megan had coffee together at a small coffee shop in Wollongong Mall. Amelia noted that the building they were in dated back to when she was first alive. The sign over the door, "Bean Joy!" was the same. It hadn't faded because it had been repainted many times over the decades since it was first put up. This told Amelia that there was a value put upon the look of "Bean Joy!"

As in the past, the coffee shop was small, with only thirteen tables. Back then, people called this number a baker's dozen. Amelia put the term to Megan, and she wrote it down.

"A baker's dozen is a new one on me," said Megan. "Why not just say thirteen?"

"That was considered bad luck," replied Amelia. "One of my social studies teachers once told me the baker used to bake twelve loaves of bread for the customer and then one for himself, hence the baker's dozen. "

"That is strange." Megan scribbled the explanation down on a pad she carried.

"Yes," agreed Amelia. "I suppose it was."

Amelia looked around. The walls were covered in the fake panel wood that was there in that earlier period she had come from. Back then, the fake panelling was there because anything real was far too expensive. Now, she suspected customers enjoyed the "ye olde" look of the place.

The tables and chairs were made out of reconstituted pine. There was a process of taking leftover bits and pieces, turning them into sawdust, then somehow super-gluing it all together, in various shapes, to create tables and chairs. Some of the tables had warped because of spillage, and no doubt that added to the "ye olde" look. Amelia knew from experience that reconstituted pine tended to buckle when water was applied. She once had reconstituted pine furniture, so she knew the signs.

The waitress who served them reminded her of a waitress of long ago. She had on an apron and a plastic smile that added to the generally fake atmosphere. Her fingernails were painted in various colours, not one fingernail the same as the others. Some of the words she spoke were older English than what was now commonly spoken. Megan had to smile at the silliness of it all. At a time when you can do better in terms of design and general appearance, you go in for nostalgia instead.

"They have real coffee here," said Megan. "It comes from a plantation in Mexico. They grind it here themselves."

"It's all right," Amelia replied.

"Real coffee isn't found in every coffee shop," said Megan. "Sometimes they have substitutes such as chicory or combine coffee with chicory. The chicory they use comes from Canada."

"So chicory is less expensive?" asked Amelia.

"Oh, yes!" cried Megan. "It's fortunate you and I can afford the real thing. Not many coffee plantations survived the last major war, hence the reason why coffee is rarer than it should be and a luxury item. There are plans to start coffee plantations on Queensland's Gold Coast."

"How much are two cups of coffee then?" asked Amelia.

"A dollar fifty." Megan shook her head at the cost.

"That's not much." Amelia expected it to be a thousand times more.

"Your thinking about how money was back when this place first started up," said Megan patiently. "Inflation was so bad a dollar was virtually worthless. Well, after the Great Goddess showed the way, inflation was ended, and costing was rolled back."

"From what I learned in college, a dollar fifty would have been a high price to have paid for coffee, say, back in the 1920s. Of course, that would have been in America. Back in the 1920s, in Wollongong, according to one of my history teachers, it would have been pounds, shillings, and pence but still roughly the same." Amelia had mouth-widening amazement for a dollar fifty being thought of so highly. She was amazed she had remembered so much from her history lessons.

After this conversation with Megan, Amelia became more aware of the difference between money in the time she came from and money now. Asking around, she found out that a room for the night at a good hotel was five dollars, and this included breakfast.

Strolling along the mall, she learned that admission to a movie house was ten cents per person, and live-action theatres cost a whole two dollars fifty to attend. It seemed that inflation here had truly been beaten to a pulp. This wasn't just in Wollongong but elsewhere as well. The money used was the same throughout the world, or so Megan told her. Wages reflected these changes.

A couple of days later, Megan met Amelia at the same coffee shop. They sat down on reconstituted pine chairs and talked.

"I got my first allowance from the university the day after you bought me coffee," said Amelia. "Up to then, I was simply given food and reading material. Soon I will fly for a living and get my pay from flying."

"That is good news," replied Megan.

"At first, I didn't understand only getting five dollars fifty pocket money from the university per week," said Amelia. "It made more sense when I went shopping with money in my pocket. It doesn't sink in, the difference in time, until you have money to spend. In this age, you can get a lot for five dollars fifty. While shopping, I discovered that bread is ten cents a loaf and a bottle of excellent wine is two dollars. Beer is twenty cents a glass, and Scotch three dollars for a night's entertainment. "

"I told you as much when we were earlier having coffee here," replied Megan, adjusting her glasses. "The dollar fifty for coffee should have been a clue."

"Oh, it was!" assured Amelia. "It just took having my own money to have it come together. Just how was inflation stopped?"

"Zero growth in the human population and it's done. The population doesn't go up and doesn't come down. The priestesses manage it for the good of all." There was pride in Megan's voice. This was obviously one of the shining accomplishments of her people.

"How's that done?" asked Amelia.

"It's something the priestesses do. Only so many males get to be mavericks, and the rest are knights." Megan was unemotional in saying this. The cost in knight lives to maintain this, and, no doubt, other benefits didn't seem to mean anything to her. Amelia suspected all the other maidens she had seen that appeared to enjoy fights between knights and dragons had the same attitude.

"I think I am beginning to understand," said Amelia uncertainly because she didn't want to believe in this lack of humanity in someone as intelligent as Megan. For a moment, Amelia made a sour lemon face. She hoped Megan hadn't picked up on that. It seemed that prosperity rested on what happens two months every year in arenas and theatres everywhere. She was sickened by this revelation.

"I heard you beat up a dozen rampaging dragons," said Megan, changing the subject. She didn't want to dwell on something she felt might, for some strange reason, be upsetting Amelia.

"Really? I did that?" This put Amelia in a slightly better mood.

"Not a very maidenly thing to do." Megan felt this should be pointed out to Amelia. Knights rescued maidens and not the other way around.

"I kicked one dragon in the head and hit another with a mace, one of those metal balls on a stick," corrected Amelia. "Where did you hear that other stuff?"

"It's getting around," said Megan. There was amusement in her voice.

"It seems Malcolm, my pilot friend, has a big mouth and tends to exaggerate. I'll have to watch what I say in front of him." Amelia shook her head at the thought of Malcolm blabbing. Her eyes then became distant, as if remembering something. Her smile changed, becoming softer. Her thoughts turned to Dreadnought praising her. She couldn't imagine Dreadnought saying anything other than what really happened, and even then, he was not likely to say anything at all. She shrugged her shoulders. Dreadnought wasn't the talkative type, whereas Malcolm, being a maverick, was.

"There seems to be lots going on in your head," said Megan.

"Oh, yes." Amelia laughed.

Megan ordered coffee for two, waited for it to arrive, then got her recording device out of her pocket and clicked it on. This time, she felt the pad and pencil she had on hand at the coffee shop were not good enough. The business with Dreadnought she'd just touched upon was fascinating in its own right. Still, it was about time she got back to exploring Amelia's earlier existence.

"Now, let's talk about your past," said Megan.

"Will this pay for my coffee, room, and board?" ventured Amelia.

"If you like, though your allowance covers that. I suppose this makes your allowance viable financially to some members of the university." Megan thought Amelia should know this. She took a sip of coffee.

"Very well, now, where shall I begin?" Amelia sipped coffee and looked expectantly at Megan.

"Anywhere you like." Megan wanted Amelia to choose where to begin.

"A man landed on the moon in 1969. That was before I was born, but it's still significant." Amelia was simply telling it like it was. She sipped more coffee.

"How so?" Megan felt that this was a strange place to begin but didn't mind. She knew there was a lot about space travel that needed to be rediscovered.

"It was a human landing on another part of our solar system. My grandfather told me people were so excited by it they couldn't talk about anything else for months. And Australia played its part in tracking the brave men of Apollo, those who dared what was once only science fiction. Then there was the expectation of a man landing on Mars, but it wasn't to happen in my grandfather's lifetime."

"How sad." Megan sounded unemotional.

"It did happen in my lifetime, though. Europe was in chaos, and Southeast Asian nations were on the brink of collapse. Still, the Americans landed a man on Mars." Amelia smiled at this revelation.

"It must have been something." Megan tried to imagine what it was like. The world in turmoil and yet a Mars landing deemed so essential it went ahead.

"Oh, yes! It was one of the reasons I took up flying. I was hoping the American space academy would take me on, and I'd become an astronaut."

"Did it happen?" Megan wanted to know.

"No. The Americans did start a Mars colony, though, but after that, civil wars intensified. My government needed fighter pilots, and so I joined up." There was a touch of sadness in Amelia's voice.

"We have some records of a Mars colony, but we have had no way of contacting them for over half a century." Megan's voice was matter of fact.

"So they could still be in existence in their domed city?" Amelia sounded hopeful.

"We just don't know. We lost a lot of knowledge during the dark times. Some of it has yet to come back. This is where we hope you can help." Megan was sincere. She took off her glasses, cleaned them with a tissue, and put them back on.

"I'll do what I can," offered Amelia. "But I don't know what I can do. I was never an astronaut."

"Are there places where knowledge might have been hidden, kept safe?" asked Megan. There was hope in her voice and in her eyes.

Amelia thought about this. There had to have been sites protected from bombs and angry mobs, but where had they been? Then it came to her.

"The Mitchell Library in Sydney would be such a locale," said Amelia. "According to what you have revealed to me, Sydney was bombed after I went into my long sleep, but if any worthwhile thing survived, it would be in that library."

"We've been there recently," Megan told Amelia, wondering what could possibly be so important about the site. "It is a hole in the ground."

"The street-level library may have been destroyed, but what about the underground areas where special documents, artwork, and charts were kept?"

"So all we have to do is dig?" Megan said this slowly, as if drawn to the notion. At heart, she was an archaeologist.

"You may have to drill through concrete to get at those stores, but they will be there." Amelia was certain. She had been inside the library, and a librarian had taken her for a tour below the surface.

"In the final days of Sydney, I believe scientific research was kept there in that library," began Megan with excitement in her voice. "We have been told, via recordings made and kept in Wollongong library, they thought Mitchell Library would be more secure than the CSIRO labs. Now, thanks to you, we know why. We have no records of this underground complex you are telling me about. Where else would we find information?"

"Federal buildings in the USA, the UK, and Russia had underground bunkers." Amelia was plain-spoken in this.

"They're worth a look, too, once we can figure out where they are located. We know about Sydney from ancient maps kept for us at the old Wollongong library," reasoned Megan. "Our friends overseas are struggling to find such maps of New York, Washington, London, and Moscow."

"What about Number Ten Downing Street, London?"

"What about it? What is the significance of that address?" Megan was asking what she perceived as being a legitimate question. Amelia was open-mouthed shocked that Megan didn't already know the answer.

"It was the address in residence of every Prime Minister of Britain that I know about."

"And what is a Prime Minister?" Again, a legitimate question from Megan that left Amelia open-mouthed shocked that Megan didn't already know the answer.

"A Prime Minister is the leader in a free world. In my time, the British had a Prime Minister. In Australia, we had our own Prime Minister. During the Second World War, a bomb shelter was constructed under Number 10 Downing Street, London. It was built for Prime Minister Winston Churchill." Amelia said this slowly as if talking to a child. She still found it hard to believe Megan didn't already know all of this.

Amelia paused for a moment to gather her thoughts. "I can't tell you exactly where it was; number ten, I mean, other than that address, but it was in the heart of London not far from the Thames River."

"What do you think we might find there?" asked Megan.

"I don't know. Maybe dead flies left over from the Battle of Britain and phones no longer in service. Then again, it may have been where all sorts of useful items were stored in the last days of London." Amelia sounded hopeful.

Megan clicked off her machine and ordered two more coffees. Then, after the coffees arrived, she clicked the machine back on again.

"Tell me about war," asked Megan.

"What do you want to know?" countered Amelia.

"Why did people do it?" asked Megan.

"That's difficult to answer." Amelia stopped a moment to gather her thoughts. She drank coffee. "I'm no expert but, just before I went into my long sleep, people had been fighting for at least a decade to defend their way of life against those trying to take it all away." Amelia wanted that explanation to be the right one and that it would be well received.

"Why were these other people trying to take it all away?" Megan sounded puzzled.

"They wanted their own culture and religion to take its place. They were coming into Europe, Britain, Canada, and Australia and making unreasonable demands." Amelia remembered how some people coming in wanted to make slaves of women, and that had to be fought against. She sighed, thinking that mentioning the threat of slavery to Megan would be too much for her to take in. Maybe she would bring it up at a later time.

"Why not live and let live?" Megan was blunt.

"That was tried, but it didn't work. My people wanted our holidays, such as Christmas. Those coming in wanted to do away with them. It was all so bizarre. A political party urged the newcomers on. Even when the newly arrived showed signs of wanting to live in peace, this political party made sure there could be no peace. It got complicated very quickly." Amelia was trying to relate to Megan what her grandparents had passed on to her. She wondered if she had remembered it all correctly.

"So religion played its part?" Megan wanted to understand about the old religions and how, unlike her faith, they seemed to be all pro-war.

"Religion? Play a part? I suppose it did at that. Funny thing is not everyone born here in Australia back then had a religion, or for that matter, wanted one. We certainly didn't want someone else's beliefs forced upon us." It was the forcing upon us that Amelia emphasized.

"Did you have a religion?" Megan leaned forward for the answer. She imagined a fighter pilot would have to be religious.

"Not as such. I believe there is a greater being, but I didn't belong to any church. It just wasn't my thing, and I didn't care to be pushed into someone else's faith." Amelia emphasized the word pushed.

"Were they doing that?" Megan wanted more details on this matter.

"They were starting to do so. You were either a Christian or a Muslim. You had to pick sides. I hated it. I thought it was wrong, but I went for Christian because it offered me more freedom, and it was something I was more familiar with." Amelia emphasized the word freedom.

"What about the Martha and the Goddess?" Megan was hazy on when the belief in the Great Goddess began. Was it before, during, or after the last Great War?

"That's new to me along with knights, dragons, and mavericks." Amelia shrugged.

"You had wars all the time?" Megan was sure of this but wanted to hear it from Amelia.

"It seems that way." Amelia's voice saddened. "In the 20th century, there wasn't a ten-year period in which Australians in uniform weren't fighting somebody somewhere. The 21st century was no better though some of the battles were fought here rather than overseas." Amelia crossed her arms and sighed.

"How awful!" Megan winced. One thing she didn't want to experience was war.

"Yes, it was awful, but what you have here might be just as bad." Having said this, Amelia wanted to take it back. She didn't want either herself or Megan to get into trouble from what was being recorded. Still, it was out, and she didn't know how she could take it back without fibbing or calling upon Megan to erase the tape.

"What do you mean?" Megan didn't know what Amelia was getting at and wanted to know. She was curious rather than angry. She was almost always curious about anything to do with the past and past ways of thinking.

"You have knights battling dragons. I take it the dragons are some form of mutation. Even so, is it necessary?" Having started this line of discussion, Amelia felt it best just to plough on ahead with it, the damage already having been done.

"You still have a lot to learn. It is our way of life." Megan was firm in this; she also crossed her arms. She didn't know what a priestess would make of Amelia's words on knights and dragons, and she wasn't sure she wanted to know.

"What I don't understand is the reward system for killing dragons. Why fifty dragons? Why not make it forty or thirty or even twenty?" Now Amelia knew she was definitely out of line but felt the need to continue further.

"I don't know. I'm no theologian." Megan opened her arms and shrugged her shoulders, wondering why Amelia thought she, Megan, should have the answers to things only priestesses would know. Then again, Amelia didn't seem to know much about priestesses and their function in society.

"This has to do with theology?" Amelia sounded puzzled. She opened her arms. It was apparent that theology was far from her thoughts.

"Yes. Knights are meant to slay dragons, and the good ones are rewarded in Heaven; the very exceptional are rewarded here on earth. I will see you get a copy of the Martha Chronicles. It is written by an eminent priestess, so maybe that will help you with your understanding." Megan was being matter-of-fact.

"I am sure it will." Amelia tried to sound convincing for the recording but didn't feel that way. The emphasis was on the word *will*. She thought she had already gone too far with her brand of honesty and hoped this last bit would get herself and possibly Megan out of strife. Going against other people's beliefs, even merely questioning them, she understood, from her earlier time, could be extremely dangerous.

Megan switched off her recorder. They finished their coffee and left the coffee shop. Both were deep in thought. Megan walked Amelia back to her residence in silence.

CHAPTER FOURTEEN

Amelia was open-mouthed surprised at all the attention. Even though Megan had warned her about this, the amazement of being considered extraordinary was there in her widening eyes. She was a barbarian, an oddity from a time when the world was very different. Yet she was a maiden who had chosen a knight many respected for his feats against the dragons. Her look of astonishment at being an instant celebrity, however, didn't last long. She wouldn't let it do so. She did not want to appear frightened.

"She can't be all bad if Dreadnought is beside her," commented a maverick journalist. This remark strengthened Amelia's resolve to be brave.

The crowd was kept at bay by robots stationed at the lower steps of the university library building. They had their guns holstered, their arms spread out, forming a chain of metallic limbs. All those gathered understood, having been brought up with these mechanical wonders, that if some fool caused a disturbance or lunged toward Amelia, the guns would quickly come into play. One would hope they would be loaded with rubber bullets or gas pellets. They could just as well contain lethal rounds. What's more, the robots were designed to be experts in the use of firearms. It was far better to respect the positioning of the robots and to keep one's distance than be responsible for what might otherwise follow.

The podium and the speakers were above the robots at the entrance to the library. First, Jens spoke and then Dean Renate.

"For those who believe Amelia has come from a backward century," began Jens in a cold voice, "there's not much I can say to change your minds, so I won't bother. Amelia, however, is not backward in any way." Jens smiled, and so did Dean Renate.

Jens paused for a moment to let what she had just said sink in. There was murmuring among the gathered maidens and mavericks. Expectations among those looking on, including the journalists, were running high. Jens waved her hand for silence before continuing, and there was silence.

"Much has been lost to us during the days of widespread destruction before we found the true path," held Jens. "We know little about how our wonderful Marthas, our priestesses came to be or how Rome was eventually rescued from savagery. Perhaps Amelia can fill in some of those details. She is currently aiding us in getting some of what we lost back, and for this, we should all be grateful. I now hand you over to Dean Renate."

There was applause for Jens and also for Dean Renate. Then there was the shuffling of feet. All had come to hear the barbarian speak and not Jens or the dean. Still, they knew they had to be patient.

"We live in enlightened times." Dean Renate waved her arms as if to encompass the times of which she had spoken. The shuffling feet stopped. "Wollongong and Kiama are thriving. We still mourn for Sydney and Melbourne, but we must look forward as well as back." The dean bowed her head in mourning for the lost cities, then raised her head and smiled for the great future she could see for her beloved Wollongong.

There were sounds of approval among the crowd for what the dean had just said. Jens waved her hand for silence, and the sounds melted away.

Dean Renate continued, "Philadelphia has become the social, financial, and political centre of the old USA. Liverpool and Oxford have taken over from London. Lyon has replaced Paris. There's not much left of the Middle East, and Bali is all that remains of Indonesia. It is hard to take in the fact that there used to be billions of people living on our planet. What happened to them and why has been debated many times. Now, thanks to Amelia, we have an eyewitness to the build-up of what ultimately went wrong. She is a treasure, yes, and also a warning from long ago. I give you Amelia."

There was much applause as the dean left the podium and then silence that seemed to stretch for an age. When it came to her turn, Amelia was almost paralysed with nervousness. Once again, it hit her where she was and what she was expected to do. She was, however, willing to push herself forward, knowing that the first words she uttered would break her out of her nervousness. Amelia had felt this way before when giving talks to large groups. She understood that retreat was no good, whereas forging ahead, with lots of adrenalin pumping through her system was best.

The microphone on the stand looked old-fashioned to her, almost comical in the simplicity of its design. It was a two-hand rectangular unit with wires attached to an adjustable metal stick. It reminded her of the microphones they had in World War II movies she saw when she was studying history. Somehow the absurdity of it comforted her. Not everything in this future was as perfect as it might be. The microphone was another sign that this civilisation she was now in had made great strides in some areas of technology, such as the guardian robots. But it had drifted backward in other areas such as this device she was to talk into. There was the click and whirr of cameras and sound recording devices. They also smacked of going backward instead of forward. Just looking at them, she figured there had been better cameras and audio recording devices in the era in which she had grown up.

Amelia looked out over the crowd and saw maidens, priestesses, and mavericks. No dragons or knights were in attendance.

"I am glad to be here," began Amelia. There was applause. She waited for it to die down before continuing. Jens helped by lifting her hand for silence. "It's true. I was rescued from a life capsule. I was a fighter pilot, and now I will fly for either your government or commercially. I now have a future." There was more applause, which eventually came to an end. Here, Jens felt it best not to interfere by putting up her hand. *Let the crowd enjoy themselves.*

"Megan has helped me to come to grips with new challenges. Jens has also been of assistance. I have a charming home, and I hope the university is learning enough from me to make my stay both memorable and useful.

"From what I can gather, bombs no longer fall on cities. This is a good thing. I have been told by Megan that the world's human population is currently at around fifty million. This is a much more manageable figure than was in play the year I was born. Scientists tried to warn the powers that be that the human population going up and up by the billions every decade was not good for the planet, but they either wouldn't or couldn't listen.

"Population increases were one stimulus for war. Before I went into deep freeze, cities I knew growing up were already in ruins. London, a hole in the ground, New York reduced to shattered skyscrapers, Paris a wreck, and Washington virtually non-existent. The enemy also suffered enormous losses.

"It was mostly the enemy who had a religion which told them to have as many children as possible. Thus, they were selfish, destructive, and intrusive. They were slow to come to terms with what was then modern science and, therefore, quick to die from it. Even now, I can't feel sorry for them.

"Retaining and sustaining fifty million people is quite an achievement. Not out-growing resources, I agree, is very important. From what I have seen of your world so far, you have done well. Do you have any questions?"

There was silence for a moment while the crowd gathered their thoughts.

"What do you think of our mavericks?" asked a maverick reporter.

"I'm still getting used to the idea of mavericks," replied Amelia.

"What's there to get used to?" the reporter persisted.

"The way men are divided up is still a little strange for me," said Amelia, "but I'll adapt."

"Mavericks are strange then?" questioned the reporter.

"That's not what I meant!" Amelia glared for a moment at the reporter, then told herself not to lose her temper.

"What did you mean?" pressed the reporter.

"We didn't have mavericks and knights. We just had men."

"I don't understand," said the reporter.

"Neither do I," retorted Amelia, shaking her head, "but I am learning."

"Does anyone else have other questions for Amelia?" asked Jens.

"What were men like in your century?" asked a maiden.

"Different. I can't explain just how different." Amelia was thinking of the crazy coloured shirts and pants worn by the mavericks in the audience but felt it best not to say anything about that. She also didn't want to say she felt better in the company of men and women in Australian air force uniform than civilians in bizarre clothing.

"Why did you pick Dreadnought to be your knight?" asked the same maiden.

"He was the most suitable candidate. He's brave and has a good brain."

Some of the crowd looked shocked at this revelation, mouths dropping and heads shaking. Not many considered the possibility of a smart knight. Amelia could see it in their faces and their frowns, and so could Jens and Dean Renate.

"A good brain?" questioned the maiden.

"Yes, that's right," said Amelia.

"That's enough for today," pressed the dean. "Interview over."

There were more questions, but Amelia was hurried away before she could think to answer them. Dean Renate, with Jens' help, was spiriting Amelia into the library and out of the view of the public.

You were doing so well, Amelia, thought Jens. *Then that last bit of nonsense!* For a moment, she had on a lemon sucking face, profoundly regretting not having Megan prepare Amelia better for this occasion.

The look of momentary, though rather intense sourness on Jen's face came close to unnerving Amelia. The dean was stony-faced, unsmiling.

Amelia didn't know what she had said that could have sent both Dean Renate and Jens into such a tailspin. Megan would no doubt explain it to her later.

****

The next morning, the headline of the Wollongong Express read: "Maiden from Past Soft on Dreadnought."

There were innuendos about how close Amelia really was to her knight and whether it was proper or not. Dreadnought's thirty-nine official kills got a mention. There was also an update on just how tragic the world was before the first Martha discovered the Goddess.

Dean Renate was not happy; her voice was sharp, brittle, and to the point like an ice pick. She phoned Jens with one instruction: "Fix this!"

"How?" asked Jens.

"Get Megan to help Amelia write a suitable statement for the newspapers and television," said the dean. "Dreadnought is now too much the celebrity. The board and the High One of Wollongong have already been onto me about this.

They need assurance that Dreadnought won't be getting any more unwarranted publicity."

"I don't understand!" cried Jens, feeling set upon and not sure why.

"What don't you understand?" asked the dean frostily. "I will clarify it for you if I can."

"I still don't understand what the problem is with Dreadnought. His thirty-nine kills alone have made him popular." Jens knew she was sticking her neck out but felt she had to understand the full extent of the mess she and the dean were in. She felt if she didn't know everything she needed to know, then more mistakes might occur down the line. She didn't want to lose her position.

"Dreadnought's thirty-nine kills have made him popular, but with the knights and not so much our maidens," seethed the dean in sharp, freezing-the-blood-of-the-listener tones. "Amelia may change that."

"But what is it about Dreadnought that has you on edge?" asked Jens.

"With any luck, you will never know," said the dean, making each word sound like it came in its own ice block, and hung up.

CHAPTER FIFTEEN

Amelia was intrigued by the booklet she was given on the care and maintenance of knights. *What strange ideas*, she thought.

She had flipped through the booklet before going horse riding with Dreadnought. Now, she had sat down and read it from cover to cover.

I'm supposed to sing to my knight, learn to play a musical instrument for him, tell jokes, cook, and generally jolly him along, Amelia thought after reading the first chapter. *I'm a geisha*, she concluded, smiling. *That's what I am, and Dreadnought is my client.*

Amelia had studied Japanese culture when she was younger and knew geishas were entertainers and not prostitutes. She grinned at the notion that, during the Korean War, when Japan was a stopover to and from Korea, American servicemen no doubt went into geisha houses ending up with a bit of Japanese culture they didn't want and none of the nooky they craved.

Holding hands was acceptable, but kissing was out. Sex would lead to the maiden's disgrace, months of being shunned by other maidens, and the knight's execution. *I wasn't planning on going there anyway*, she thought.

The men here are damaged, she concluded, *the knights and dragons physically and the mavericks psychologically.*

She did not want someone who was destined to die for no good reason, someone whose body was no doubt a mess of stitches. On the other hand, a scaly reptilian being whose ancestors were human wasn't her idea of a catch.

That left the maverick whose need to please was just too sickening to consider. Malcolm was an excellent example. He was a man when he was talking about the technical issues of handling a flyer but became less so when he tried on the old charm.

If the men are not what they are supposed to be, reasoned Amelia, *what then the women?* They displayed a streak of cruelty that was reminiscent of her grandfather's stories of the women who frequented the old disco clubs of Sydney and Wollongong, only ten times worse. They enjoyed seeing men get dismembered way too much.

A passage in the knight's booklet, in chapter two, recommended a cup of your knight's blood for when you are not feeling well. It should be collected when he has sustained a blood-gushing wound or upon his death. *Wonderful!* Amelia thought. *Now I'm a vampire!* She had too much respect for Dreadnought, plus knowledge of what might be found in someone else's blood, to ever go there.

She laid aside the booklet and tried to get some sleep for the following day's activities. Before climbing into bed for shut-eye, she fluffed her pillow.

The next morning, she got her pilot's licence off Malcolm and her first assignment from the government. With the licence came the weekly salary of two hundred dollars. This payment was considered, by maidens and mavericks alike, to be quite a sum.

For her first outing as an official pilot, she was to fly Dreadnought and four other knights to England for a bout with five English dragons. Megan would go along to provide company for Amelia, other than Dreadnought, and to prevent any international misunderstandings from getting out of hand. Megan and Amelia decided to stop off in Hawaii before going on to Liverpool.

Why give such a long trip to, by all accounts, a relatively inexperienced flyer pilot such as Amelia? Megan wondered, joining Amelia, Dreadnought, and the other knights at the airfield. Megan wanted to say something about this to Amelia, warn her that things may not be right, but couldn't bring herself to do it. She knew from previous conversations how much Amelia enjoyed flying. Still, Megan reasoned, there had to be some differences between the kind of military jet Amelia used to fly and a modern flyer. Also, she suspected that the skies were not as friendly as they once were in that earlier time.

I am an inexperienced pilot on a flyer, Amelia thought as she greeted Megan and the knights on the airfield. *Why have I been given such a long trip? I thought they'd start me off on small hops such as a trip from Wollongong to Kiama. Malcolm's free, and I bet he's already done this long trip plenty of times. Surely, he is familiar with the hazards I might face. Still, I am thrilled at the prospect of being in the air for such a long period. Ah, well, I haven't questioned it or turned it down, when maybe I could have, but I do wonder why me and not someone more knowledgeable.*

Dreadnought also harboured doubts. *A crash landing at sea would be the perfect way of getting rid of both myself and Amelia,* Dreadnought thought grimly. *How this might come to pass would not be looked into in any great detail if certain maidens and priestesses had their way.*

Amelia was smart enough to look over the engines and the general structure of the flyer for problems before takeoff. This was something she had been trained to do as an Australian air force pilot on fighter aircraft. She insisted on being able to do so with the flyer when she was in training with Malcolm. Everything checked out perfectly.

One of the maverick airfield mechanics made sure there was plenty of fuel, and Dreadnought and two other knights kept an eye on him for signs of betrayal. In particular, they watched the hands of this maverick to make sure he didn't sneak in contaminants such as sugar or soil into the feed. They knew enough to realise that if you put something in an engine that shouldn't be there, it could result in disaster. Dreadnought had once seen a maiden put sugar into the engine of a car to stop a maverick from winning a car race. Dreadnought didn't tell anyone why that engine conked out; it wasn't his place to do so. But the knowledge stayed with him, and he passed it on to his fellow knights.

Dreadnought told the maverick handling the fuel that if it was discovered they suddenly ran out of power, or there were elements that shouldn't have been there in the mix, a knight who had not gone on this trip would cut his throat. The maverick took this threat seriously; Dreadnought could see it in his eyes.

Once in the air, Amelia plotted a computer course for Honolulu. She turned the radio on for information about tides and wind direction. There was talk of a storm front building up that offered a rough ride halfway to their first stop, but she considered this nothing major to worry about.

"The flyer's built to handle heavy rain," Amelia told her passengers. "She won't melt."

"What about a lightning strike?" Dreadnought asked.

"They're rare," said Amelia. "If we were hit by one, it would fry our computer control and our radio, but we'd still be able to fly."

"How do you know?" asked Megan.

"I've read the flyer's manual," said Amelia, wondering just how accurate the manual happened to be.

It was a beautiful, sunny day when they left Wollongong air space. Bad weather didn't seem much of a possibility despite what she heard over the radio. Over the ocean, all was calm without a ripple on the water or a cloud in the sky. The blueness of the water almost matched that of the air to where it took a sharp eye and computer information from the console to tell them apart.

There's a growing vacuum, thought Amelia, *It's the so-called calm before the storm. This vacuum, this calm, needs to be filled by something, and it will be by thunder, lightning, and a lot of rain. I can sense it from my days as a military pilot flying over Bass Strait. Now I am not in doubt about that radio warning of approaching severe weather.*

When, according to the fuel gauge, they were too far out to turn back, dark clouds formed. Amelia did her best to avoid flying into the centre of what was eventuating. Still, it was nearly impossible to work out just where the heart of the climate monster was when it continually shifted. Then they were in the darkness looking for a way out, the rain pelting down. White fluffiness to Amelia's left, which might have been a cloud, offered the best option until it turned out to be a giant albatross, which was also, no doubt, looking for an escape from the blackness.

It was the biggest damned bird that those aboard the flyer had ever seen. It was larger than the flyer, unlike a typical albatross from Amelia's earlier life. She gathered the beak, solid looking and no doubt powered by jaws that could snap tight, was capable of ripping up their craft without much effort, and she was now flying right at it. She veered away in time not to come into contact with it, but not before the bird took the flyer to be a threat. It was at this moment Amelia wished she was in her old fighter jet with missiles at the ready. Lightning lit up the face of the albatross, and it looked angry, eyes narrowing.

Amelia put some speed between her craft and that of the albatross and, just when she thought she had lost it, that giant feathered creature struck. A massive claw thumped down on the roof, causing the flyer to totter. It struck again and again. Amelia put the craft into a climb to get away, but the bird was in close pursuit. There was every chance it could out climb the flyer. Amelia levelled off, and the flyer was struck once more, causing it to drop, almost to fall into the water below. It took every effort on Amelia's part to avoid the flyer ending up a sinking wreck. "It can't take much more of this," cried Megan. "Do something!"

"We can't run," said Amelia.

"So it's hopeless?" cried Megan, picking up her fallen glasses and putting them back on.

"Not hopeless," said Amelia.

She flew the craft in a tight semi-circle then tilted the flyer until it was in a vertical position. The flyer was generally oval-shaped with jets and swept-back wings for added manoeuvrability. Along its centre was a hard steel joint Amelia felt could be of use. As the bird came at them again, she sped at the creature's stomach. The impact jolted everyone aboard, but it also gave the albatross a tummy ache it would not soon forget. The bird backed off, and the flyer was free to resume its course.

"When you can't retreat, you attack!" cried Dreadnought.

"That's it," said Amelia.

"No offence," offered Dreadnought, smiling, "but you would make a marvellous knight."

"How rude you are, knight," Megan admonished Dreadnought coolly as she put her glasses back on after having had them jolted off her face. "Especially coming after she has just saved our lives."

"My apologies," said Dreadnought. He didn't feel much like apologising but, at the same time, he didn't want future trouble with Megan.

"No need." Amelia sighed. "I know it was meant as a compliment."

"I have the right maiden," Dreadnought mused. He wondered if it was all right to say that with Megan around, but he meant it. The other knights smiled and quietly nodded in agreement.

Hawaii, from the air, was everything Amelia remembered it being. It looked like paradise. As she came into Honolulu, there was little turbulence and not much traffic.

A reporter at the airport, with black, slicked back hair, wanted to know more about Amelia and Dreadnought. She walked up to Amelia first and then Dreadnought, hoping for exclusives for her paper and possibly the weekend magazine put out by her publisher.

"I have nothing to say," Dreadnought said, waving the reporter away.

"No comment," Amelia told her and walked on.

At the restaurant where they were to have their first meal, Megan found shark mentioned a couple of times as a main dish. "Why is shark so popular here?" she asked a knightly waiter. He told her that shark, prepared one way or another, was the main dish at most of the restaurants in Honolulu.

"I'm not surprised," said Amelia. "Most of these restaurants are seaside establishments, and various types of shark have been around a lot longer than humans. What's more, they are likely to continue to be around long after humans have gone for good."

The memorial to the USS Arizona was still there, but no one knew what it meant since the memorial plaques had been eroded by age and saltwater. Amelia was able to fill Megan in on details of America's entry into the Second World War, and Megan taped the information for Wollongong University.

"Americans were reluctant to enter that war?" asked Megan.

"Yes," said Amelia, "but after being bombed by the Japanese here in Hawaii, they felt they had no choice."

"Now we are free of war," enthused Megan.

"Yes," agreed Amelia. "I suppose we are that if nothing else."

Maidens bathed along the beach in either bikinis or one-piece bathing suits. A local maverick tourist guide told Amelia and her companions that there had once been fierce fighting to preserve this right and other rights.

"Some people who came from Malaysia wanted our maidens in chains," the guide told them, "but our knights changed their minds for them. They thought they could sneak in after dark and take our women away with them without a fight, but they were wrong. It was the start of those civil wars between Nationals and Globalists that are in the history books. Well, our knights, time and time again, thrashed those Malaysian Globalists, and that's the truth."

"I bet they did," said Amelia, looking at Dreadnought,

who was clearing his throat. It was then Amelia got the impression that at least one knight didn't care for mavericks telling such stories. No doubt, he felt they were not entitled to do so since they didn't fight. The other knights preferred to look away from the guide. They didn't want to betray their feelings on the matter. They wanted to remain neutral.

Amelia found the local beer weak, but she didn't say anything. She had no desire to offend anyone. She drank it anyway. It was virtually tasteless, so no sour face, just a sigh. It was hot, and she longed for the kind of brew that used to come up from Victoria on those long, sweltering summer days to quench the thirst of those serving in the armed forces in New South Wales. In Australia, the art of making good beer had survived in Wollongong but not further south in Melbourne and not north in Queensland.

She remembered reports of London breweries and pubs being closed down because of religious fanaticism. The result was rioting to the point where the rebels took over and kicked out the fanatics. That happened months before London was devastated. The bombing was an object lesson to those who wanted to be free. The people of Australia, who had connections to the British rebellion, took it hard and wanted to help the remaining English rebels any way they could in their fight. *It was all such a mess*, thought Amelia, *and the fault of the so-called United Nations of the day, which was soon disbanded. What were they thinking? Whatever it was, it was wrong.*

The flight out of Honolulu was uneventful. The repairs needing to be done to the flyer because of the giant albatross were completed with care and efficiency. A few dents had to be straightened out for it to be airworthy. Dreadnought and two of the other knights had kept a close eye on the maverick who was putting the fuel in, but they knew they couldn't make any threats that would stick. Even so, they did make the maverick nervous. They knew, by the fear in his eyes that he wasn't going to put any contaminants in while they were watching him.

Amelia did a flight check, and they were off. There were clouds in the sky but no sign of rain or dangerous birdlife. Seagulls followed them out for a short distance before turning back.

From Hawaii to St. Louis was about the same distance that they had already travelled. The manual said it could be done with fuel to spare, and so far, it had been right. Still, Amelia knew it was not wise to be running close to empty when coming into an airfield or landing pad. There might be several aircraft coming in, and you might be placed in a landing queue. With this in mind, she climbed and levelled off at a height where there would be less wind resistance and, therefore, better fuel consumption.

Soon clouds gathering below them cut into their ability to see the waves. Then the radio started cutting out, words from the Hawaiian radio station went missing, then there was nothing but static. Amelia tried to pick up mainland USA, but that was also no good. She switched the radio off, pronouncing it useless. "I'll try it again later," she told Megan and the others.

Amelia began to rely more and more on her computer for information on direction. This was a mistake. When a mountainous island appeared out of the soft, fluffy white, she understood they had gone off course for the USA and were no doubt going toward Mexico. She headed in what was, in all likelihood, north with her fingers crossed, hoping the clouds would clear again. They cleared once, showing a landmass, but there was no indication of where they were.

"What's wrong?" asked Dreadnought.

"While we were sightseeing, someone tampered with the navigation centre of our onboard computer," said Amelia. "I tested it all before takeoff, and it seemed okay. I take it they loosened things up so that enough motion from the flyer would result in the situation we're in. At any rate, my best guess. Also, the radio's now completely dead. I tried it a moment ago and it's gone, not even a static hiss. I imagine a slow-acting acid might have been the trick here. Megan, Dreadnought, everyone, look for landmarks when I descend. We need information the computer can no longer provide."

It was a risky business diving down below the cloud layer. There was the possibility of running into a hill, a bridge, or a building. Still, it had to be done. On the first try, Amelia narrowly missed a weather balloon. On the second go, she almost hit a tree, but Megan was able to garner some information from nearby housing.

"We're headed for Lake City," said Megan. "We can put down there. They have an airfield."

"Good," said Amelia, "we will keep going in our present direction."

The clouds eventually left them, and Megan was able to fix the radio with electrical tape kept in the pilot's glove compartment well enough to send and receive a message. Amelia was surprised at Megan's ability to do this. "I have learned a thing or two from Malcolm," she told Amelia. This was followed by a canny smile.

The area around Lake City airfield was cleared of traffic as Amelia made an emergency landing. They refuelled at Lake City, had both the radio and computer repaired, and paid a late visit to St. Louis where they spent the night. They found the hotel they had been booked into; all but two of them drifted off to sleep to the sound of jazz playing in a cafe below them.

Two of Dreadnought's companion knights decided to stay in the flyer overnight to make sure there would not be any more sabotage. They gave up more comfortable accommodation to keep everyone safe. Dreadnought was proud of them and said so to Amelia. She agreed with him and, at the same time, regretted not having had much to do with the other knights. In truth, she couldn't help it. It was the fear of forming close attachments to those not long for this world.

Amelia wondered if it was a good idea to get too close to

Dreadnought. Even so, she couldn't help but imagine holding his hand and even kissing lightly the scar on his face as if a kiss could make it better.

The flight from St. Louis to Liverpool, England, went without incident. To everyone's relief, both the computer and radio worked the way they were supposed to.

England was different from what Amelia thought it would be. "Where are all the buildings?" asked Amelia as they were coming into Liverpool.

"What buildings?" Megan wondered what Amelia expected to see.

"Never mind," said Amelia.

Their flyer taxied to a stop, and everyone got out. They were greeted by representatives of the Liverpool Gaming Board and were told where and when the knights had to report for the scheduled battle with Liverpool dragons.

"For now, you are all free to explore our wonderful city," a maverick in bright reds, oranges, and whites told them, waving his hands about.

After securing her flyer in a hanger, Amelia joined the others in the airport lounge for coffee. Megan had a guide to the city booklet she had gotten off a newsagent and was studying it. After Amelia had bought a coffee for herself and sat down, Megan switched on her tape recorder. "Now tell me what Liverpool is supposed to be like."

"Reports from my time had Liverpool as a grimy, overly industrialized city. Its economy collapsed when the shipbuilding and repair trade fell off, and warehousing wasn't enough business to keep the major players going."

"How sad," Megan sighed. She looked at her guide but found no references to this.

"There had been improvements made to the city in the early 21st century. It had thrived for a time, but that came to an end when civil war broke out."

"That was the business between the Nationals and the Globalists?" asked Megan. There was mention of this in the guide booklet.

"Yes," said Amelia. "Through all of that strife, the legend of the Beatles kept the tourists coming, or so I have been told. I admit I was somewhat sceptical about this in history class. I wonder if those tourists were really coming and are still coming to Liverpool."

Megan leafed through the guide and was open-mouthed surprised to find a reference to these Beatles.

After a pause for a sip of coffee, Amelia asked, "What does that booklet tell you about modern-day Liverpool?"

"In this new age, Liverpool has gone back to shipbuilding and warehousing in a big way. Goods from Britain and Europe are once more flowing back and forth to America and further south to Australia and New Zealand. The population is half the size it had been, but it's comfortably busy and prosperous."

"That makes sense," said Amelia. "What about all the buildings I was expecting to see as we came in?"

"With the population not growing, old buildings that have no historical significance have been pulled down. Strawberry Fields, a place made popular by the Beatles, has been extended to where it is now a much more magnificent park. A statue of the Beatles is at one of the entrances. Here, the wildlife is flourishing, including the famous blackbirds and also the liver birds the place was originally named after."

Megan put down the booklet and smiled.

"Why not find out about Liverpool for ourselves instead of just relying on that booklet?" suggested Dreadnought since he and the other knights had drunk their coffee and were getting restless.

"Yes, of course," said Amelia. "We've hung around here long enough." Megan clicked off her tape recorder.

Amelia, the knights, and Megan spent half a day wandering about the docks and the new swamplands. Then they received a message from a maverick to go to their designated hotel and await instructions on the upcoming match everyone was anticipating.

"I wish it weren't so," said Amelia confidentially to Dreadnought.

"I know," answered Dreadnought.

The idea of flying people to their doom did not sit well with Amelia. It didn't seem real when they were travelling, though she knew what was going to happen from the start.

This is not like launching missiles and dropping bombs from on high, she thought. *This is far too personal*. It seemed so justified in taking out an enemy population that threatened your way of life. What was happening now, though, wasn't like that at all.

A judge for the contest met Amelia and her party at Amelia's hotel room with a disc she shoved into a machine for viewing purposes. The television screen lit up and showed first an old, battered ship and then its hull.

"The venue for the match is the rusty interior of a once magnificent ship," the judge in her priestess robes told them. "Everything has been taken out to give both knights and dragons plenty of room to move about. There are cameras and lighting overhead and close to the bottom plates. As you can see, there are two entrances to the hull. The knights will enter via the left, and the dragons via the right. Stairs are leading down on both sides."

Amelia moaned out loud, astonished that men were going to end their lives in such a place. When eyes were on her, she stopped making those sounds and clasped her hands together instead.

Megan seemed okay with the site. She barely glanced at it. The knights looked stoic as if made of wood or steel. It didn't seem to matter much to them where they were supposed to fight. They knew the venue wasn't up to them and that complaining did no good. They also had pride in who they were and in how they should behave. Some, no doubt, were thinking of the promised afterlife and all its riches.

"The hull will have water added," said the judge after a moment's silence. "Your knights will climb down and stand with the water up to their chests."

"Why?" asked Megan.

"Why add water?" the judge mused, her voice indicating a one-sided joke. "Our dragons are amphibians. They do best in water."

"But even in May, if the water comes from the river, it will be freezing," said Megan.

"Yes," agreed the judge. "But, our dragons are used to the cold."

"Is this what you call fair?" cried Amelia.

"You knew the conditions beforehand." The judge shrugged.

"Only just beforehand," said Amelia.

"This was agreed upon before you left Wollongong," said the judge. "The information was sent to your High Priestess and approved."

"But we personally didn't know about it until now!" cried Amelia, red-faced, fighting back the tears of outrage. Her knuckles turned white from curling up her fingers into tight fists.

"A pity," stated the judge. "If you are concerned about the visuals, I can assure you the cameras and lights situated at both the top and the bottom are waterproof so you will get to see everything from the comfort of an observation room or if you prefer, your hotel rooms. If you pull out now, this may be seen as an international incident. The Highest One would be notified."

"And what would come out of that?" asked Amelia.

"I can only guess what the Highest One would have in mind," said the judge in a playful voice. "I'd say these knights of yours, without swords or shields, would be fed to mutated nameless creatures far fiercer than our dragons."

"That's outrageous!" cried Amelia, wanting to hit the judge

but knowing that would not help.

"Shall I go on?" the judge asked. She smiled broadly at Amelia as if daring her to do something stupid.

"Yes," said Megan. "Please do." She needed to know the worst of it.

"For maidens and mavericks deemed responsible for interference in the games, the mavericks would be demoted to knights and the maidens banned from every important role in government. This would be for life. Oh, and it would be some time before representatives from Australia are invited to England again. Is any of that what you want?"

"Of course not!" cried Megan. The threat of being taken away from her work at the Mitchell Library was all too real to her. "If our High Priestess found the arrangements suitable, then we will go along with her decision."

"Good!"

The judge switched off the disc and took it out of the machine.

"Good luck to your knights," added the judge. "I believe they will need all the luck they can get."

"Our usual armour will not be suitable," said Dreadnought once the door had closed, and the sound of the judge's shoes could no longer be heard.

"We'll get you and your fellow knights wetsuits," offered Megan.

"And short spears if at all possible," said Dreadnought. "The swords and maces we have brought with us may prove to be too bulky in the water."

"We'll see what we can do," Megan assured him.

"The cold will make us sluggish," grumbled one of the other knights.

"That can't be helped," said Dreadnought, who understood what sluggishness meant in a fight. He was still wooden, in control, but there was a waver in his voice indicating that there was underlying tension he kept caged no doubt for the sake of the other knights. If nothing else, he wished to give a good example worth imitating of how he felt a knight should behave. Dreadnought knew, from lots of experience, that it is the slow movers who are generally killed off first in battle and, understandably, he was afraid of being such a knight.

The wetsuits and short spears were quickly purchased. Megan managed to find some leather vests that would not offer the same protection against knife and sword as heavier steel plate but would at least offer something. Luckily, they had the money for added expenses, and the exchange rate of currency wasn't too bad.

Amelia, Megan, and the knights made their way to the derelict ship in plenty of time.

Before they went into the hull, Dreadnought's fellow knights pinned onto their vests the tokens of affection their maidens had given them, just for this occasion, before leaving Australia. They were colourful handkerchiefs and ribbons. Upon seeing a look of uncertainty take shape on Dreadnought's face, Amelia took off her scarf and tied it around his neck. "My token," she told him. "Now, be safe."

He smiled a thank you. "I will try."

Strangely enough, Amelia hadn't noticed these tokens before when she saw knights battling dragons but, then again, she hadn't been looking out for them. She wondered how many maidens wanted their knights to come back alive.

It was a short walk along a gangway to where the knights climbed down into the water. It was just as quick a walk for the dragons. Amelia and Megan watched them in the viewing room with the judge. It was the captain's cabin converted for that purpose.

The dragons were black-scaled but, unlike the ones in Australia, had smaller tails without spikes. They also had gills and could breathe underwater as well as on land. They had cutlasses and daggers. One had a trident, and another had a net. None of them wore pain collars. Amelia gathered it was traditional to have them removed before they were expected to go into action. As the dragons took to the water, it became apparent their blackness blended in so well with the water it made them, once submerged, almost invisible.

Robots gave the knights little choice but to enter. Once in, the knights formed a circle with their spears and shields. All were breathing heavily from the chill. The dragons glided in, and it was difficult from then on to pinpoint their positions. A bell rang, and the battle commenced.

The knights did their best to follow any movement they could detect in the murk, a minor ripple being a clue to where a dragon might be found.

Suddenly, a dragon leaped out of the water, grabbed a young knight's shield, and threw it aside. Before this now shield-less knight could react with his spear, the dragon was gone back into the water. A second dragon then came at him with a cutlass and slit his stomach wide open. The young knight, bewildered by the swiftness and the savagery of these actions, gasped. His eyes virtually popped out of his head as his blood and guts coloured the artificial pool. This second dragon also went successfully into hiding in the covering depths. Meanwhile, the young knight fell face down and thus perished.

The knights closed ranks, looking for a sign as to where the next attack would come from. For too many minutes, all was calm when an old knight felt a claw grasping his left leg. He speared downwards and managed to get through the scales to the dragon's heart. In seconds, the enemy popped to the surface, spurting blood. A second thrust to the neck made sure the dragon was dead.

Dreadnought tossed his spear into what appeared to the other knights to be nothing but water. The result was a dragon coming to the surface with a spear through his right shoulder. It was amazing anyone could throw with such force with the pool hampering their effort. Even so, the wounded dragon ripped the spear out and threw it back at Dreadnought. He somehow was able to catch it in the air before it hit either his person or his shield. Another dragon, who thought he saw a chance of taking out an unarmed knight, broke surface and came at Dreadnought with his glistening daggers. Before he realized his error, this dragon was first battered by Dreadnought's shield and then ran through by Dreadnought's spear.

For at least twenty minutes, nothing was happening. The dragons must have understood that the temperature was weakening the knights and so planned to let it do so.

At last, a claw came out of the water and with it a blade. The dagger flew and struck a knight, who had let his guard down, in the chest. Two spears found the offending dragon and dispatched him. Both wounded knight and dragon soon died.

Unexpectedly, a dragon surfaced and was thus in plain sight. At the same time, Dreadnought noticed two hands wielding a trident moving toward him. A spear thrust missed the upright dragon, and a net came out of the water to entangle the knight standing to Dreadnought's left. Shield and spear were dropped, making the entangled knight easy prey for a dozen killer dagger thrusts. Meanwhile, Dreadnought watched the trident draw closer to his position.

At the right moment, Dreadnought tossed aside his shield and spear and dove for the trident. He reefed it away from its owner and stabbed him with it. Next, he picked up his shield in time to avoid a dragon's dagger. Then the trident went to work again and dealt with that dragon. This was the dragon he had wounded earlier in the shoulder but was now no more. Dreadnought gave a deep sigh when he realized that was the last of the enemy.

Slowly, Dreadnought and the other surviving knight emerged from the hull. Their lips were blue and their feet and hands a pale white. The wetsuits they were wearing only gave so much protection, none unfortunately to their hands and feet.

Amelia didn't know what to say when she met up with Dreadnought and his companion. She offered them towels she had on standby, and they took them. Dreadnought tried to say something, but he just didn't have the strength. Both knights collapsed and were taken to hospital. Neither had been severely wounded. Both knights needed warmth, hot liquids, and rest.

"Patched up again," said Dreadnought the next day when Amelia and Megan visited him and the other combatant. It didn't matter that at this time, neither Dreadnought nor the other knight required stitches.

"From that fight, you gained three official kills." Megan smiled.

"That brings my total to forty-two," said Dreadnought. "Now, there are only eight more to go."

The journey back to Wollongong via St. Louis and Hawaii was uneventful. It marked the end of May. Officially, it would be another six months before knights from anywhere would clash with dragons for the amusement of maidens and mavericks. In those months, Amelia hoped to find out more about the origins of these sick contests.

****

Meanwhile, Jens confronted Dean Renate in her office. There was fire in Jens' eyes, like the blaze from a black opal with red and blue lightning fighting for dominance in the heart of the stone. For once, she didn't give a damn about her job. Megan had been with her too long just to have her thrown away in some savage manner. For the Goddess' sake, Megan was a maiden, not a knight or a dragon!

"Did you try to have Amelia and Dreadnought killed?" demanded Jens. "If so, I did not appreciate you putting Megan and Amelia in such danger!"

"Calm down," said the dean in a soft tone, motioning Jens

to be seated before she wrecked her career by possibly threatening a superior. The dean knew there was a time to rigidly demand loyalty. And there was a time to bend a little so as not to have to break a more than competent worker. The dean knew Jens had a future and wanted her to keep it. She would put up with a little bit of emotional nonsense from Jens, but not too much.

"All right!" snapped Jens, sitting down. She leaned forward, glaring at Dean Renate. "Tell me why? Why put those maidens in such danger?"

"The incidents on the way to the match in Liverpool, England were not my idea." The dean coolly waved her hand as if brushing it all aside. "Blame members of the council for them. My hands are clean."

"You have it in for Dreadnought!" Jens was still seething.

"True," the dean agreed in a more frigid voice, warning Jens her patience did have its limits. "But I don't want the death of Amelia if it can be helped, though others might, and I certainly have nothing against your assistant Megan. Unfortunately, others feel differently."

"Can you name these others?" asked Jens, much of the fire in her gone.

"They are council members," said the dean. "That is all I will tell you. It is none of your business and shall stay that way. Oh, and by the way, don't you ever come bursting into my office like that again! It is fortunate for you I understand your feelings so well."

"The fight in England was unfair," said Jens in a matter of fact voice, understanding that her recent behaviour with the dean had been incorrect. "I can see the dragons were meant to win."

"That's true." The dean's eyes now blazed with anger and frustration. "I thought I had arranged an apt death for Dreadnought, but it didn't work out that way."

"No." Jens shook her head sadly. "It didn't. Now he has a score of forty-two."

CHAPTER SIXTEEN

On the night of the seventh of June, Megan took Amelia to a singles party hosted by a maiden and her maverick.

Knightly waiters served up oysters, prawns, and mullet cooked in a light batter, and chocolate pudding for dessert. There was a brilliant white wine with the main meal and coffee to follow.

All eyes were on Amelia, who had shown no interest in any of the mavericks she met. She was polite but abrupt. Their outlandishly colourful clothes reminded her of male peacocks or male spoonbills that put on a white, feathery headdress during mating season. Their talk reminded her of young magpies chattering away for attention. The only slight exception was Camden Miller, a tall fellow in his mid-twenties, in a black and white suit that might not have been an eyesore except for the bright orange crisscrossing it. Camden talked about the stock market. It was wonderful, at first, to hear something practical rather than flattery coming out of a maverick's mouth.

Amelia surprised Camden over coffee with her questions. She wanted to find some common ground with these mavericks since this was the world in which she now lived.

"In my past life," began Amelia, "the market relied as much on population growth as it did on any other kind of growth. Here, however, you don't have population growth. How does it work then?"

"As radiation levels recede," said Camden, "new areas open up for settlement. Maids, mavericks, and their servants are then encouraged to move out of the major cities and towns to these places. Then there are houses to be built, transport to be organized, and lots more to be done. Thus, there is growth of a sort, but not reliant on population increases."

"Won't depleting the city's population create problems?" asked Amelia.

"Not everyone will want to move. Besides, some of our cities could still do with thinning out. More parks for everyone, less built-up areas, that sort of thing." Camden smiled a devilish smile, no doubt thinking about making more money.

"There has to be more to it," reasoned Amelia. She gave Camden a half-smile to get him to talk more on the subject.

"In various parts of the world, such as Norway, Russia, and below us in Victoria, seed banks have been discovered. Varieties of plants that haven't been around for a while are making a comeback. As radiation levels drop, there's more planting and not just of species that will feed us. There are shade and beauty also to be considered." Camden returned to his devilish smile.

"So there's a different outlook on supply and demand." Amelia shrugged her shoulders and frowned slightly.

"Yes," agreed Camden, beaming and feeling very much in his element.

"And with a readymade force of slave labour, too," commented Amelia, then wishing she hadn't said that even if it was true. Camden looked shocked, his mouth opened for a moment without words coming out, and his eyes widened.

"Slave labour?" cried Camden, getting red-faced. "What do you mean? We do not have slaves! They are a thing of the past!" Camden brushed the notion of slavery away with his hand.

"The knights and the dragons fit that bill," said Amelia, feeling she shouldn't back down on this issue now that she had started. "Neither knights nor dragons are expected to live long enough to get degrees or to otherwise chase down dreams of a better life, so why not get them to do the menial tasks you would prefer not to do?"

"They are not slaves!" cried Camden indignantly, more red-faced and feeling attacked. "They have free will ten months out of the year. The pain collars on the dragons are for your protection. It is just that neither knight nor dragon is equipped for higher thinking."

"Do you really believe that?" asked Amelia. "I bet you they don't get paid nearly as much as you do for what they do."

"We all have our part to play in society," said Camden airily, losing some of his anger. "Thank the Goddess I was fortunate to have a leading role."

"Others were not so lucky." Amelia crossed her arms and frowned at Camden, who folded his arms and glared back at her. It was at this point Megan felt she had to intervene and drag Amelia out of the social mess into which she had gotten into. Mavericks and maidens were chattering in tight little groups about what was going on between Camden and Amelia. Fans held by mavericks and maidens were being waved about, and noses were rising in, no doubt, contempt of Amelia's impertinence. Slavery indeed!

"I am not a Globalist!" cried Camden huffily.

"Okay," agreed Amelia, understanding the reference, "you're not a Globalist. They prefer black to what you're wearing." Amelia thought this a cheap shot at Camden but didn't regret taking it.

"Let's go!" cried Megan, grabbing Amelia by the arm and taking her to the door. At first, Amelia resisted then, when she looked at the faces of disapproval around her, decided it was better to go along with Megan than to stay.

"Should I thank our hosts for a wonderful party?" asked Amelia as they got closer to the door.

"I don't think that is appropriate," said Megan. "As you probably know from your earlier time, there used to be slaves,

many of them female. That was back in the days of the Globalists. We know that from history, even someone like Camden.
We have lots of details missing from that period, sure, but that
isn't one of them. It would do you well to remember we do not
have slavery here anymore."

Megan knew Amelia had shocked many of the guests
and had offended at least one with her talk about slavery. Everyone there was against the traditional form, but not the current
type, as recognized by Amelia. They had lived with it for too
long to see it as immoral.

On the walk back to Amelia's place, Megan asked, "What
was that all about? Were you trying to make yourself unpopu-
lar?" Megan looked flustered. She was still taken aback by what
Amelia told Camden. She knew it would get around.

"There was a time," said Amelia, "when the truth was
such a threat to governing bodies, they made a law against it."

"So what if they did?" pressed Megan, getting her curiosity back and losing some of her fluster. She adjusted her glasses.

"When the people had to eventually face what had been
done to them and supposedly for them," said Amelia, "the only
response possible was civil unrest, mob uprisings, and, in the
end, divided nations."

Megan clicked on her recorder and beckoned Amelia to
sit down with her on a nearby park bench.

"Tell me about it," beckoned Megan. She felt that Jens
might separate her from Amelia after that party debacle, so she
thought it best to get what she could now on her tape recorder.

"Not much to tell from my point of view," said Amelia.
"In Australia, I was at the tail end of it. The big clean up, you
might say."

"And how did that go?"

"A fellow pilot by the name of Sam Grieves, who was in
charge of a military helicopter, told me all about it from his end."

"And what was his end then?"

"Not always were bombs or missiles required. Sometimes the enemy just needed to be strafed from the air with withering machinegun fire. He'd bring his aircraft in low, risking a ground to air missile launcher attack as he did so, for his gunner to get a good aim."

"Good aim at the enemy?"

"Yes. Efforts were made not to kill non-combatants, but the enemy was often not in uniform and so were hard to spot. So the gunner aimed at the black flags with the squiggly writing."

"The enemy's flag."

"Yes. On one mission, it was a road heading toward the Gold Coast in Queensland, columns of people waving those flags went down in a hail of gunfire. Later Sam, the pilot, was to learn that many of those carrying the flags were forced to do so. They were men, women, and children made over into slaves by the armed despots who did so in the name of their god. He was devastated by what he and his gunner had done. He would have happily killed those despots, but not civilians caught up in someone else's madness." Amelia sighed deeply, feeling Sam's pain all over again. The Sam she knew was gentle and didn't want to be responsible for any killing, especially when those killed were innocent. The gunner, no doubt, had felt even worse.

"But that's war." Megan shrugged her shoulders, indicating it couldn't happen in her lifetime, and it, therefore, had a certain irrelevance to today. She felt the need to distance herself from such horror, but, as someone fascinated by history, she knew she would soon get back into it. There was a lot to rediscover.

"Yes. But it didn't start that way. People saw the tragedy unfolding early enough to stop it without much bloodshed, but had their voices silenced by the ignorant fools and the power-hungry. Everything will be all right, they were told. Only everything would not be all right. And now we have your world." Amelia shook her head and smiled at Megan.

"Where war no longer exists. By the way, how did Sam find out the people he had helped kill were not all the enemy?" Megan's curiosity was climbing.

"Later on, the bodies were examined. On some were found small crosses hidden away, on others tiny bibles. Many were in chains. There were men and women dressed like Buddhist monks and a few fellows who were Sikhs by the clothes they were wearing. Making them march and keeping them in line with guns, were a few of the real enemy now dead beside them. "Amelia showed the futility of it all with her open hands.

"How awful." Megan was glad she had the tape recorder going.

"Tell me, has there ever been a knight or dragon uprising?" Amelia looked carefully into Megan's eyes for honesty in the reply.

"There was unrest among the knights when I was a girl. But that unpleasantness was easily put down by our armed robots. As for our dragons, well, they wouldn't dare." Megan was matter of fact about this, as if it was inconsequential.

"No, the dragons wouldn't rise up, not with the pain collars around their necks." Amelia's voice was cold.

"And what about your part in the horrors of the past?" Megan was getting flustered again.

"I fought for my people. Now I am here." Amelia was off-handed about this, her voice flat. Yes, she had fought for her people, and it was appropriate to do so back then.

****

The following day, Megan was called into Jens' office to review the recording she had made on that park bench. There was coffee and biscuits, so it was to be a friendly get-together.

"A picture of the past is emerging," Jens told Megan. "You are doing a good job of getting information out of Amelia. Some of it is quite disturbing."

"I am sorry about what happened at the party," offered Megan, feeling it should be brought out in the open. "Amelia wasn't ready. Camden could make trouble."

"Relax. You are still working with Amelia. I have dealt with Camden. Our university has financial interests in some of his building projects. An apology from me has proven to be sufficient. As for Amelia, you'll have to do better in tutoring her on current etiquette. She cannot be allowed to keep on insulting prominent mavericks, even if they are pompous in the extreme." Jens waved her hand as if the matter was now closed.

"Do you know anything about why our flyer was sabotaged?" asked Megan, changing the subject but also wanting to know the answer.

"No idea at all," said Jens, straight-faced in her lie. "I do regret that it did happen. I am sure it is being investigated. Even so, we may never know the why of it. Getting back to what we were talking about, Amelia was rather inept at the singles party you took her to."

"Yes," agreed Megan. "Our barbarian maiden does have a way of upsetting people and also getting them to think. She hasn't done any major harm so far from what you have told me."

"Maids and mavericks alike now see her as a bit of an oddity," concluded Jens, shaking her head and smiling. "After that party, and this may be a bonus, they won't take her too seriously as a fine catch for some maverick."

"Yes. That's what I believe, too," said Megan. "Her earlier life must have been terrible."

CHAPTER SEVENTEEN

It was the second week in June, and Dreadnought was part of a twelve-knight crew digging a ditch for a local council. Amelia walked by him on her way to the shopping centre. She didn't make eye contact as he worked his pickaxe. Other knights had shovels. Sweat glistened on his forehead as he called out, "Don't be embarrassed for me, Amelia. I must have a paying situation, and this is it. Besides, you are the only maiden I know who would feel this way."

She turned around, returned to where he was and said, "But you could do so much more given a chance."

"How do you know?" asked Dreadnought with a touch of amusement in his voice. He tried not to smile. He knew that smiling showed off his facial scar. Strangely enough, only with Amelia did he care if that scar became more prominent.

"I just know," said Amelia, shrugging her shoulders and smiling weakly since she was about to state what she thought was obvious. "You have leadership qualities. As you have told me, you train the younger knights."

"That should be nothing to you," Dreadnought told her, frowning, remembering his place in society.

"In another time and place, it would be everything," said Amelia, sighing.

"We are here and now," said Dreadnought, amusement once more in his voice, "and I have a ditch to dig."

"But are you safe?" asked Amelia, wondering for a second if it was her place in this world to care about that then deciding, even here, she was her own person.

"I am as safe as I can be." Dreadnought shrugged his shoulders at the absurdity of the question. According to every priestess he had ever met, he was not meant to have a long life anyway. Waving a hand at those around him in the ditch, he added, "I have a pickaxe for protection plus these eleven able-bodied knights I know I can trust."

"Good," said Amelia, firmly. "Will I see you tonight?"

"If that is your wish," replied Dreadnought, eyebrow raised. "There is The Noble Leaf. It is frequented by knights and maidens. It is only a few blocks from here, past the big greengrocers. Meet me at seven o'clock. The proprietor, an okay maverick, will provide us with a booth."

"Fine," Amelia said decisively. "I'll see you then."

As she walked back toward her shopping, she wondered what she could possibly do to make Dreadnought's station in life a little better. A song wouldn't do it. She had a terrible singing voice. She remembered air force personnel begging her to stop her interpretation of a popular song.

Poetry was out. For the most part, Amelia detested it. Where it wasn't hearts and flowers, it was dirty limericks; neither appealed to her. Where it had something to do with Nationalism and pride in one's own country, city, town, or air force base, it was acceptable to her since it called you to fight for what you believed in.

Amelia didn't see why Dreadnought would want anything to do with any poetry. She knew she couldn't swap dirty limericks with him without getting red-faced about it, and that would never do. Hearts and flowers just seemed wrong. She thought it would be more a maiden and maverick thing than a maiden and knight thing. Those who wanted to could drown, for all she cared, in soppy poetry, but definitely not Dreadnought and herself. Her previous military standing wouldn't let her sink that low and drag Dreadnought down with her. As for patriotic poems, Amelia believed Dreadnought really had nothing to be patriotic about. Dancing was not on because she would feel too silly doing it in front of him. *I make a lousy Geisha*, she thought wryly.

Amelia turned up at seven at The Noble Leaf with a pack of cards she got from a novelty shop. She knew a couple of games, including twenty-one. It was the best she could come up with.

She was ushered to where Dreadnought was waiting for her by a knightly waiter.

Dreadnought looked at the deck, shaking his head. "I'd rather not play." He gave no explanation. Perhaps, in his mind, he linked cards with gambling, and he didn't like to gamble.

"You don't have to play if you don't want to," Amelia said after a pause in the conversation. "It was just an idea. I take it I pay for the meal?"

"That is the custom," said Dreadnought, dryly.

A knightly waiter came by, and they put in their orders. Dreadnought decided on a steak with chips and salad, also an orange juice and a black tea to follow. Amelia went for the same.

While they waited, Dreadnought took a paper napkin and folded it in various ways. Amelia looked on in fascination. Within minutes, it was a paper crane.

"It is origami," said Dreadnought. "A Japanese knight taught it to me. He told me it helps clear the mind before battle, and he was right."

"It's ancient," Amelia told him. "It goes way back to a time before there were knights and dragons. Samurai warriors used to do it for the same reason. I tried it a few times but could never get the hang of it."

"I will teach you," said Dreadnought, coolly with a hint of amusement.

"I will be happy to learn," mused Amelia, "but I thought I was supposed to be entertaining you."

"Let us drop that foolishness. It ill becomes either one of us."

"Very well," agreed Amelia, wondering where they could go from there.

The food came, and they dug in. To Amelia, it was typical pub fare.

"No fear of being poisoned?" asked Amelia, suddenly aware of that possibility.

"Not here. I know all the waiters and cooks. They are all knights, and they want me to live. The proprietor may be a maverick but, if he tried anything, he'd end up on the menu the next day salted and seasoned."

After a while, the remnants of the main meal were taken away, and the tea arrived. There was silence for a few minutes before Amelia decided it was time to find out what she could really do for Dreadnought.

"So how can this maiden make your life better?" she asked.

"I don't know if you can, but I have always been interested in flight. Before I was officially designated a knight, I used to go bird watching with my parents. I miss those days. Every now and then, I feel I have lived too long."

Amelia understood combat fatigue and thought she might be seeing it right now in Dreadnought. Sometimes, leave didn't help when the man or woman knew they were going back to risk their lives and that this risking of life would happen again and again. She understood Dreadnought had had years of being expected to fight with time in between to think about it. She didn't believe he was suicidal, just fed up with it. The real danger she felt was he'd go gung-ho in some future clash with dragons and get himself killed that way. To go into battle with passion but without the brain in gear, Amelia knew, had put many a man and woman in an early grave.

"Do you get to see much of your parents?" asked Amelia, thinking perhaps his parents might be of better help to him than she could be.

"No," said Dreadnought, taken aback by the question. "Once we are pronounced a knight, we are not supposed to have contact with them. It is best that way. They mourned my loss at the time of my knighthood. This way, they are not affected later on by my death at the hands of some dragon."

After a pause, Dreadnought continued, "I have known knights that had tried to reunite with their parents; neither parent would acknowledge them. If they were persistent, they were whipped in the town square. If that failed to discourage them, then they were put up against a wall and shot. Robots are good at that. It is also a disgrace for parents to have anything to do with sons made over into knights. I have not wanted to put my parents in the situation where they would lose, for a time, their standing in our society."

"And I am supposed to be compensation?" asked Amelia.

"I suppose so," said Dreadnought, "though I've never heard it put that way."

"We can talk about flight and about birds," mused Amelia.

"Can I go up again with you?" asked Dreadnought.

"I can't see why not," said Amelia, "but I'd have to clear it first."

Dreadnought took another paper napkin and fashioned a bird. This time it was a seagull. He handed it to Amelia.

"This is for you."

"Thank you." Amelia smiled at the bird and then at Dreadnought. He couldn't help but smile back his crooked smile, the scar crinkling as he did so.

"I must go, a busy day tomorrow." Dreadnought sounded gruff but didn't mean to. In a short time, he had revealed more to Amelia than he had to any other maiden. He wondered why.

Dreadnought got up and left. Amelia paid the bill but, before she departed, the waiter who had served them tea approached her and said, "Please look after him."

"I'll do my best," replied Amelia, and the waiter nod-ded. Dreadnought was indeed important to other knights. She suspected his legend was growing.

Amelia took the paper seagull home and put it on her bedroom table. It was something she could admire. No doubt, the paper crane either went home with a knight or was placed in a commanding spot in The Noble Leaf's kitchen. One could imagine it overlooking food preparation and flexing its wings.

Amelia was given a short flight to the Gold Coast in Queensland, where she delivered some necessary medical in-struments to a doctor. It was half a day there and back in the fly-er. She asked if she could take Dreadnought along, but was re-fused permission.

The next day, Amelia went to the Wollongong universi-ty library, looking for information on birds for Dreadnought. She found a few books that might amuse him. She had only re-cently been issued a library card.

Amelia asked if many knights used the library, and a young librarian said, "Heavens no!"

"Why not?" asked Amelia.

"They don't have library cards," replied the young librar-ian, looking puzzled that someone Amelia's age wouldn't know that.

"Why not?" persisted Amelia

"I'll get the head librarian to explain," said the young wom-an and ran off.

A few minutes later, a stern-looking, no-nonsense wom-an came up to Amelia and said, "Can I help you? Do you have a question relating to our services?"

"Why are knights not allowed library cards?" Amelia asked. She took the person she was now faced with to be the head librarian, a woman in her early forties with a long nose suited to looking down at unruly customers.

"We don't normally discuss such matters," observed this

pompous, nose drooping woman, "but since you have asked, we don't expect knights to be able to read all that well. Also, if they die suddenly, there would be the difficulty of getting books borrowed before death returned."

"I see your reasoning," said Amelia, sickened by it. She wanted to pull a face but knew it wouldn't be appropriate. Too long, the need to be courteous had been part of her military existence, and it was something she couldn't always shake.

"If that is all you wish to know, I'll leave you." The head librarian's nose was still tilting down at Amelia.

"Yes. Thank you." Amelia was glad to see the head librarian go.

While Amelia was there in the library, she decided to find out all she could about the robots. So far, she only knew that they guarded events involving knights and dragons and, when not guarding such events, shot disobedient knights. As it turned out, the university library had several books on robots which she was allowed to borrow.

Over the next two weeks, she poured over the texts to get what insights she could. She discovered there were two thousand robots in Wollongong alone, and they were all involved, in one form or another, in law enforcement.

According to one book, a group of Norwegian scientists, headed by Professor Olga Swenson, had created the prototype robot over two hundred years ago for the men and women then journeying to Mars.

What's more, during the last of the civil wars, they were mass-produced in the USA and also in Japan and Australia for the protection of non-combatants. Then they were used as machines capable of dealing harshly with those who wanted to keep on fighting. Women did most of the programming. Now, in a more enlightened age, only high-ranking priestesses were given that task.

Their silvery faces and red eyes gave away the fact they

were not human. Also, they were stronger than the average knight or dragon and better armed. Ordinarily, they couldn't harm priestesses, maidens, mavericks, or children. If a priestess, maiden, maverick, or child broke the law, however, the robots were programmed to arrest and, if attacked, only shoot to wound. This leniency was not given to knights and dragons. If a knight or dragon were to be seen to do something unlawful, they could be shot dead by a robot, and no one in power would bother to look into the matter. The walking automatons were capable of independent thought. However, they could not deviate from the instructions and directives fed into them. *More slavery*, thought Amelia as she read on, *though of a different kind*.

There seemed little wrong with getting soulless machines to do what you want them to do. The question of morality, however, came when those mechanical men formed the continuous strong-arm required by an unjust civilization.

Amelia still didn't quite understand how the cult of the Goddess first took off or how it continued, but she could now see how the robots fitted in. Their existence meant there was no need for a human army or a large police force (maiden officers were in charge of the machines). The divisions created between humans need never end while those machines were around. Some maidens and mavericks had learned martial arts, but only for sport and physical fitness. They would not cope with knights and dragons that were used to fighting for their lives.

None of the books Amelia had borrowed went into any detail as to how to put together a robot or the finer points of how the artificial brain operated. No doubt, the priestesses involved were smart enough to keep such items of knowledge to themselves.

Amelia gathered from her reading there were factories, large and small, in cities such as Wollongong, Liverpool in England, Detroit, Lyon, Moscow, Shanghai, and Tokyo. Some made things such as refrigerators, cars, and aircraft, while others made certain robot parts. She wasn't surprised she couldn't find out from books where the assemblies or the maintenance for the robots took place. Where the programming centres in every city and major town were, however, was common knowledge, and robots guarded them well.

CHAPTER EIGHTEEN

On the twelfth day of July, Amelia took a maverick diplomat to Christchurch in New Zealand. The name of the city, she understood, dated back to when there were Christians there. The survivors there had just lived through a massive earthquake. It was up to the diplomat to assess the damage and recommend to the Wollongong city council what might be done to help the New Zealanders to rebuild.

Amelia packed medicine and bandages for the flight with the notion that the local hospital over there might be overwhelmed with casualties and lacking in supplies.

The diplomat's name was Abdul Kahn, and he reminded Amelia of the people she had fought against long ago. The fact that he wore a predominantly black suit with a few white and yellow stripes didn't help much. The black raised alarm bells in her mind. *Get a grip*, Amelia told herself, *I have nothing against this man. His ancestors may not even have been Globalists, and even if they were, that's not necessarily who he is. He probably has no idea why I would find black on him disconcerting.*

Amelia did her best to make sure any signs of discomfort in being near Abdul didn't show on her face. After all, he deserved the benefit of the doubt.

Then he made certain remarks while they waited for the maverick refueler to finish up on her flyer so they could be on their way.

"What are those clods doing threatening that maverick refueler with disembowelment if he tries anything to harm your flyer?" Abdul chuckled. "They're knights after all! Since when do knightly ground crew dictate to a maverick?"

"They're friends concerned about my safety." Amelia didn't like the way Abdul was sniggering at those knights as if they were foolish, and it was beginning to show in the narrowing of her eyes.

"Don't they know what would happen to them if they did carry out those threats?" asked Abdul of Amelia, humour still in his voice.

"They know," said Amelia coolly, "but they would do it anyway. They live with death."

"But what are you to them?" asked Abdul, wondering about the connection.

"I am Dreadnought's maiden," said Amelia proudly.

The take-off was smooth. The turbulence over the radioactive remnants of Melbourne and the unruly Bass Strait was expected and at least acceptable to Amelia.

"Do you know how to fly this thing?" asked Abdul as they went past the outskirts of what had once been a major city.

"We'll be fine," answered Amelia coldly. She hated having her piloting skills questioned.

Over Bass Strait, Abdul said, "I am not accustomed to being buffeted about like this!"

Amelia went red-faced. She wanted to reply but felt it best not to do so since what she would say would not be kind. She almost wished for more turbulence to rattle Abdul. In any event, there wasn't much she could do about the discomfort of flying into areas where the weather was always bad.

Tasmania was lush, beautiful, and worth seeing from on high for Amelia, but not Abdul. "All that bush and jungle needs clearing," he said, pointing down at the greenness of it. *Spoken like a true Globalist*, Amelia thought. *They were out to destroy everything natural until we stopped them.* She felt like sneering at him but knew it was best to be as polite as she could be since he was on an important mission.

Abdul barely glanced at Hobart, the city in amongst all the trees. "A touch of civilization in the wilderness," he called it. "Not good enough as far as I am concerned."

As they came into the landing zone outside Christchurch, a large flock of seagulls and terns made their appearance in the air. Amelia put the flyer into a vertical position and ascended rapidly to avoid the birds. It worked but not without giving Abdul a shakeup he didn't appreciate.

"Couldn't you have just ploughed right into them and through them?" cried Abdul in exasperation as Amelia righted and levelled off the craft.

"Yes," agreed Amelia. "That might have been all right, your idea of smacking into them. On the other hand, a couple of our feathered friends could have been sucked into an engine and done real damage to our flyer."

"Best not to take chances then," agreed Abdul as she brought the craft in for a landing.

"And besides, they're beautiful creatures. I didn't want to hurt them. I prefer live and let live whenever that is at all possible, don't you?"

"Now you are absurd," said Abdul huffily, crossing his arms as they taxied to where hover cars were waiting for them. Wheel-less and supported by artificial air pockets plus anti-gravity modules, these modern marvels could safely run above the most dilapidated of roads.

Abdul wanted to keep the medical supplies onboard while negotiations with the Christchurch city council took place; but against his wishes, Amelia unloaded what they had to the delight of the drivers who knew what the medicines and bandages meant for their people. "Nothing like goodwill," Amelia told Abdul as they headed toward an intact building that overlooked the devastation.

They spent two days in Christchurch before flying back. Abdul proved to be a smooth talker who could, when pushed, show sympathy in hand gestures and smiles for the earthquake victims, though he wasn't about to go anywhere near the sick and dying. Amelia suspected he was afraid of picking up a virus or something equally nasty from those who had been hospitalised.

"I'll organize for more medicine, accompanied by doctors and nurses, to be flown in before reconstruction commences," Abdul told the Christchurch authorities. "Of course, this will have to be cleared by my people in Wollongong, but I am sure I can hurry that along." *By hurry along, you mean take credit for it,* Amelia thought, trying not to show anger toward Abdul. She suspected he might even slow things down if there was a way of promoting himself by doing so. *Am I being fair here?* She wondered.

A short, middle-aged maiden council member stepped forward to address Abdul. She said in a warm voice, "We're pleased with what you have already delivered, though it is not nearly enough to tackle all the suffering. It was, after all, from one lone flyer."

"There will be more. Rest assured, there will be more." Abdul failed to mention that the medical supplies that had been received so far by the people of Christchurch were Amelia's idea.

Abdul tried small talk on the return journey, but Amelia just wasn't interested. She gave short answers only and dirty looks until he gave up. This time Abdul didn't complain about rough winds over Bass Strait or Melbourne. He felt he had said or done something to offend Amelia but could not think what that might have been. It was this maverick's disregard for those seagulls and terns that continued to irk her. To be reasonable, Amelia realised upon reflection on the journey back, Abdul was doing his best to get along with her. She might have had the same attitudes as him toward nature and fellow human beings if she had grown up the way he had. In that regard, she could see that what he was wasn't entirely his fault even though what he was happened to be appalling. Would he keep his promises to the people of Christchurch? She didn't know but suspected that he would since she couldn't see, offhand, any advantage for him in not doing so.

It was the following day at The Noble Leaf over tea, when she told Dreadnought about her experience over Christchurch. He was pleased with her actions.

"Terns, with their blacktop feathers, remind me of youngsters with bad haircuts," said Dreadnought wistfully. "Seagulls sound like so many kids squabbling on a playground at lunchtime."

"They didn't mean to get in my way," said Amelia.

"I know," agreed Dreadnought. "I just wish I was there to see the panic in that maverick's eyes."

"He was so afraid," said Amelia. "I suppose he's never been in a tight spot before."

"But we both have, and that makes all the difference."

"He did his job well enough," said Amelia. "I'll give him that."

"But you don't like him?" ventured Dreadnought.

"How can I," said Amelia, "when he has no feeling for birds?"

For the first time, she heard Dreadnought laugh.

Amelia's behaviour on the New Zealand flight was mentioned by Abdul to first Jens and then to Dean Renate. He deemed it unmaidenly.

"Amelia's attitudes toward knights and birds are bizarre," Abdul had told Jens over the phone.

"She's still adjusting to being here," offered Jens in response.

"She had better adjust faster," snarled Abdul.

Dean Renate was less polite toward the diplomat. When he started in on Amelia's reaction to birds over the phone, the dean asked, "Don't you like seagulls and terns?"

"That is not the point!" groused Abdul.

"I think it is," said the dean and hung up on him.

The next morning, Megan had Amelia come to the centre for scientific research at Wollongong University to identify an object she thought was a mobile phone.

"So what is it really?" asked Megan, handing over the object.

"A mobile phone," said Amelia, rolling it around in her hand and then giving it back to Megan. "Americans called them cell phones. I have no idea why."

"The towers came down ages ago," mused Megan, "so I don't suppose we could make a phone call."

"Where was it found?" asked Amelia.

"Buried not far from where you were found," said Megan. "We're still digging in that general area of old Sydney."

"The battery would have to be dead by now, but your scientists might still be able to get the phone operational again."

"What's the point?" Megan shrugged her shoulders. "No reception, remember?"

"I know this model. It has a top of the range memory chip. It might contain downloads from the internet and photos taken by whoever owned it."

"So it was more than just a phone?" Megan's eyes lit up, and she adjusted her glasses.

"Much more until they went out of service. If you can get it working again, you might find lots of stuff of interest."

"By the way, I heard that you didn't get along with that diplomat you took to Christchurch," said Megan after a pause in which to gather her thoughts on the subject. "You have to be more careful."

"I don't know how I can be with someone like Abdul

Khan," admitted Amelia, crossing her arms and pouting.

****

Over the next couple of days, a maiden electrical expert was able to get the mobile phone running long enough, several times, to show images as well as recorded text. The maiden wrote down the text and got an artist to draw from the images. She was able to show Amelia and Megan her findings before they faded away forever.

There was a recipe for caramel slice and another for Pavlova. Amelia loved both and said as much to Megan.

Also, there happened to be two letters from a boyfriend plus a draft notice. The person the notice was addressed to was Sue Tang, who was born in Melbourne but whose parents moved to Sydney when she was young. She was to become a private in the army. Whether or not she did serve in the military was something that could not be discovered from the mobile phone. *There were lots of people who were drafted*, thought Amelia. *I hope she was a good soldier.*

The photographs, however, caught Amelia's attention. They were a reminder that the civil wars that erupted across many parts of the world, including Australia, were never about where a person's ancestors came from but about numbers.

One collective was all about keeping the human population down and thus protecting the planet as much as possible from humanity's destructive ways. *Poorly organised, we can be rather awful*, thought Amelia, looking at a photo of a lone tree near a park bench and knowing that human population growth at the time, no doubt, only allowed for one lone tree. The better collective, as far as Amelia was concerned, was for having enough for everyone to eat plus plenty of room for suitable housing and wildlife. Then there was the other, which she could just imagine Abdul Kahn being part of. They were about their God and their right to go crazy increasing their numbers. Amelia noted in her mind that there had been more than one God plus a handful of holy books getting in the way of what she thought at the time was progress.

Amelia had been with the collective out to reduce humanity or at least stabilize numbers because she wanted more parks and more trees. She would like to believe Sue Tang felt the same way. She probably did. The photo of the lone tree had been taken by her or a friend of hers.

Amelia had wanted to breathe in fresh air and watch a possum climb to a topmost branch in some park larger than one that had a single tree and bench. She had believed these were things worth fighting for. Her collective had better weapons and greater scientific know-how, but the others had proved to be better con artists before everything went wrong and so had gained some useful knowledge before everyone had to choose sides. A tear rolled down Amelia's cheek as she continued to stare at that tree.

"What are you thinking?" asked Megan. "It's only a tree."

"It's a beautiful tree from long ago." Megan wiped away another tear.

According to the draft notice, it was definite that Sue Tang had been on Amelia's side.

One photo was of a hospital scene where a man in his early twenties was bandaged up and being visited by a young woman. Sue most likely was the photographer of this as well as the others. Three photos were of a Christian wedding in the Blue Mountains. It was at a small chapel Amelia recognised. The people who had worshiped there had believed in her cause. Not all religious types at that time were mad. Having children was okay just as long as the couple didn't overdo it. There was a photo of a space rocket being prepared for launch somewhere in the USA, going by the military uniforms. Another portrayed an Australian Aborigine in an army major's uniform being saluted by two privates.

"They're your people?" asked Megan upon reviewing the photos.

"Oh, yes!" answered Amelia. None of them had worn anything to indicate they were the enemy even though she knew the enemy was good at infiltration.

Near the end of the month, Amelia had her phone installed in her cottage. She noted that the very next day, Megan invited her over to her place to watch television and to have a chat. Amelia gathered, by Megan's voice, that something was up.

"I don't care much for television," Amelia told Megan. "I doubt if it has improved over time. I was always more active and preferred being outdoors. One thing I can't stand is the relentless day soaps dealing with this maiden and that maverick. It's the kind of brainless crap I ended up watching in hospital before I went into the deep freeze."

"How about reruns of battles between knights and dragons with highlights of special kills, injury to the eye moments being very popular?" Megan offered. "There's one episode of a trendy show featuring Dreadnought. It, no doubt, reminds everyone he has only eight more kills to go."

Amelia winced visibly. "No thanks!"

On the evening news, as Amelia and Megan ate their TV dinners together, there came a report on a boy who had stolen candy from a candy store in Lyon. His sister claimed that she had done the stealing, and her brother had merely pocketed what was taken, but that wouldn't wash with the authorities.

"Poor kid," said Megan. "He'll have a record now."

"Does that matter?" Amelia wondered why it would matter.

"It will matter in a couple of years from now. He has just reduced his chances of being designated a maverick. See the maiden with him? That's his mother. Now you know why she's in tears."

"Yes. I get it. Best not to swell the ranks of mavericks with thieves, even reformed ones." Amelia shook her head.

"Now I want to tell you something important," said Megan, switching off the television screen.

"What is it?" asked Amelia.

"You know you don't have to keep seeing Dreadnought. You may have chosen in haste. You can break it off with him at any time. Just tell him so in front of a witness or two, and it's done." Megan was very matter of fact, but Amelia gathered there was an important reason why she didn't want Amelia to spend time with Dreadnought anymore.

"You and Jens urged me to take a knight. You said it was my maidenly duty." Amelia was cool about this. She had done what was asked of her, and she was happy being in Dreadnought's company. She couldn't see anything wrong with that.

"Yes. All that is very well, but it may be a bad fit." Megan adjusted her glasses, a sign of nervousness.

"How so?" pressed Amelia.

"You have Jens and Dean Renate worried." Megan wanted Amelia to figure it out for herself.

"Worried about what?" Amelia asked.

"I don't know precisely, but it has to do with unrest." Megan sighed, feeling awkward. She was not good at politics, and she knew it. "You are upsetting the wrong people!"

"Revolution?" Amelia asked, surprise in her voice.

"Yes."

"Really?" Amelia asked, dumbfounded.

"Yes."

"That's crazy. We are just two people." Amelia shook her head in disbelief and smiled sheepishly.

"Dreadnought isn't like other knights." Megan took off her glasses and waved them at Amelia before putting them back on. "He's special."

"In what way is he special?" asked Amelia.

"I don't believe even Jens knows for sure, but there are priestesses in high positions who are afraid." There was a tremor in Megan's voice. She was venturing into an area she felt she had no business going into, a dangerous place.

"Has this to do with the fifty dragons?" asked Amelia.

"That's part of it, but only part of it." Megan rubbed her hands as if trying to wash them.

"And the rest?" Amelia asked.

"There's you and your inquisitive mind and a mystery that began decades ago." Megan stopped rubbing hands and sighed deeply.

"When Dreadnought was born?" Amelia asked.

"Yes!" The word came out as a sob.

"And they don't want certain secrets to get out?" Amelia asked.

"That's why Dreadnought must never reach fifty. No knight, especially that one can obtain the golden number. And that's all I can tell you."

****

On the first morning of August, a package arrived for Amelia at her home. This was most unusual. She wasn't aware up until then that there was a postal service. The messenger maverick who handed it to her wore a postal uniform and so looked genuine enough. But who would send her a gift? Could it be Dreadnought?

She was tempted to rip open the packaging and find out what was inside but hesitated. Instead, she phoned up Megan to ask her opinion.

"Fill a basin with water," advised Megan. "Then, put the package carefully into the water."

"Why?"

"Just do it! I'll send someone over right away."

Three men came by. They were all wearing white dust

coats as if they had just come from a lab. One introduced himself as Professor Longer from the Dangerous Chemicals Research Subdivision at Wollongong University. He told Amelia his assistants were knights with some lab experience.

"Please leave," said one of the knights in a calm voice so as not to rattle Amelia. "We'll let you know when it is safe to return."

As she walked away from her cottage, Amelia noticed the knights barring the entrance to it. She saw the professor enter her home. Amelia imagined him stepping cautiously toward the water-filled basin in her bathroom and the object of concern. *That package, it can't be what I think it is*, thought Amelia. Minutes later, a great explosion shattered windows for three blocks and reduced the cottage to a burning wreck.

Flying debris injured the knights, and the professor was killed outright. His body was barely identifiable. Amelia experienced a ringing sensation in her ears that would persist for days. The soak in the water hadn't worked. It was fortunate Amelia had not tried to open the package herself.

It got on the news and made the newspapers. Reporters came upon the scene before an ambulance hovercraft, gliding in on compressed air and anti-gravity modules, could take away the wounded. Pictures were taken. Amelia was interviewed via a pad and pen.

Reporters wrote down their questions, and Amelia responded by writing down her answers. She made it clear that it wasn't an accident, and that someone was out to murder the maiden from the past. She also noted that Dreadnought was also in danger for merely being a better than average knight.

Jens was not happy about the bombing or the interview. She phoned Dean Renate, who also concurred that higher-ups had made a grave error. "It was supposed to be blamed on a gas leak or some such thing," said the dean regretfully. "I know Amelia had electricity on rather than gas, but it could have been fudged that way. If not for Megan's interference, those who sent the bomb might have gotten away with it."

"Megan doesn't know much about what's going on," Jen told the dean. "I don't know much more than she does. If there is another attempt at Amelia's life, there could be civil trouble."

"I know that." The dean sighed. "But believe me, none of this was my idea."

"If Dreadnought dies outside of combat with dragons, there could be an uprising of knights, maidens, and mavericks," warned Jens. "It could spread across the globe. He has become that popular."

The doctors at the hospital informed Amelia that her hearing would soon come back, but no taking to the air for at least a month. Otherwise, at high altitudes, she might black out.

The hospital staff looked after her, and knights friendly with Dreadnought kept guard day and night, in shifts, to make sure there wouldn't be a successful attempt on her life.

Time in a hospital bed gave Amelia time to reflect. It had dawned on her that the people she was fighting with and fighting for when she was a fighter pilot may have been instrumental in the eventual creation of the society she now lived in. Her side probably did win the final war. If that was so, she wondered how long it had taken them.

Amelia was in a "maidens only" ward. Elsewhere, there was a ward where the injured knights were in recovery. She hoped they were getting good treatment.

Dreadnought visited her and informed her of a plot against him. A young knight turned traitor tried to stab him in the back with a dagger while he was exercising in the gym. Fortunately, two other knights had observed the would-be murderer and gleaned his intent from his body language. They grabbed him before he could act and rested the blade from his hand. He received a swift blow to the head issued by Dreadnought that put his lights out.

"Did you kill him?" asked Amelia; her hearing had returned.

"No need," said Dreadnought. "When he is working during the day, there will always be someone keeping an eye on him. At night, he will be in chains. He will not survive the November season of battle. No knight on his own can do so, and he will be on his own."

"Did he tell you who put him up to this?" asked Amelia.

"He said the head priestess of Wollongong. I don't know if that is true."

"It sounds about right. Religious zeal can be powerful. He probably thought the Goddess wanted him to do it, and he'd have a grand palace in heaven. Whoever wanted it done needed our deaths to be quiet and untraceable. Now that the media knows about the attempt on my life, they may back off for a while."

"I hope so." Dreadnought shook his head and smiled a smile that barely touched upon his facial scar. Amelia could tell by this he was doubtful.

"Megan visited me earlier and says she has a new cottage for me to live in for when I get out." Amelia wanted to be positive.

"She is a good maiden." All real friends were good as far as Dreadnought was concerned.

"One of the best." Amelia smiled a disarming smile.

Dreadnought had taken a napkin from the hospital cafeteria earlier and now fashioned it into a paper pelican. He handed it to Amelia.

"This may bring you luck," he told her before leaving.

The following day, the knight who tried to kill Dreadnought died under an avalanche of bricks at the building site where he was employed. It was recorded as an accidental death. *Someone is covering their tracks*, thought Dreadnought when he was told.

CHAPTER NINETEEN

When the doctors deemed it was safe, Amelia resumed flying. Malcolm, who had been her maverick instructor, joined her on her first flight after recovery just to make sure she was all right.

The mission was a short hop to Adelaide and back to deliver a parcel to the mayor of that city who turned out to be a thin, black-haired maiden. It was done in a day, and Amelia was glad to reacquaint herself with Malcolm. He was surprised anyone would want her dead even if her talk was sometimes strange for a maiden.

"It was on the news about your home being blown up," said Malcolm to Amelia on the flight back to Wollongong from Adelaide. "I'm glad you weren't badly hurt. You seem fine to continue flying. But why would anyone do that?"

"I don't know." Amelia smiled and shook her head. "It may have something to do with me seeing Dreadnought."

"Maybe you should drop Dreadnought then." Malcolm frowned. "He is, after all, only a knight."

"No. I won't do that." Amelia was firm on this. She wondered why. Then it came to her that Dreadnought was as close to being one of the men she had known in the Australian air force of long ago as she was going to come across in the world she was now living in. He didn't wear a uniform, but he did fight, and he did have a cause, those fifty dragons. Fellow knights now depended on him to make fifty to give them hope.

September and October are spring months in Wollongong. Autumn hadn't been harsh around the time of Amelia's awakening from that capsule, but she didn't expect it to be. She knew winters in even the southern part of New South Wales, Australia were never like those people have always had to endure in the northern countries such as Canada or further south, where New Zealand was once famous for their skiing holidays. *Were there skiing holidays in winter now in New Zealand?* She wondered. The last war had stopped that sort of thing. There was now no reason for such delights not to go ahead.

Amelia hadn't thought much about the seasons, though she did love the spring months. *Some things weren't screwed up by the last war,* thought Amelia one morning as she woke up to the harsh laughter of at least a dozen kookaburras calling out in nearby trees. If anything, life had improved in Wollongong since the priestesses took over. That was true for some people. It was apparently good for local wildlife.

In October, Amelia was sent several times to Houston in the USA. There she experienced a mild autumn. With land to do it in, a place to house aircraft, and warehouses in which to store vital equipment plus a structure close to completion that might soar among the stars, scientists were making efforts to revive the space program. Amelia carried schematics with her, some retrieved from the rubble of Sydney, while others, she was told, had been taken from private collections.

Amelia gathered from her visits that what was planned would be a one-way trip to Mars for some lucky maiden and maverick. At any rate, the trip was being advertised as lucky on the radio. Just how fortunate, Amelia knew, would depend on how well the rocket being built could fly, plus conditions on Mars.

It was on the news that the space vehicle under construction was being equipped with radar that would keep the maiden and maverick in contact with the Earth, but for only a short time. Then they would be on their own. The dish in the centre of New South Wales had been repaired. It was staffed by three maidens and three mavericks to allow longer contact with the astronauts and for use in future space exploration.

According to the news, the spaceship would contain a capsule to be sent back to Earth with information about the Mars colony. What could be collected would be gleaned from space as they approached the red planet, photographic records and, if possible, transmissions from the surface of Mars. It would then go on its way back to Earth so that the people back at Houston would get something for their trouble, and so ventures into outer space would continue.

It was planned that the spaceship would land close to where the dome was located. The astronauts would bring extra canisters of air and oxygen as well as spare food packages for the Martians. They would also carry information about modern Earth. There were to be translator devices so that communications would be less difficult since it was known that language does change over time.

"Do you think there are people still alive on Mars?" asked Amelia of a maiden scientist on her first trip to Houston.

"Honestly, we don't know," the scientist told Amelia. "We have gone through what records survive of the construction of the dome and the ecosystem within. It was impressive work that took decades to get right. The water we suspect to be under the Martian surface may have helped sustain them. Minerals we know are on the surface could also have been of help in keeping them going. Our prospective astronauts may find corpses or a flourishing new world."

Amelia met a dozen fit, young maidens and mavericks in astronaut training. They were eager to talk to her about her past life and also about Dreadnought.

Each time she set off for Houston, she wondered why she was making the journey and not some other flyer pilot. The flight meant a short stopover each time in Singapore to make contact with researchers studying the stars and pick up newly made star charts from them. Next, Amelia headed for and spent a night at Midway Atoll. Then overnight at Houston before heading back to Midway Atoll, Singapore, and finally home to Wollongong.

Singapore was a fascinating city. Back in the early twenty-first century, efforts had been made to incorporate greenery and other forms of nature in with the steel and glass necessary to build skyscrapers for a growing human population. With the human inhabitants at a more respectable number, many of these structures sheltered wildlife alone. They were magnificent to visit for that reason.

Amelia had time on her first trip to go on a nature walk with a local guide who was Asian but spoke perfect English. Her name was Camilla Yen, and her long, black hair was the most memorable thing about her. Amelia wondered if she should grow her hair longer rather than continue to have it cut short military style.

"There are places where we can't go," advised Camilla on the walk. "Some structures given over to our wildlife have become too fragile over time. They remain okay for the birds nesting but not for maidens and mavericks walking around in. I am glad to be able to show you what is safe to experience."

Amelia was taken by the variety of birds she saw. She suspected other visitors also felt the same. The birds were in large numbers with plenty of plants around to provide food.

"There are cheeky bulbuls with blue faces, java mynas, horrid in their blackness, oh over there! There's a greater green leaf bird, magnificent in his greenness." Camilla was beaming with pride. "I only wish you had a camera with you to capture these delightful creatures living the way the Great Goddess no doubt intended."

"You're so fortunate to have all this beauty." Amelia smiled at Camilla, and Camilla smiled back.

Midway Atoll remained a nature reserve with shearwaters, petrels, terns, and other birds making a nuisance of themselves on landing and takeoff. At Houston, a city being funded by several other cities to once more head interplanetary research, one hotel employee was full of zeal.

"Please tell us about Dreadnought," asked a knightly bellhop in blue. He leaned close to Amelia to get her response.

"What do you want to know?" Amelia wondered what she could say to this fellow who was bursting with enthusiasm, a great big grin on his face.

"Everything!" the bellhop enthused. Amelia understood hero-worship when she saw it, and she was looking at it right now.

"He's taller than you and has a scar on his face," said Amelia. "What else would you like to know?"

"Will he get his fifty?" asked the bellhop. "He has only eight to go!"

"I don't know." Amelia felt it best to be honest. Not even Dreadnought could know that. It was a shame he had to try to kill more dragons and risk death, but that was how this world operated. Amelia didn't like it but couldn't see what she could do about it.

"Are you helping him?" asked the bellhop.

"I am doing all a maiden like me can do," replied Amelia.

"Bless you then!" The bellhop walked away happy. No doubt, he would have loved to have hugged her, but that wasn't permitted. He was, after all, a knight and not a maverick.

Later, at the hotel bar, two mavericks asked her what she thought of the time in which she now lived.

"It must be so wonderful to get away from all that violence they had in the past," said a fellow in eye-watering colours where pink and violet met and ran screaming from each other.

"Yes, you must be so relieved to get away from all of that," offered another with a star map on his vest and white stripes on his sleeves. At least, he was easier on Amelia's eyes.

"I had cancer, and your modern science cured me," said Amelia, smiling. She finished the vodka cocktail she had been sipping and left. Anything worthwhile knowing about where she had come from, she wanted to give exclusively to Megan. Her successful treatment for what should have been a fatal disease was already common knowledge.

On the final trip to Houston, Amelia was granted permission to take Dreadnought along with her. This was unusual. Megan and Malcolm also decided to go along. Nothing of a disturbing nature happened. Even so, Amelia, Megan, and Dreadnought felt something was going on they didn't yet know about.

Dreadnought was asked to test some scales at Houston, and so was Amelia.

"Why do you need us to do this?" Amelia asked a maverick technician in a dust coat and a sickeningly bright red, green, and purple tie.

"Oh, we're just making sure the equipment works." The technician made some notes on a pad and left. Neither Megan nor Malcolm was asked to test these scales.

At the hotel in Houston, Dreadnought got to meet the bellhop, his biggest fan. Unfortunately, the bellhop was too tongue-tied to ask him anything. He smiled sheepishly and looked at Amelia for help.

"Say something to him!" Amelia was insistent.

"Good lad," said Dreadnought warmly and patted the bellhop on the shoulder. The bellhop beamed so brightly he lit up the hotel entrance.

On this trip, Dreadnought was amazed at the birdlife he encountered, his eyes wide, taking in all he could. *I wonder if he dreams of flight, of being one of those feathered creatures*, thought Amelia when they were at Midway Atoll on their way back to Wollongong. She knew he liked the wildlife in Singapore, but she had to admit the wildlife was a tad wilder at Midway Atoll.

Does Dreadnought imagine an end to the brutalities of May and November? Amelia thought and realized she had to be right. But they would only end for him and no other knight if he was successful in gaining those fifty kills. The May and November slaughter would go on without him because that was what many of the priestesses, maidens, and mavericks wanted and expected.

Birds, Amelia understood, were solace for Dreadnought as he continued to do the bloody bidding of those in charge. If successful, she wondered what years of involvement in these games would do to him. Already, they had taken a toll. Dreadnought was one for burying his emotions because all of those fellow knights he grew up with and got close to were now in a knight's cemetery.

Megan and Malcolm got on well during this final journey and so decided to go out together afterward. *I can't blame Megan*, thought Amelia. *Of the mavericks I have known, he is the least soppy, and he does know his way around flyers.*

CHAPTER TWENTY

In the last week of October, Jens and Dean Renate were summoned to Wollongong's great temple to meet with the High Priestess. It was the third time in a decade that Jens had been so invited.

The corridors are so long and wide! Over there and there, we have statues of Mary praying to the Great Goddess, thought Jens, awestruck by the wonders of what she was seeing. She felt a little intimidated by such splendour. *Some carvings are of baby Jesus in Mary's arms, no doubt depicting the marvels of motherhood. Over there are smaller statues of knights slaying dragons or being slain by them.*

Dean Renate walked with even footfalls, determined not to succumb to everything she was seeing. There were high ceilings, and robots guarded the huge doors. *Everything about this building is geared to intimidate those unused to the surroundings,* she thought. *Here it is cold, passionless. The masses view this whole structure as a gateway to the good beyond, and so they should.*

With rising trepidation, Jens couldn't help listening to the click-clack echo of her footsteps on marble. They sounded like the sound of her heart beating faster as she approached the one door with a golden handle amongst the whiteness of the painted wood around it.

Two robot guards stopped them and asked for their names. Once given, the door was opened for them, and they were bidden to enter. Resting on a lounge was an athletic-looking forty-year-old woman dressed in white with a white cowl. Jens recognized her as the High Priestess. Next to her was a coffee table, and on it was an assortment of sweet biscuits, a sugar bowl with a spoon, a steaming coffee container, and three cups with spoons. Two empty chairs were positioned near the coffee table.

"Come! Sit with me," said the High Priestess, and they obeyed. "Do you know why we import coffee?"

"It must be because we can't grow it ourselves," said Jens. The High Priestess smiled at this answer.

"It is actually to make coffee more for the elite," said Dean Renate. "It is the case of the price of it being an import making it a luxury item. If we wanted to, we could grow it in northern New South Wales and Queensland. Most maidens, of course, don't know this."

"Bravo!" cried the High Priestess. "It is about weights and balances. It is how we maintain order. Some cities need us to import their coffee so we can export goods to them."

The High Priestess looked at Jens with penetrating eyes. "Do you know why we allowed your Megan to interview Amelia and to keep records of those interviews?"

"Scientific research is our area of expertise," said Jens. "There is much about the twenty-first and twenty-second centuries we either don't know or don't understand."

"That's right," agreed the High Priestess. "Besides, too many maidens and mavericks knew about how you discovered Amelia to keep her a secret forever. We wanted her to be gradually introduced to the public while you and Megan taught her about how we live."

"That was the plan," said Dean Renate. "The university board members agreed, though some had their doubts."

"At first, the priestesses under my care were wary." The High Priestess waved her hand in a dismissive gesture as if, all along, she knew better than her subordinates. "Amelia might have been highly religious, but she wasn't. Perhaps her military background explains this, though many of our knights and dragons who face death two seasons in every year are very religious."

"It is a comfort for them," said Dean Renate.

"Amelia was curious about our ways, which is understandable," continued the High Priestess in a matter of fact tone. She could have used a much stronger word than curious, but that was not her way. "She stirred up some controversy when she spoke, but those she addressed tended to regard her as either naive or foolish."

"We did gather information from Amelia about the past," Jens told the High Priestess candidly, palms open. She wondered if she and the dean were in serious trouble. There was no indication that this was so on the High Priestess' face, but that face wasn't giving away much at all.

"And a great deal of the information you have gathered has been useful," said the High Priestess. "It will keep the academics busy for years to come."

"But that changed?" prompted Dean Renate, feeling it was time to get to the heart of why this meeting was taking place.

"Amelia should never have met Dreadnought." The High Priestess punched out the word never and glared at Jens in a way that made her blood run icy cold, acknowledging what happened and what was happening was all Jens' fault. "Amelia should not have taken Dreadnought to be her knight. That was most unfortunate. It added to his fame and popularity. He became known, not only in Wollongong but elsewhere as a potential maverick and the companion of the maiden from another time."

"And that made him more difficult to dispose of?" asked Dean Renate.

"I did not sanction those attempts on either Dreadnought or Amelia's lives," replied the High Priestess. "They were clumsy and born out of fear and desperation. Thanks to those ill-considered actions organised by my fellow priestesses, however, nothing more can be done until the next combat season takes place in November. Thanks to the foolishness of those priestesses, the balance has been badly disturbed here and in other cities. The most High Martha, the Priestess of all Priestesses, is displeased."

"If either Dreadnought or Amelia were to die tomorrow," reasoned Dean Renate with a slight shiver in her voice, "the very next day, there would be rioting in the streets and a general refusal of knights to participate in the seasonal culling."

"The knights believe in the fifty because Dreadnought is close to gaining his fifty," said Jens. She was beginning to understand the High Priestess' concerns and how badly she, Jens, had messed up. "If Dreadnought is then to pass away before November and his chance to become a maverick thus evaporates, knights, maidens, and even mavericks will cry foul. Even harming Amelia to demoralise Dreadnought will be seen as not playing the game right."

"Our robots would rip into the rioters with their lead pellets, but at great cost to human life," spoke Dean Renate with some passion. "Maidens and mavericks would be slaughtered by rampaging knights who feel they have nothing to gain and therefore nothing to lose. The knights would die, but they would certainly take some prize citizens with them before the robots could act."

"You are correct in all of this," said the High Priestess. There was sadness in her eyes. "Now it is time you knew why Dreadnought is such a menace."

The High Priestess poured the coffee out into the three cups while contemplating what she would say next.

"What I tell you may shock you," she informed them after a moment's hesitation. "What I reveal to you must never leave this room. Do you understand?"

"Yes, High One," said Jens, taking a cup and then a sip.

"If that is your wish, High Priestess," agreed Dean Renate, picking up a cup.

The High Priestess took up a cup, drank deeply, and then said, "You have all read the book of the Martha?"

"Yes," answered Jens. Dean Renate nodded.

"It is all true," spoke the High Priestess soothingly, "but certain items known only up to now by the priestesses add new dimensions to our civilization. As you know, it was the first Martha who decided that there should be knights and mavericks. The knights were to be the warriors who fought and died to keep us safe from war. The original intent was that they fought each other. You know the other purpose of the maverick. Legend has it the first Martha picked that name for them to denote their boldness and incorruptibility. It happens to be true that maverick, in the old American English tongue means, unbranded and free."

"Mavericks are not like that," said Jens, and realized she was being too brazen with someone as powerful as the High Priestess.

"And knights do not fight knights," added Dean Renate, hoping to defuse any displeasure from the High Priestess headed Jens' way.

"The nature of mavericks changed," said the High Priestess offhandedly, "As did the requirements of knights. There was plague and radiation sickness. Maidens, a name that once meant single woman but came instead to mean not married to the Great Goddess, started giving birth to creatures that did not live for very long. In too many cases, they writhed with agony during their short time, and the painkillers of the day could do little for them. Babies, male and female, with their hearts or their brains showing, noses not properly formed, and arms and legs horrid stumps. Out of this was born the first dragon. He was black with scales and a tail. He clawed his way out of his mother's womb, causing her death as dragons still do today. He was free of pain and lived to a good age. I believe he was in his sixtieth year when he passed away."

"And then appeared other dragons," added Jens.

"But not the way you imagine," said the High Priestess. "The first Martha concluded that it would be better if knights battled dragons rather than fighting each other. So she urged a scientist to take DNA samples from the one living dragon and dose certain pregnant women with the dragon's essence. Thus, these maidens dutifully ended their lives by bringing dragons into our world."

"Dutifully?" asked Dean Renate, incredulous, shaking her head.

"Unwittingly would perhaps be the better term," reasoned the High Priestess flatly.

"That's monstrous!" cried Jens, once more forgetting her place.

"It explains a lot," said Dean Renate, sadness in her voice. "It was hard to believe that dragons being born today were the result of plague or radiation since we have been free of both for generations."

"Most people simply think of it as the will of the Goddess." The High Priestess shrugged her shoulders. "And in a way, it is. We, the priestesses, choose the maidens who will produce dragons. They are of low stock and considered expendable."

"There are tests?" asked Jens, leaning forward, anxious to know.

"Of course!" cried the High Priestess. "It is all scientifically evaluated."

"And we've been tested?" asked Jens, still leaning forward, anxious.

"Yes," said the High Priestess. "The tests in terms of the mind as well as the body are carried out without any fanfare when you are in your early teens. There are exams in language, art, science, leadership, and culture in general. All part of the school curriculum. Then there are notes taken by priestesses of how each maiden is progressing in their field of activity after their schooling is over. I suppose I shouldn't say this, but you have both passed, and if you fell pregnant, you won't be having dragons."

"Is that why, at a certain age, we're to choose either the possibility of pregnancy or the priesthood?" asked Dean Renate.

"Yes," said the High Priestess. "A life of celibacy and contemplation, however, is not for everyone. Surprisingly, many maidens would rather remain maidens than take the vow I took long ago. They take their chances and hope for the best. Only high-ranking priestesses are told how the gamble those maidens take actually works."

"What about Amelia?" Jens asked.

"That has yet to be decided." The High Priestess' face was like stone, and the words were a little too noncommittal the way they had been delivered. Jens suspected that if Amelia did team up with a maverick, it would be the end of her for sure.

"What is it then about Dreadnought that priestesses find so disturbing?" asked Dean Renate; she had to know.

"I'm getting to that," said the High Priestess. "As you know, not all dragons now have black scales. Some are silver, some in Japan are dark blue, and there are those in Greece that are a deep crimson. Why these anomalies came about we don't know. Still, a dragon is a dragon, and we left it at that until an anomaly eventuated that was set to rock the foundations of our society. And it happened here in Wollongong."

"What happened?" Dean Renate prompted.

"A dragon child clawed his way out of his mother," said the High Priestess. "It was such an ordinary delivery. The maiden died, and the black-scaled beast was covered in her blood. Then something extraordinary happened. As the nurses were cleaning off the blood with a washcloth, some of the scales came off, revealing perfectly healthy white skin. Over the next few days, more and more scales left the creature until he appeared to be not a dragon at all. Even the claws and the tail disappeared within a month of him being born. This has never happened before or since. Usually, the scales, claws, and tail of a dragon are permanent. The scales and tail, if removed by accident, even grow back, but not for this particular creature. Now, do you understand?"

"The dragon child who lost his scales, claws, and tail, and never got them back was Dreadnought," said Dean Renate contemplatively.

"We should have had him killed then and there," said the High Priestess. "Instead, he spent his first few years in an orphanage and was adopted by a nice, respectable couple. They had high hopes for him, which we dashed. When the time came, we designated him a knight, despite his quick mind and extraordinary reflexes. That couple thought their adopted son was going to be a maverick, how sad."

"Why not a maverick if he was smart and strong?" asked Jens.

"Think on it," said the High Priestess. She smiled a Cheshire cat smile. "As a maverick, he might have gone on to sire a creature like himself, and we couldn't have that. It is still doubtful it would happen because of him. However, if the secret of how dragons are made ever got out, it may well be the end of all we have built up over the years. Anything that could put doubts about the order of things into the minds of ordinary priestesses, maidens, and mavericks is dangerous. What's more, if knights and dragons are ever seen to have too much in common, they might choose not to fight one another, and then the wars their battles prevent could start all over again. A half-dragon and half-knight is a menace to us all."

"And you have kept the secret of his birth all this time?" asked Dean Renate.

"Yes," said the High Priestess. She frowned and then continued, "Only a handful of priestesses ever knew about the scales falling off and the claws and tail retracting. I was the one who made the fateful decision to let him live. I have followed his exploits as a knight ever since. I was surprised when he made it to twenty kills and shocked when he got over forty. I believe he can get into the minds of his opponents, but he is far from invulnerable. He may fall in November before he can reach the golden fifty."

"What if he doesn't?" asked Jens.

"We know he will never be accepted by mavericks as one of their own," said Dean Renate philosophically, her arms folded. "There would be protests and Goddess knows what else."

"You could have cities split over the rights of one individual. After all, it isn't every day a knight turns into a maverick," reasoned Jens, seeing the immensity of the problem.

"Precisely," agreed the High Priestess. "But I do have a plan for this contingency. If Dreadnought makes it to fifty and is designated a maverick, we must make it so that this causes as little stress to our people as possible. For what I have in mind, I will need the help of you both plus the aid of Megan, who need not be briefed the way you have in this matter."

Jens and Dean Renate listened, nodding in agreement where it seemed appropriate to do so as the High Priestess spoke. Deep involuntary sighs indicated they had to agree with what this High One had come up with. It might work and need not necessarily lead to the deaths of either Dreadnought or Amelia.

CHAPTER TWENTY-ONE

On the second day of November, ten knights from Wollongong, including Dreadnought, were sent to Rome to battle ten dragons in the Colosseum rebuilt ten years ago. They departed in two flyers. One was piloted by Malcolm and the other by Amelia. Once more, she was irked by the notion of possibly flying Dreadnought and the others to their doom but knew she had to do it to at least assure them they would get there in reasonable safety if nothing else. Their first scheduled stopover was Hawaii, then St. Louis, and finally Rome.

Halfway to Hawaii, there was a storm at sea. Rain splashed and then drum-rolled both vehicles. Thunder grumbled overhead, followed by flashes of lightning that reminded Amelia of journalists with their cameras. Turbulence tossed them around, and black clouds had them relying on their onboard computers more than they would have liked. Then it ended, and out of the shadows ahead of them came two giant albatrosses. *Now we're in for it,* Amelia thought, but she was wrong. Upon sighting the flyers, the birds took as much action to avoid contact as did the pilots. *Someone remembers a sore tummy,* concluded Amelia, smiling.

In Honolulu, reporters made a fuss over Dreadnought and the possibility he might someday soon become a maverick. "What will be the first thing you do if you ever reach that exalted position?" asked a young maiden with a recorder. "Stop fighting," was his answer.

Dreadnought took a walk after dinner and stopped by the statue of King Kamehameha. He had seen it before, but somehow the statue now held more meaning for him. *This was a war-*

rior who fought for his people a very long time ago, he thought. *Am I now fighting for my people?*

"It is an amazing look," Amelia said as she joined Dreadnought. "It is as if he is reaching out to us from long ago."

"He is reaching out to me," spoke Dreadnought. "Perhaps he is also doing the same for you."

On the journey across the Pacific Ocean to mainland America, the waters were calm. The Pacific was peaceful. Nothing stirred until a great black beast, larger than any whale Amelia had ever seen, lunged out of the water at her flyer. It had rows of jagged teeth and beady eyes that were fixed on getting a meal. It could not, however, leap high enough to score one flyer for lunch. This was the second time she had seen a monster from the deep, and it had shaken her. There was a tremor in one of her hands; Amelia suppressed it by placing the other over it. She took a deep breath and slowly let it out. She did this a couple of times. It was military training on how to deal with stress. After a short while, her hand stopped shaking. The others, no doubt having confidence in her or not caring too much how they died, remained calm, and this made her less fearful. Dreadnought looked amused; he was smiling in her direction. *What are you thinking?* Amelia wondered. *Do you do something similar to what I was doing to get over a big scare?* Dreadnought said nothing, and Amelia found she didn't want to broach the subject with him. She had her dignity to consider.

At St. Louis, more reporters were out to get a story from Dreadnought. He had nothing to say to them except he would do his best in Rome.

The flight from St. Louis to the seven hills overlooking Rome was uneventful until Amelia caught the flash of something rushing in her direction. She moved her craft out of its way, but it hit and exploded against the second flyer. It was a ground-to-air missile. The attack happened so fast it was tough, if not impossible, for Amelia to take in all the ramifications attached to it at once. The back end of the second flyer was damaged, ripped apart, so two knights fell out onto hard ground. No doubt, they died from multiple injuries. One landed on softer ground and so might have survived. Inside the craft, knights were being battered about by the shaky flyer as was the pilot. Amelia imagined Malcolm fighting what remained of the controls to bring the plane down safely. It had to be a crash landing, and it took place not far from the gates of the eternal city.

Luckily, Malcolm's flyer was low enough when the missile struck for decompression not to be a problem. He was piloting just beyond the hills when it happened and his flyer was losing height for his landing approach to the airport. Still Malcolm would have been extremely fortunate to be able do anything with his controls considering the state his craft was in.

By the time Amelia set her flyer down, a motorized hovercraft ambulance, operating on cushions of air and anti-gravity units in place of wheels, was on its way, its crew to look after any survivors. Malcolm and two knights had walked away from the disaster with minor injuries. One knight was badly hurt, and two had been killed by the fall from the craft.

"Welcome to Italy," said Amelia, a half-smile on her face, as she taxied to a landing near some transport.

"Glad to be here in one piece," replied Dreadnought.

Hours later, the maverick responsible for the missile launch was hunted down and caught. His name was Hugo Forgeron, and he was from Lyon. The launcher still in his possession had been the giveaway. He pleaded guilty and said he had done what he did for Lyon and good mavericks everywhere. The sentence imposed on him was swift. He was stripped of his maverick status and made to compete as a replacement for the knights he had murdered. He was to wear a dragon pain collar, made suitable for a human by maverick technicians, up until he was required to go into the arena. The collar would mean he would not be able to have any contact with a maiden. Even holding hands with one would result in a nasty shock.

"We don't want him," said Dreadnought to Amelia when he heard about the decision, "but I suppose that isn't up to us. He will not be, by any means, a good replacement for any of the knights we have lost."

Everyone from Wollongong received translators to wear for half a day to understand the Italian language. Officials made apologies to Amelia and Malcolm for the incident in the air. The wounded knight, the one who had landed on softer ground, would spend as much time as required for his recovery in hospital with the local council footing the bill. In two days, the other knights would be needed for the arena.

"It will now be seven Wollongong knights plus one outsider versus ten Greek dragons," said the official to Amelia in her designated hotel suite. "We got in touch with your officials, and they said this was acceptable."

"Yes, I suppose it would be to them," agreed Malcolm, who was there at the time. He was, after all, only one of the Wollongong pilots, and this was the closest thing to a protest he felt any official would listen to from someone without much diplomatic status. Amelia had nothing to say.

The press was not allowed to interview Dreadnought and the other knights. Dreadnought was glad of this. "I have nothing to say to maidens and mavericks who want my words before a battle," he told Amelia. She touched his hand, but he didn't respond. She sensed he was toughening up for what was to come. This, she understood. When she was a fighter pilot, there were occasions where she divorced herself from everything except the mission. Some reporters tried to get a statement from Amelia and Malcolm but without success. Even so, the attack upon the flyer made for screaming headlines about bad sportsmanship and Dreadnought's right to try for the golden fifty.

Amelia spent a day walking around Rome with Dreadnought and the six other knights, Malcolm, and a local guide. There were still ruins where the Vatican had once been. The reason for this was evident to the guide and the people of this city. "We don't want the old religion coming back," he told them. "Abandoning the site forever sends a clear message we continue to be free from its influence."

Strange statues of naked men and women stood everywhere, along with ornate fountains. Amelia was taken aback by a female in bronze, without even pants to wear, with a spear in hand. *I'd put clothes on first if I were going to fight anyone*, thought Amelia. There was a fountain where a little marble boy was pissing into the water. *Too weird*, thought Amelia, dismissing it. The Arch of Constantine caught Dreadnought's eye with its great battle scene. "This has always been a place of warriors," he told Amelia.

The rich history of Rome impressed Amelia more than it did the others. *I read about the glory of Ancient Rome in one of my history classes*, she thought. *Mind you, I didn't find much beauty. The ancient Romans, however, were brilliant architects, and their brilliance is still here to be seen and admired. All of these fountains and statues, however, were created during the renaissance with capital from various popes and other higher-ups. That doesn't make them any less impressive or bizarre.*

She stopped every so often to admire a building that held remnants of the past or a fountain that gave some indication of style at play—a pretty face here, a monstrous one there. She then had to catch up with the others.

Amelia had known about the gladiatorial games and how they went. It had been all about spectacle and the bloodthirsty nature of the crowd. It seemed to her, after centuries of finding other ways to amuse people; it had gone back to that form of amusement.

The Colosseum from the outside rose above the other nearby structures. Amelia could only imagine how it looked from the inside. For a very long time, it had been a broken tourist attraction. Now, it was once again much more.

The morning of the games arrived. Around seven o'clock, the knights were taken from their hotel rooms by robot guards to a holding cell below the arena. They were not locked in but guarded by these mechanical creatures, as were the dragons that had been placed collarless in a nearby cell. Two sets of stairs led up to where the fighting would commence. The knights would take one and the dragons the other.

Around nine, Amelia and Malcolm were taken from their hotel to the Colosseum by their guide. He left them once they were seated. There they discovered there were seats in this modern version of the place for one hundred thousand maids and mavericks. All the seats this day were taken, and mavericks were sitting on the aisle steps. The first row with white, cushioned seats and excellent views of the coming action was reserved for the Highest of High Priestesses, her entourage, and dignitaries from all parts of the world. Malcolm was all smiles, feeling honoured to have a place there. Amelia felt no such thing. She was trying not to frown, knowing that any sign of disapproval here would be hazardous.

The Priestess of Priestesses was in her late forties and dressed in a plain white robe with hood. What differentiated her from the other priestesses around her were a golden crown and a pearl ring. The crown was a simple gold band, but it was something no one else could or would wear until her passing. She expected to live a long time and to make sure her brand of faith persisted long after she was gone. Amelia looked into this woman's eyes and saw nothing but cold steel.

"The arena floor is made of hardwood imported from Africa," said a minor priestess to Amelia and Malcolm. "Sawdust has been thrown down to absorb the blood."

"How nice." Amelia was sickened. She was being sarcastic, but the priestess didn't take it that way.

"Yes, it is," enthused the minor priestess. "We are so fortunate to have this venue. There are cameras strategically placed and view screens here and there so you won't miss a thing. Plus, there's a replay. Fifty cities will be tunning in. There are six events. Yours will be the last, and I suspect, the best."

"All knights versus dragons?" asked Malcolm.

"Heavens, no!" cried the minor priestess. "There will be one lion and one tiger that have been starved for the occasion pitted against one another for the prize of a lone goat. The goat, of course, doesn't stand a chance. Following that will be three mutant bears trained to dance for us. It should be exciting. They're imported from Lexington in Kentucky. Oh, and a couple of bouts with other knights and dragons before those Wollongong knights make an appearance. Also, a music recital from our famous Roman choir made up of young maidens and mavericks. That should be a treat."

"Anything else?" asked Malcolm.

"We have a grim clown with a black cowl, grinning face mask, and everything including balloons for the children," said the minor priestess. "The grim clown is a resident knight who carries a big, wooden mallet. Both contestant knights and dragons are expected to walk on and off our battle site without assistance. If any of them happens to be incapable of doing so because of sustained injuries, the grim clown steps in. Whack! Whack! You get the picture?"

"That's horrible!" cried Amelia, forgetting herself with that outburst. She breathed in and out to steady herself, knowing that another mistake like that might have severe repercussions. *I am supposed to be here to enjoy myself*, Amelia thought, *and that is what I will pretend to do!*

"Horrible? Yes, it is, isn't it," agreed the minor priestess whimsically. "Oh, and there will be a comic-opera performance in the lobby of where you are staying tonight. *The Mikado* by Gilbert and Sullivan, I believe. It's being put on by visiting Liverpool members of some English theatre company. Yum-Yum as they say."

"Yum-Yum?" wondered Amelia, thinking in terms of cannibalism.

"You know, the character Yum-Yum out of the comic-opera," said the minor priestess.

"Oh, right!" Amelia had never heard of Yum-Yum or *The Mikado* but felt it had to be better than what she was about to witness. Comic-operas were not a specialty at any military base where she had ever been stationed.

The preliminary events went slowly for both Amelia and Malcolm. Amelia couldn't bear to watch the contest between hungry wild beasts and the lone goat running here and there, trying desperately to escape. She left for the toilet, and when she returned, she was told the tiger had gotten the goat and had eaten most of it. Some was left for the lion. The tiger and the lion were allowed to take the bones and the leftover meat of the goat back to their cell below.

Chained bears with a second row of teeth were made by knightly trainers to dance and jump through hoops. Those that were slow to obey were, to the crowd's delight, whipped into being more obedient. *Animal mistreatment has returned*, Amelia thought. She would have liked to have gone back to the toilet but felt she had better not do so. It would give too bad an impression.

Four new layers of sawdust were added to the arena floor over the coming hours to prevent slippage by contestants before robot guards brought out Dreadnought and his knights. With them came Hugo Forgeron, the ex-maverick. The audience cheered at the sight of the Wollongong knights, then booed when the dragons made their entrance. A maverick vendor sold Malcolm a bag of peanuts and a soft drink. Amelia wasn't hungry or thirsty. She declined the offer of both. "Your loss," said Malcolm shrugging.

Amelia wondered if the soft drink might not be a good idea. It could settle her stomach and stop her from throwing up. "I've changed my mind," she told Malcolm. "I will have a soft drink. Can you make it lemonade?"

"Not a problem," said Malcolm, smiling. "Hey! Vendor! A lemonade for this maiden, please!" Coins were exchanged for the carbonated drink.

Two of the knights had short spears, three including Dreadnought had swords, and the rest maces to bash in heads. All carried daggers and shields. They wore chest plates and leather leggings for added protection.

The dragons had shiny red scales. All but two of them had battle axes. What those two had was, for the moment, a mystery. Suffice to say, metallic backpacks were the key.

Dreadnought formed a circle of mutual protection with his fellow knights. He didn't want to do it but thought it wise to invite Forgeron, the dishonoured ex-maverick, to join them.

"No! I will not help you!" cried Hugo Forgeron. He dropped his mace and shield then knelt to pray.

Dreadnought looked at this small, weedy man with the large nose and thin moustache and wondered what had ever made him so much more worthy than himself to be rated a maverick. It just didn't make sense. *No, you are not better than me,* he thought, *or my knights.*

"And here we have the final event for today," spoke a maidenly announcer over the speaker system. "The brave Wollongong knights versus these tough Spartan dragons. As a bonus, with respect to the tradition of the Greek and English legend of Saint George slaying the dragon, we have a surprise I know you will enjoy. But now, at the blast of the horn, let this game begin!"

The horn sounded, and Dreadnought made a decision. He broke ranks and advanced on Forgeron. "You will help," he said as he took the fellow by the scruff of the neck and by the seat of the pants and hurled him into the advancing dragons. Two went down with Forgeron on top of them. As the felled dragons scrambled to their feet, two blades from two knights sped through the air, getting one dragon in the neck and the other in the chest. Both fell and died. A battle axe from another dragon then came down swiftly onto Forgeron's head with a great crack sound like a coconut being split. Dreadnought thought he heard Forgeron squeak like a mouse caught in a trap before he expired.

The dragons stopped within twenty feet of the knights. The two with the strange backpacks that had tube and nozzle attachments, moved forward a few feet then also halted. Dreadnought got back into formation, waiting for whatever was to happen next.

"These dragons don't breathe fire like the dragon that took on Saint George," said the announcer, "but they do the next best thing ... with flame throwers!"

Buttons were pressed, and flames shot out of the nozzles at the knights. Shields held. On the second twin burst, the dragons aimed for the feet of their opponents and caught two knights out that way. They screamed at having their feet scorched even through their boots and dropped their shields. A press of two buttons and third twin burst ate them up. They moved away from the other knights so as not to set them aflame. The crowd clapped and cheered. Amelia thought she could smell burning human flesh, and it disgusted her. Sipping her lemonade did help a little. Thankfully, it wasn't long before the flaming men crumpled up and became nothing more than ash and bone. The dragons who had started this gave the men a fourth twin burst possibly as an act of mercy to send them more quickly on their way.

During a momentary respite from the use of the flame throwers, Dreadnought threw a dagger that punctured a tube of one of the devices. It seemed such an insignificant action until the dragon with the hole in his tube pressed his button to fry

Dreadnought. Instead, the resulting escaping gas from the tube caught on fire, causing the wielder of the flame thrower to then become a living torch. The other dragon with the flame thrower, being too close to his companion, also lit up. Seconds later, there was one exploding backpack followed by the other. More clapping and cheering from the crowd ensued.

Apart from the flame thrower wielding dragons blown to bits, two had their legs cut into by debris from the explosion. They fell and were not able to rise. Later, the grim clown would come along and end their lives with his mallet. The knights were able to hide from most of the hurling metal and human bone fragments behind their shields.

It took a few moments for the remaining dragons and knights to take in what had happened. Then a dragon snarled and came at the knight next to Dreadnought with his battle axe raised for action. He was forced back by the attacked knight's shield, and Dreadnought finished him off with a sword thrust.

Then three dragons threw their battle axes. One got past the shields and brought down a knight. The others bounced harmlessly off metal. Moments later, the two knights with spears used them, thus eliminating two more of the enemy. The two remaining dragons ran at Dreadnought, yelling and waving their battle axes. One was dealt with by a sword blow from another knight. The other managed to plant his weapon in Dreadnought's left shoulder before being slammed by Dreadnought's shield and then having his throat slit by Dreadnought's sword.

The dragons all dead, including the two the grim clown took care of, the horn sounded, and the remaining knights bowed to the applause of the onlookers. Dreadnought came close to falling and becoming a victim of the grim clown. Still, he managed to stagger out with the rest, and two of his fellow knights helped him down the stairs.

Dreadnought did not have the axe removed while he was still at the Colosseum. He waited for it to be done at the hospital.

He realized there would be blood loss and wanted to be where he could get a quick blood transfusion and other necessary care. Also, he feared that too much nerve damage might cost him his arm. The blade of the axe was only four inches across but had sunk deep.

The next day, a maiden nurse told him that he had officially made four more kills, bumping his overall total up to forty-six. Amelia and Malcolm made five visits to his hospital room before heading back to Wollongong in the flyer with the other remaining Wollongong knights.

Amelia didn't want to leave Dreadnought, but she was given no choice. She was required back at Wollongong, and it would be too much a risk to Dreadnought's health to have him fly home with her. She was assured by the Italian priestesses that there would always be a robot guard on the entrance to his room while he remained in hospital and that only the best doctors and nurses would see to him.

She was told that the severed nerves found in Dreadnought's shoulder would be repaired via microsurgery. It was a newly rediscovered technique and given the blessings of the Highest of High Priestesses in her infinite wisdom. Still, months would go by before Dreadnought would be fit for travel, let alone be capable of slaying more dragons. This saddened him and other knights.

"So close," he told Amelia the last time she saw him in Rome.

"I know," replied Amelia, clasping his right hand and then letting go before departing. Dreadnought thought he detected a tear rolling down her face as she walked away.

Throughout the world, newspapers and periodicals covered the Colosseum games. The highlights were the victories by Dreadnought and his wounding. He was too important now to knights everywhere, not to be allowed to survive. Any possibility that he would die from inadequate hospital care or poisoning had to be eliminated at all costs to prevent hundreds of thousands, possibly millions of knights from running amok. If he were to die in the future, it had to be somewhere he faced dragons in an attempt to gain the golden fifty. Malcolm told Amelia this as they headed home.

Malcolm took the controls for the flight from Rome to St. Louis because Amelia wasn't feeling well. "That lemonade at the games didn't sit as well as I hoped it would," she told him. She was feeling queasy, and, though she hadn't upchucked, there was still that possibility even though she hadn't eaten much for dinner.

At St. Louis, reporters wanted to know about Dreadnought's condition and his plans. Amelia and Malcolm had nothing to say. Amelia was getting over what she said must have been a touch of the flu, but she knew it was really her reaction to all the cruelty she had recently witnessed. What helped was a message from Rome she received informing her that Dreadnought's operation had been a complete success, and he was no longer in immediate danger from his wound. Via a reporter on a radio station, Amelia and Malcolm learned that the knight who was injured rather than killed falling out of Malcolm's broken apart flyer was also on the mend.

From St. Louis to Honolulu, they encountered rough weather. A storm engulfed them, and for three solid hours, they flew more reliant than either Malcolm or Amelia wanted to be on instrumentation.

After too long in the dark with spears of lightning, now and then, brightening up the nothingness outside, Malcolm said, "I need a visual sighting; I am desperate for a visual sighting." He strained his eyes to see something, anything. His sense of reality was slipping away. It was as if the only people in existence were there with him in the flyer as it rocked with turbulence. Amelia could see what was happening to Malcolm and the others. It was also getting to her. The engulfing blackness and the threat from gusts of wind were challenging their sense of being. Only the knights seemed unaffected, possibly drawing strength from how they thought Dreadnought would behave.

Amelia broke the spell created by the blackness by getting Malcolm to talk about his Megan. She kept him talking about her until they were out of those heavy clouds, and the sky was clear. "Thank you," said Malcolm, after the nightmare was over, realising how thinking about Megan had centred him and prevented panic. "I needed that."

The onboard computer did not let them down, and they safely reached Honolulu. There, reporters bombarded them with more questions, and this time Amelia told them all she knew about Dreadnought's condition and his chances of fighting again. She mentioned microsurgery, and that made the newspapers. Some of the medical journals also picked up on this and ran with it in more detail, making some of the doctors and nurses at Rome's hospital overnight celebrities.

It was on a calm morning when they took off from Honolulu with Amelia at the controls for the final leg home. Terns and seagulls flew with them for about an hour before turning back. They noticed movement from time to time in the waters below and took it to be signs of those black monsters that are best avoided.

Touchdown in Wollongong was smooth, and cars were waiting to take them wherever they wanted to go. The knights went back to their barracks in one vehicle. In the other, Amelia and Malcolm decided to go for drinks at the nearest watering hole before each heading to their respective dwellings.

"You're too close to Dreadnought," Malcolm told Amelia over drinks at The Great Grape, a local bar near where the flyer landed.

Amelia looked around. Maidens and mavericks were sitting at the bar with their glasses of wine. The walls, tables, and stools were all in light pastel colours. Malcolm did not impress with the glass of white he was gently sipping.

The maverick barkeep had to dust off a bottle of scotch just for Amelia. She wasn't, however, in the mood for anything weaker. The subdued lighting and smooth jazz helped her feel better, happier with where she was, but it wasn't enough. She was so glad that jazz, in at least one form, couldn't be killed by time, but this wasn't her scene.

"So what if I have feelings?" asked Amelia, downing a glass and then motioning the barkeep to fill it up again. He shook his head as he did so.

"It's amazing anyone can swallow that awful concoction," murmured the fellow. "It's only fit for dragons if you ask me."

"So why do you have it on your shelf?" asked Amelia.

"The previous owner thought mavericks might get a taste for it." The barkeep shrugged. "He was wrong."

"Getting overly emotional about someone whose life can easily be snuffed out isn't good," said Malcolm.

"But as a maiden, I am nevertheless supposed to spend time with my knight," reasoned Amelia.

"You're still not used to our ways." Malcolm fetched a sigh. "We grew up knowing knights and dragons don't last long. You have found that out as an adult."

"I sure did," agreed Amelia.

"Dreadnought could have died in Rome but didn't," said Malcolm. "Next time, who knows? But that's life and death."

Amelia tossed down her drink and put the empty glass on the bar. She shook her head when the barkeep went to refill it. She plunked down some coins. "Let's get outta here and find a livelier spot," she said, and they left.

Not more than a street away, they found Demons, a place that served dragons. The décor was very different from The Great Grape. Everything was either red or black, making Amelia think of Australian black widow spiders. They didn't stay long. It was full of silver and black dragons who would have cheerfully murdered them if only their pain collars were removed. The music was disjointed and harsh, which was no doubt a reflection on the way they lived. Hard liquor was everywhere and cheap for customers who couldn't afford much.

"What a dump!" Malcolm cried. As they reached for the swinging doors, an empty bottle sailed over his head to smash against a crimson wall, and a dragon screamed horribly as his pain collar took effect.

Across from Demons was a notorious pub for knights known as The Spear and Shield. Amelia ventured in, and Malcolm reluctantly followed her. It was a place of browns, greys, and blacks. Country style music was playing. In one corner, there was an old, beat up lounge where injured knights rested. In another, a dozen knights were playing a game Amelia took to be similar to pool. What caught Amelia's eye, though, was the dartboard against the wall in the centre of the establishment. It had a privileged location, and yet no one was making use of the darts.

Most of the knights were drinking beer, which suited Amelia fine. She went up to the bar and asked the knight behind the counter what he recommended. "I recommend The Great Grape," he told her. "I am sorry maiden, but we don't have any wine on the premises."

She pointed to a knight that was drinking something black with a frothy head and said, "We'll have whatever that knight is having."

"Both of you?" asked the barman, looking both Amelia and Malcolm up and down.

"Yes, of course," said Amelia.

"It's good, strong stout," warned the barman.

"We'll take our chances," said Amelia.

The barman knight skilfully poured them the two drinks they had asked for and waited for their reactions when they drank. Half the customers looked on. Malcolm winced at the bitter taste, but Amelia smacked her lips, grinned, and got stuck into the grog. She finished the glass, paid for it, and ordered another for herself. Malcolm gingerly put his nearly full glass on the counter and reluctantly handed over coin for something he thought was ghastly.

"Anyone up for a game of darts?" Amelia asked the crowd of knights who had taken an interest in her and Malcolm. The background music stopped.

"You play darts?" asked a heavily built knight.

"Why not find out?" offered Amelia.

All went quiet. Knights looked at each other in surprise. Malcolm looked uncomfortable, shrinking away from those surrounding him, but not Amelia. The knights were a scruffy lot in their grey or blue clothing, but they still reminded her of air force personnel she had known. *Wimping out on an air force base was never recommended*, thought Amelia, *and it's not recommended here.* She had to admit that Malcolm, in his zigzag black, gray, and red suit, looked silly in such company.

"Very well, maiden," said the husky knight, "but I play to win."

"You should always play to win," said Amelia.

"Maidens are not supposed to act this way," whispered Malcolm in Amelia's ear. He was looking at the door and, no doubt, thinking about a fast getaway.

"I don't care," she whispered back.

The music started up again, and they played. The heavily built knight was good, but Amelia was better. They had three games, and she won each time.

"You're not letting me beat you, are you?" asked Amelia when they stopped for drinks.

"Oh, no!" cried the husky knight. "This is our place. We leave all that nonsense outside."

"I hate a false win," said Amelia. "Not much fun."

Then there was a hush that frightened Malcolm. By this time, everyone in the establishment was looking at Amelia and the maverick she was with. Malcolm expected a pool cue up his nose at any moment, or a glass smashed against his head. His eyes moved this way and that from one brute to another. Sweat trickled down his forehead as he realized an attempted dash out of there might be regarded as an insult to every knight in the establishment. He knew he wasn't all that fast, especially dragging Amelia away with him. Instead of violence, however, the knights burst out laughing in good humour.

"I could learn to like a maiden like you," confessed the heavily built knight.

"I'm sure you could," agreed Amelia, "but Dreadnought is my knight."

The music stopped. There was dead silence. Suddenly, the darts on the dartboard looked deadly to Malcolm. He knew he couldn't make a successful dash for the exit with Amelia without getting killed by them.

"No, you're not!" cried the heavily built knight. "She wouldn't be seen dead in The Spear and Shield."

"I am Amelia Warren, former Australian air force fighter pilot," she announced, "and I am Dreadnought's maiden. And what is so wrong with The Spear and Shield?"

The heavily built knight blinked, looked around, and wondered what he should say. True, it wasn't where maidens and mavericks were supposed to hang out, but to put it down might get him kicked out. "Nothing at all, maiden," he finally said.

Then the atmosphere changed, and there were a lot of eager questions about Dreadnought that came Amelia's way. She happily answered them as best she could. Everyone wanted to shout her beer and talk about the golden fifty and how she might help Dreadnought get there. The word got out, and more knights came in to see the famous maiden from the past and glean her connection to their most celebrated warrior.

"What made him decide on you?" asked a young knight.

"He doesn't like soft maidens," responded Amelia and was cheered by the mounting crowd.

"And how did you end up with her?" a knight with only one eye asked Malcolm.

"Just lucky, I guess," said Malcolm meekly. This revelation was greeted with laughter.

As dawn approached, the crowd thinned to where Amelia and Malcolm could get away. "Before you leave," said the heavily built knight, "I want the barman to give you back the money you have spent here. I will pay for your drinks in respect for Dreadnought."

"No, you don't," said the barman, handing coins to Amelia. "I pay for her drinks and not you in Dreadnought's name, and for the extra customers she's brought in tonight."

"This is too kind," said Amelia, who wanted to refuse the money.

"We will take it badly if you don't take it," grumbled the barman.

"Anything for Dreadnought and his maiden," concluded the heavily built knight.

Amelia took the money and left with Malcolm, who was glad to get out alive and in one piece.

"Now that was lively," commented Amelia as she hailed a pay-as-you-go transport.

"Please don't ever do that to me again," said Malcolm, slumping slightly, hands shaking. "That was insane!"

"Lighten up," replied Amelia, who was feeling great. "Now, I ask you, why can't we enjoy ourselves every once in a while?"

"That's enjoyment?" questioned Malcolm sarcastically.

"You bet!" replied Amelia.

"You and Dreadnought deserve each other," concluded Malcolm in resignation. He shook his head sadly and then smiled. Megan was more suited to him. She was someone with whom he could sensibly plan a future.

"Kind of you to say so," replied Amelia. "Are there pubs and bars where only maidens hang out?"

"I wouldn't know," said Malcolm. "I suppose there must be. Do you want to go to one?"

"Probably not," Amelia mused. "I can't imagine them being very exciting."

How she was feeling, she knew, was in part due to the alcohol she had consumed and in part from all the good wishes showered onto her by well-meaning knights. *I must remember to drink a glass of water before sleep*, she told herself, *to avoid a hangover.* This she failed to do, but that was all right, considering the night she had just had.

She had almost forgotten what too much drink the night before with too little food was like. It was brutal. Her bedroom that morning would not stop spinning for what seemed a long while but was probably only an hour or so. She managed to get to the bathroom before throwing up. That was a blessing. She felt she needed to apologise to Malcolm over something, but she couldn't think what that might be.

Amelia felt heartless at not still feeling bad about the horrors she had witnessed in Rome. She realized, however, that if she let such things continually get to her, she would become useless to Dreadnought, who needed her to be strong. But what could she do for him?

Birds were one answer. Amelia went to a book shop and bought a dozen books on local avian wildlife. She then posted them to the hospital in Rome addressed to Dreadnought. What else? She began a diary and mailed off selected pages she hoped would not be too dull. She mentioned her adventures in The Great Grape, Demons, and The Spear and Shield in one of them.

She had to wonder if he had ever hung out in The Spear and Shield. He replied to her that he hadn't in a very long time and that he wasn't much of a drinker.

For two weeks, she had nothing much to do; then, she was given the job of transporting five dragons to Tasmania for a battle with five Hobart knights. She wanted to turn it down at first; then, she thought maybe it was time to reacquaint her mind with dragons, even the ones she was taking to their doom. That time in their barracks plus five minutes at Demons hadn't told her much about them. It was too easy to slip into seeing them as just the enemy. She knew they could talk. The question was how much they would be willing to say to her on a short trip?

CHAPTER TWENTY-TWO

A robot guard accompanied the five dragons Amelia took to Hobart. Three dragons were silvery, and two were black-scaled.

Amelia wondered what good the guard would be if, despite the pain collars, the dragons went crazy while they were in flight. The gun carried by the robot was formidable on the ground, but if fired in the flyer at a high altitude, it could prove fatal to all onboard. One small hole made in the side of the craft that reached the outside could destabilize it and cause it to crash. A robot fist accidentally smashing into the controls or causing a crack in the superstructure would be just as disastrous. It was, however, standard procedure to have it aboard while transporting dragons. Knights were considered more trustworthy and so didn't need this added security.

Once in the air, a silvery dragon pulled a book out of his satchel and began to read. Amelia noticed it was *1984* by George Orwell. She was amazed it was being printed. It had been banned when she was a little girl. She couldn't imagine why it wasn't forbidden now. Perhaps it was a pirate copy.

A black-scaled dragon reached into a bag for a Chess set and played a game with the other black-scaled dragon. Chess was one of the games Amelia had enjoyed at flight school back in her RAAF days. The remaining two dragons started a conversation about gardening. Apparently, one of them was a rose expert, and the other knew a lot about orchids. Because of their forked tongues, they hissed as they spoke. Amelia had no particular interest in flowers and found them easy to ignore. She concentrated on the flight. What they were saying was simply background noise.

Powerful winds swirling up from the ruins of Melbourne knocked the flyer about but seemed to be of more concern to Amelia at the controls than to the others. The reader dropped his book, but he took little time in once more finding his place. The Chess pieces were scattered about, but the players patiently put them back where they were so they could continue. The two talkers had stopped for a moment but then had continued their conversation. It seemed that aphids were more of a worrying topic than what might have happened to their transport.

Once the danger had passed, Amelia looked at the dragons and said, "Can we talk?" All stopped what they were doing and saying and blinked at her.

"What do you want to talk about?" asked the dragon who liked roses.

"History?" suggested one of the Chess players.

"Art?" suggested his companion in Chess.

"What is it like to be a dragon?" asked Amelia.

"If you wish to get under our ssskin," replied the book reader, "you will have to get past our scales first."

"That's a joke," said the orchid fancier. "We do like to pretend we are human."

"It's only pretend?" asked Amelia.

"What else could it be?" The art lover hissed in a whimsical tone. He shook his head and smiled. His forked tongue poked out a few times as if for emphasis. "You couldn't do what's done to us if we were human."

"Humansss don't have tails." The rose fancier pointed this out by raising and lowering his tail slightly but not enough to get a reaction from the robot. "Though I do believe humans have tailbones."

"What good are tailbones without tails?" contemplated the book reader, smiling. "I know! Those tailless wonders must be jealous!"

"That's the answer!" cried the history buff with a great big grin. "Give everyone who doesn't have them tails and scales."

"Problem solved." The orchid fancier threw up his claws as if in surrender and then aimed a curved nail at the controls. "Now turn us around, and we'll go back to our barracks and pack for a better life."

"Can't you be serious?" asked Amelia.

"What's the point of that?" The art fancier shook his head, and then his tongue poked out.

"No point at all," concluded the history buff, his tongue coming out and going back in. "Had enough talk?"

"Ever been to Demons?" asked Amelia.

"Demons?" There was the wow factor in the art fancier's voice. He was surprised she knew that dive existed.

"You do mean the drinking hole not far from the airport?" asked the history buff.

"That's the one," said Amelia.

"We're not all the same," announced the book reader. "There isn't a mould we all come out of."

"I went to Demons once," said the rose fancier. "I had one drink and left. It's a good place for wallowing in ssself-pity and getting blotto. I thought I might be into that, but it's not for me."

"It's rough." The orchid fancier closed his eyes in remembrance and then opened them again. "Even though we're dragons, some of us wouldn't last five minutes in there if our pain collars were removed."

"Does that ever happen?" asked Amelia.

"You know where it happensss." The book reader growled, tongue coming out and going in rhythmically with each word spoken as if trying to get the taste of an ugly truth out of his mouth. "We're going there, and you are taking us there. Now, if you don't mind, I'll get back to my reading."

"Please do," said Amelia, taken aback by the book reader's sudden show of passion. "No more questions."

The book reader took up his book again and was pleased to do so.

Amelia then realised how young these dragons were. All five were probably in their late teens and had never been in combat before. If they lived a year or two longer, Demons would be their future. For now, they were not quite hard and cynical enough for that dump. What they had, no doubt, been doing aboard her flyer was trying to take their minds off the upcoming game. She now felt guilty taking them to where they were going. She wondered how many, if any, would survive and need her services to return to Wollongong.

Over Bass Strait, the air and sea were calm. Nothing stirred below. The sky was clear and would remain so the rest of the way to their landing site. It was a smooth run into Hobart's airfield, where officials met them.

Amelia was taken to a hotel, and the others, including the robot, to a cell for the night.

The next morning, Amelia was asked to inspect the stage where the fighting would occur. She thought this strange, but the owner of the theatre and the announcer informed her that, because she was the only viable representative of Wollongong around, it was up to her to see that everything was done fairly from the Wollongong side. She was also told the Wollongong ambassador had urgent business elsewhere in Hobart and couldn't attend to this himself.

Since Amelia was only asked to look, surely there couldn't be any harm in doing so. She looked and nodded.

Amelia knew she didn't have any reason to say no to the whole damned thing that the maidens and mavericks of either Hobart or Wollongong would understand.

Sand had been laid down, and the cameras put into place. The theatre had enough seats for an audience of only two hundred maidens and mavericks, but the action would be televised.

Late in the afternoon, the dragons were taken to the back area of the theatre and then issued with maces and battle axes. Their pain collars were removed under the supervision of the robot. The knights had chest plates, short swords, and shields. The knights came on stage first, followed by the dragons. Both sides, to Amelia, seemed too young to be doing what they were about to do. She wanted to protest, but she knew no one would listen.

"I'm looking forward to this," said a stout maiden in her forties dressed in a loud purple outfit. She sat in a row below where Amelia was seated.

"I'm betting on the knights to win." An elderly maverick in a yellow suit with orange sleeves rubbed his hands together in anticipation.

"They look like a poor crop of dragons." A maiden in a green frock with a girl child wearing a similar outfit waved a dismissive hand. "I hope they won't disappoint."

Amelia told herself they were just dragons she'd transported from Wollongong and nothing more. Still, the woman's comment didn't sit well with her. She wanted to look away from what was going to happen but couldn't. She sighed deeply, wondering what had become of her humanity.

A horn sounded, and the dragons moved toward the knights. Neither side seemed to have a plan involving their teammates. One of the knights scooped up sand with his shield and flung it in the direction of the dragons. It blinded the rose fancier and the book reader, who were then run through with swords. The orchid lover used his tail to knock a knight off his feet then planted his axe in the fellow's chest.

The two chess players slammed away at two knights' shields with their maces to little effect until a knight tripped over his own feet and fell, taking the other one down with him.

The two maces then descended hard on the skulls of the clumsy knight and his friend.

The remaining two knights came at the orchid dragon, running him through with two swords. The chess players howled when they saw this and hurled their maces at the offending knights. One bounced harmlessly off a shield, but the other got through and hit the knight in the chest, winding him. Before the knights could counter-attack, one of the remaining dragons picked up a fallen knight's sword and shield. His companion grabbed a battle axe.

"Is this in the rules?" asked a maiden in a blue jumpsuit. "Are dragons allowed to use knightly weapons?"

"Yes," said her maverick friend, who was in a Hawaiian style shirt and blue jeans. "So long as the weapon is abandoned, it's all right."

"I suppose a dead knight has no use for sword or shield," grumbled the maiden. "It just doesn't look right."

The chess player, with sword and shield, slammed away at the knight with the aching chest and damaged chest plate until his opponent was accustomed to the idea. Then he used his tail to grab the fellow by the left ankle and bring him crashing to the stage floor. Two sword thrusts in the neck, and then the stomach ensued. Before long, despite the gurgling of the throat and the shaking limbs, the knight was dead.

Unfortunately for him, the last knight had paid too much attention to the death throes of his final companion. His shield was knocked aside, and an axe split his skull. It stayed in because the dragon couldn't get it out. Blood fountained as the knight collapsed into a puddle of his fluids. He had also urinated.

A horn sounded; the chess players bowed and left the stage. There was clapping and booing. Backstage, the robot saw to it the pain collars went back on, and the weapons the dragons had on them were handed over to waiting authorities.

Amelia once more stayed in a hotel overnight while the remaining dragons languished in a cell with their robot guard. The next morning, they headed back to Wollongong in the flyer.

On the journey across Bass Strait, three giant albatross saw their craft and followed it for a while before turning back.

The chess players were careful to hold onto their chess pieces and board over Melbourne. There, this time, debris was channelled upward by hot winds, and some of it collided with the flyer. Amelia was able to avoid the larger chunks that would have done considerable damage. Even so, she suspected by the pinging sound of minor hits, that the front of the flyer had gotten at least one dent that hadn't been there before. A smashed window might have let in radiation and been fatal to all.

Amelia had been told avoiding Melbourne also had its hazards with unsafe forests containing monstrous wildlife. The beaches teemed with predatory creatures that were once harmless. If the pilot flew too low to conserve power, hit a tree, and went down, those onboard might well be eaten by the terrors born of radiation. Some of the things that haunted the sands could leap great distances and so, with their flabby bodies and springy legs and arms, strike a flyer in flight.

There was also the question of fuel consumption. Getting around Melbourne cost fuel. Amelia had to be careful how much she deviated to avoid running out of fuel. If she had to fly to Hobart again, she would try to find a better way of making the journey.

Just before coming in to land at Wollongong airport, the history buff said to Amelia, "Can I ask you a question?"

"Sure." Amelia shrugged. "What have you got on your mind?" She had been avoiding talking to the remaining dragons most of the flight back. Seeing the world from their point of view had been just too much of an eye-opener and rather unsettling.

"The whole time you have been with us, you haven't asked us our names." The history buff leaned forward, his eyes downcast. "Is it your belief we don't have names?"

"I don't doubt you do have names," said Amelia.

"But you don't want to know them," concluded the art fancier.

"No, I suppose I don't." Amelia shrugged her shoulders and smiled weakly. She wanted to say that knowing their names would make their deaths too hard to take but knew, in this society that would not be deemed appropriate. No maiden was supposed to care about dragon fatalities. Amelia then considered Dreadnought and what he had to do. It was all wrong. *Dragons should be brainless brutes,* thought Amelia; *only then would this knight versus dragon thing make sense.*

"I understand," the history buff mused, turning away. "Namess would only get in the way and make us all too human."

The art fancier then took the book out of the book reader's satchel and handed it to Amelia. He winced slightly from a shock by his collar. He wasn't supposed to get that close to her. The robot shifted, perceiving a possible threat, and then shifted back. It was there chiefly to protect Amelia from the dragons.

"He would want you to have this," the art fancier said. "If he died, I was to pass it on to someone who would live a long life. I have been informed you weren't brought up here. Perhaps that is a good sign. This book will hopefully continue to exist long after we, the dragons before you, have all gone. It is not a gift as such but an obligation I wish you to take on. *Nineteen Eighty-Four* is an important work, or so my dead comrade has informed me. It does not deserve to expire when we do. Read it and try to understand what it can tell you about usss and about yourself."

This revelation on the part of the art fancier brought Amelia close to tears.

The landing was flawless. Within minutes, the dragons with whatever they had with them and the robot guard were out of her hands. She watched them go, hoping never to see them again.

Amelia had gotten to know those dragons too well and didn't desire to have them maimed or die before her eyes in some future battle. She didn't want them killed by Dreadnought but knew that was a possibility.

Amelia would start reading *1984*, the book just given to her, as soon as she got to her new cottage. She felt she owed it to her now former dragon passengers to do so.

CHAPTER TWENTY-THREE

Dreadnought received a lot of mail while he was recuperating in Rome's hospital. He had fought in the Colosseum already, not long before he had met Amelia. Back then, he was one of the thousands who had gone through the place. His only fame being back then that he had survived the ordeal the same as hundreds of others had done. Now it was all different.

Once out of surgery and on the mend, he was treated like royalty by the entire medical staff. He was asked about his favourite foods for when he was off the drip and the light diet recommended by his doctors. No one was surprised when he mentioned steak. There were those taken aback when he said strawberries. Whoever thought the brute would like them for dessert?

Healing, even with top-rate medical treatment and an excellent constitution, was a slow process. Near the end of January, he knew, physiotherapy would start. Muscles no longer used to activity would throb when given tasks to do. Getting the promised movement back was one thing; being able to grip a sword or hold a shield another. He was determined to be fit enough for battle next May.

Dreadnought realized he couldn't fight again that year, let alone that month, and this saddened him. He didn't like putting himself in peril, but all he needed were those four kills to fulfil the lifetime dream of every knight.

On the 26th of November, he received a letter from Amelia. She had been asked to identify yet more artefacts from the site where she was found. The digging there had continued.

What Megan thought might be some kind of plug-in ray gun turned out to be a broken hairdryer. A hard, red ball made of cork that fitted into a small canon was, in fact, a cricket ball. *Poor Megan*, Amelia wrote, *she expects every strange object to have something to do with war, and she is so disappointed when they turn out to be otherwise.*

There was, however, a small case found with a cyanide capsule inside. Amelia remembered carrying such a case on her fighter pilot missions. If capture was imminent, it was better a quick death than a slow one through torture. The enemy particularly hated women in uniform, and their captors were prone to show no mercy. It was part of their culture to look upon women as being less than men. This was something Amelia found hard to explain to Megan, but Dreadnought, reading the letter, got it right away.

She didn't write much about her trip to Hobart, but she did send him a book she got from that journey she thought he might like. She had read it and found it fascinating. She thought, though, that some priestesses, maidens, and mavericks might not care for its contents, so she informed him it was best not to show it around too much.

Dreadnought wrote back but, in writing, found he had little to say. He was getting better, but it would be months before he would be ready to go up against a dragon with any hope of winning. In late January, possibly early February, he would be well enough to travel. He thanked her for the correspondence, the books on birds and the novel, and said it would be good if she could write some more. He noted that the other Wollongong knight who shared the same hospital ward with him was likely to go home in late February and be ready for action in early May.

Meanwhile, on the twenty-fifth of November, Megan was having an early morning coffee with Jens at her favourite coffee shop when the subject of Amelia and Dreadnought came up.

"You don't think Amelia has gone further with Dreadnought than she's supposed to, do you?" Jens asked.

"No," said Megan. "She's strange, but not that strange. Look at the scar on his face. The rumours are ridiculous!"

"If true, Dreadnought would be executed." Jens frowned and crossed her arms. "Amelia would be in disgrace."

"Amelia knows it would be wrong, and so does Dreadnought." Megan cupped her chin with her hands, nudged her glasses with a finger then said, "I don't think Amelia would be that stupid, and Dreadnought is too close to winning every knight's dream without making it null and void at this juncture."

"Some maidens would love to believe Amelia is having sex with Dreadnought because she's so unmaidenly." Jens unfolded her arms and waved a hand as if in surrender.

"True," agreed Megan.

"No one is going to act unless there is proof." Jens drank her coffee before continuing. "Even then, the authorities will only do so if it is made public. Too many knights and maidens would see it as an awful cheat on our part if Dreadnought died anywhere but in a venue against dragons."

"I'm so glad work has started at last on the search for the underground remnants of the Mitchell Library," said Megan, happy to change the subject. "There's this great slab of concrete the team assigned on the dig has to get through, but they're confident they'll do it before the end of December."

"One of our best archaeological teams has been put to work on the project and is now getting results." Jens paused to look at Megan's reaction to this news. "I'm sorry you couldn't be involved. The dig on that other site goes on."

"They've used ultrasound equipment to determine there are hollow spaces down below where the surface library stood so, when they do break through, they're bound to find something of interest." Megan was informative, but Jens sensed she would have loved to have been there. "For once, a team has been authorized to use robots. The concrete is at least a foot thick, so they will come in handy."

"It took some doing, but I got the authorization," said Jens with a touch of pride in her voice.

"We can thank Amelia for this discovery," enthused Megan after taking a sip of coffee. "We need to know more about what went wrong in the 21st century to prompt the wars of the 22nd century that devastated our planet."

"Of late, has Amelia enlightened you in any way on the subject of what did go wrong?" asked Jens.

"Amelia told me about the September eleven attacks." Megan wanted to make it clear that Amelia was still of great value. "Her grandfather said it was the start of everything that went wrong. It happened in 2001. You see, the USA, a vast and powerful country, was attacked on its home soil. Lots of ordinary people died when these planes ploughed into these New York buildings."

Megan paused a moment for effect, to let what she had said sink in. "There were also incidents elsewhere, but it was these planes destroying those buildings that did it." She stopped to gulp down coffee and to study Jens' reactions to what she had already told her. "Outrage swept the USA, and there was retaliation on a massive scale. Religions that were not so important suddenly developed greater and greater importance. Men who didn't want to take up arms had to do so. Over time, things just got worse and worse. Amelia was born into that craziness."

"She should be relieved then to be in the here and now," said Jens, shaking her head at the madness of the past.

"She should be, but I don't know if she is." Megan sighed. "What she needs is a maverick."

"You'd better find one suitable then, "said Jens. "It would crush any notion she was doing anything illegal and immoral with Dreadnought."

"Yes, it would. So, I'm back to getting her to socialize more then." Megan shrugged her shoulders and smiled, knowing it was going to be a difficult task.

****

A day later, there was a meeting between the High Priestess of Wollongong and Jens. It took place over tea and scones in the High Priestess's private office.

"More pieces are fitting into place concerning the lost century," offered Jens.

"Yes," agreed the High Priestess. "Even so, our holy books still ring true. There was an imbalance, and it spilled over into bloody chaos."

"Amelia tells us through Megan that greedy businessmen kept the workers in the poorest countries continually poverty-stricken while also keeping the peasant workers in the richer countries just above the poverty line. For some insane reason, the poorer people in the poorer countries thought having more children was the answer to their condition. Even the peasants in the richer countries knew better than that."

"Another form of imbalance." The High Priestess sighed. "Overpopulation inevitably leads to unrest and the need for conquest. And people being conquered will resist."

"They did resist. According to Amelia, governments tried to stop them from doing so, but it was inevitable. First, there were civil wars. Then religious wars."

"Amelia doesn't seem to care much about religion," observed the High Priestess. "Does that make sense in all of this?"

"No, it doesn't make sense," agreed Jens. "It's rather complicated. There were people, such as Amelia, with no real interest in religion. They went along with the Judaic Christian front to avoid being forced into other religions that were more hard-line and less likely to tolerate their lacklustre approach to faith. Also, Amelia wanted to protect her culture and way of life against the intruders who were not Judaic Christian."

"According to what you have learned so far, who won?" asked the High Priestess.

"I'm not sure." Jens frowned for a moment. "I suppose Amelia's people. They, for the most part, had superior weapons, but the others had higher numbers."

"We won," asserted the High Priestess. "We made a peace that would last, thank the Goddess."

"Yes," agreed Jens. "Thank the Goddess."

"No more poverty, no more overpopulation, and wasted resources," said the High Priestess, "and no need for war."

****

A week later, Megan talked Amelia into going to the dullest of dull parties. It was set in the home of a happy, well-to-do couple who had three small children. There were more single mavericks invited than maidens, so Amelia had plenty to choose from. She winced at the idea of forming any kind of relationship with any of them.

The eagerness of unattached mavericks to please, and no doubt escape being demoted to knighthood, was irritating. Amelia understood it was why they dressed like peacocks on magic mushrooms and had exaggerated mannerisms. A few bad words from a displeased maiden or priestess to the right authorities and they were facing the terror of the arena. Marriage wasn't mandatory for mavericks, but it had to be better than being single. At least that way, a maverick could prove that at least one maiden wanted him. A divorce, however, had to include the maverick becoming a knight.

Amelia understood the maverick need to avoid combat and death. She knew that if she were in their shoes, she would probably act the way they were acting. Still, she couldn't help but think how genuinely spoilt for choice she was in the RAAF when it came to real men.

The la-de-da clothes the mavericks wore also didn't do much for her, although all of them kept in good shape. Again, she was aware of the fact they didn't dare do otherwise, and that also spoiled their look. She gathered from her observation that it wasn't until they reached a certain age they could safely let go and be themselves. By then, they had played the game so long they had no idea who they were and what they were really like. Once a maverick was over forty, Megan told Amelia in confidence; it would be difficult to downgrade him unless, of course, he did something foolish.

Amelia tried to draw the mavericks out to discover what they thought of her and themselves. It was a useless exercise. Young mavericks were not willing to put their necks on the chopping block for her or anyone. The older ones also knew better. Dainty compliments from men who should be decidedly less genteel and manlier did not sit well with her and never would. They were all Sir Percy when what she wanted was The Scarlet Pimpernel.

"We have some of the most prominent mavericks here," whispered Megan, taking Amelia aside. "Do try."

"I will," Amelia whispered back.

She decided to try harder for Megan's sake. Amelia looked around, found a maverick that wasn't wearing a puffy shirt or an earring, and homed in on him. She ignored the bright colours of his outfit, including the multicoloured boots.

"Hi!" she called out to him. "I'm Amelia!"

"I'm Brian," he replied. "You're Dreadnought's maiden, aren't you?"

"That's right," said Amelia.

"How can you stand to be near that brute, if I may ask?" returned Brian dismissively, waving a handkerchief.

Amelia would have liked to have given Brian a backhander or maybe a spanking but knew that wouldn't sit well with Megan. Instead, she said in a meek fashion, "I try."

"I know you must, poor dear," ventured Brian, again waving the handkerchief.

I want to strangle this dipshit, thought Amelia, but diplomatically asked, "What do you do for a living, Brian?"

"I'm in manufacturing. You know, I deal in swords, shields and spears. We'll be branching out into maces next year. When it becomes legal again everywhere to have morning stars, the maces with the pointy edges in the games, we want to be ready. There were recently given a successful trial run here in Wollongong. I have a small factory on the outskirts of Wollongong. We have a staff of about twenty knights and dragons. It's all good quality gear, only the best. But I don't want to bore your pretty little head too much over the details."

"Bore away," said Amelia. *You are a la-de-da monster*, she thought. *And you have the people who are going to be hurt and killed by your so-called gear making them.*

"We sell to Newcastle and Hobart," Brian told her, "but the biggest market is Rome. We hope to crack that with Dreadnought's help. He does use our swords and shields, doesn't he?"

"I am sure he does," said Amelia. There was a punch bowl close by. She wanted to dunk his head in it but refrained from doing so. *Why am I such a coward?* She wondered. *Just do it!*

Then Amelia thought about consequences and realized what would, no doubt, happen to Megan if she followed her best instincts and so continued to refrain.

Amelia suspected that if she played up bad here and now, Megan would have to lose some of her standing as a knowledgeable archaeologist capable of understanding someone from the past. Someone else would be assigned to be Amelia's minder, possibly a less friendly maiden. What else might happen to Megan she didn't know. She felt that was more than enough to stay her hand.

"Would Dreadnought endorse my product?" asked Brian.

"You could ask him." Amelia would like to see a meeting between Brian and Dreadnought.

"Couldn't you do that for me?" Brian smiled weakly. He was apparently not eager to meet Dreadnought, just use him.

"Would you provide him with a morning star?" Amelia had it in her mind Brian being hit on the head by a mace with sharp points that came out of his factory. She smiled broadly at the notion, and there was a twinkle in her eye. Brian took this to mean she was happy to be with him.

"If and when morning stars become available, that could be arranged." Brian smiled back. Amelia tried not to show her revulsion.

"Good," grunted Amelia, and began walking away from him. "Let me know when that will be, and I am sure Dreadnought will comply."

Amelia felt dirty being in the same room as this Brian character. Still, from what she knew about medieval weapons, she figured a morning star in Dreadnought's hand would give him a better chance of survival against the dragons than a sword come May and his struggle with the remaining four kills.

"You seem to be getting along fine with Brian Tiller," Megan told her.

"Yes, we understand each other," said Amelia. *Or at least I understand him*, she thought.

"Good!" Megan enthused. "Now, there's a fine couple over here I want you to meet."

Just shoot me! Amelia thought, *right between the eyes. There's a good girl. I don't even need a blindfold. Anything to get me out of here!* Amelia had had enough of pompous mavericks and stuffy maidens for one night. Regardless, she went along with Megan. The food was superb, even if the company wasn't up to the higher standards of the mess at her old RAAF headquarters. *I need to get the good old days out of my head*, she told herself, but it was so difficult to do so.

Amelia drank too much to ease her discomfort at being with those people and woke up the next day with a hangover. Megan phoned to see how she was.

"Did you drink water before sleep?" asked Megan.

"No," croaked Amelia, "but I did get through that party without embarrassing you too much."

"I think you made a friend," said Megan.

"You mean Brian?" Amelia wanted to laugh but felt that if she did, her head would fall off.

"Yes," replied Megan.

"Good for me," said Amelia, and was surprised to discover she meant it. Brian was a scumbag, but a potentially useful one.

"You could cut down on your drinking," advised Megan

"Any more of those events on the horizon?" asked Amelia. She knew she didn't sound too eager.

"You made a better impression this time, so I am sure more will turn up soon."

"Great!" cried Amelia and hung up. *Just what I need*, she thought, *to be popular with monsters, parasites, and yes men.*

CHAPTER TWENTY-FOUR

Amelia hadn't seen much of the religious life of Wollongong, and that was in part her own doing. Back in her RAAF days, she was happy to be a token Christian. Her main goals were to protect her customs and culture as well as her people, and nothing more. Fellow pilots understood this. Some agreed with her. It was the enemy, the Globalists, who were the hated fanatics.

Here, on the twenty-fifth of December, in this more futuristic setting, that was in some instances backward and in other ways more advanced, a carnival spirit took hold. In the early hours of the morning, a parade consisting of priestesses with statues of the Virgin Mary carried on their shoulders, followed by maidens and mavericks, and then knights made its way through the streets to the main beach. There, as the sun rose, the statues were bathed in salt water and flowers cast onto the waves. The High Priestess then gave a speech praising the Goddess and asking for her blessings in the name of Mary, the first Martha.

Hours later, Amelia caught some of this on television. She had no interest in participating, though she was expected to attend services at the small temple nearby at a more reasonable time. Not to attend would make maidens and mavericks think she didn't care about the Great Goddess, and she gathered, from a short talk by Megan, that might mean fewer people would want to travel in a flyer piloted by her.

Although the dragons were not permitted to participate in the walk to the sea, they could and were in attendance in the temple. Even the lowest of the low had their place on this day of days.

Unlike the Christmas of Amelia's youth, Jesus barely got a mention. It was almost all about Mary and the Goddess. The cross had been replaced by a fish which, strangely enough, was also an early sign of Christianity. Amelia could smile through all of this symbolism without showing outward contempt. She did it in the past, and she could do it now.

Gifts were exchanged. Amelia got an owl necklace made of silver from Megan.

"This is beautiful." Amelia held it up to the light to see it sparkle. "Does it have a special meaning?"

"Long ago, the Athenians thought owls were the eyes and the messengers of their goddess."

"Yes. I remember." Amelia thought of Athena and how, no doubt, Athena was now the Great Goddess. History studies had not been a waste of time.

"You like birds, don't you?" pressed Megan.

"Oh, yes."

Jens saw to it Amelia, at last, got a computer. It looked like something out of the 1980s, but surely it couldn't be that simple. Jens plugged it in for Amelia at her cottage and said it was all ready to go.

"Does it have the internet?" asked Amelia.

"What's that?" asked Jens, clearly puzzled, her eyebrows raised.

"A worldwide network of communication," said Amelia, thinking it might now go under another name.

"No," said Jens, further puzzled. "Nothing like that exists. I can't imagine it ever did."

"Does it have email capabilities?" asked Amelia. "Can I send messages to whoever I want?"

"No. But it comes with a printer." Jens was frowning.

"Well, it does have a printer, so I can type up letters to Dreadnought, and they have to be more legible than my handwriting." Amelia felt she had better find something positive about this machine or be considered ungrateful to someone in power.

"Look!" said Jens. "You can get our regular television and radio stations on computer."

"That is marvellous." Amelia felt she had to be positive and struggled not to grimace. At least, it was more than just a glorified typewriter.

Amelia remembered how the internet had been heavily censored in her earlier timeline, so it did make sense someone would take it that one step further and ban it altogether. Getting rid of emails also made sense.

"Thank you," said Amelia at last to Jens. "This is a wonderful gift."

"You're welcome," replied Jens.

When Jens had gone, Amelia tried lifting the computer screen and found it heavy. *This isn't very portable,* thought Amelia, *hence another sign that in some ways, this civilization is less advanced or perhaps, one should say, more controlled than the one I came from.*

Amelia, knowing the custom still held from talking to shop keepers, had bought Megan silver earrings in the shape of autumn leaves.

"I do love autumn," said Megan after receiving them. "Do they have a special meaning for you?"

"They look nice," replied Amelia. "Sometimes, something just looks nice."

"I agree." Megan smiled a broad smile.

Jens got a cookbook off Amelia.

"How do you know I like to cook?" Jens sounded suspicious.

"I just asked around." Amelia shrugged her shoulders and smiled.

A week before the holidays, Amelia mailed off a letter to Dreadnought together with a fruit loaf which was the closest thing to a Christmas cake or pudding she could find. *Oh well, he'll enjoy the fruit loaf*, she thought.

The service in the temple was a drag for Amelia, but she enjoyed the gift exchanging and the barbeque and swim afterward. The swimming, especially the cool motion of the waves on a body on a hot day, took her back to an earlier time of fun in the surf and sun.

She remembered being one of the young women one year who wore a yellow bikini on a Sydney beach in summer in defiance of the enemy. When a lifeguard wearing a silver cross on a chain around his neck told her and her friends to put more clothes on, she cried: "I am not a fucking Globalist, so you can stick it!"

He was taken aback by this, but grinned and said, "As you are then ladies. I could run you all in, but I won't. It's just the higher-ups that get antsy about bikinis. If any of them turn up, I am afraid I will have to act. Until then, have a lovely time."

"Let them get antsy; it will do them good." This came from a young woman, also in yellow; Amelia was with at the time.

"No black bikinis here," said yet another young woman in yellow. "No Globalists here, no friggin' way. See? I have a little silver cross on a chain. It's like yours. Do you like it?"

"Yes," said the lifeguard. "Charming."

"Want to come in for a swim?" asked Amelia, smiling.

"Not right now," said the lifeguard. "I'm on duty just in case anyone's drowning, fighting, or I see an enemy periscope on the horizon."

"Suit yourself." Amelia and her friends got back to the swim.

Amelia wondered why she recalled that particular scene with that lifeguard, and then it came to her how free she had felt.

Now at futuristic Wollongong, maidens dressed in different ways on the beaches in absolute defiance of no one and nothing. Even so, she had bought a yellow bikini and wore it proudly for old time's sake. *No one here knows how much not wearing black can mean to both body and soul,* thought Amelia. *Maybe it's just as well they don't know.*

There was surfing and volleyball. She wasn't surprised, though, to find the beaches divided into zones. There was a place for maidens and mavericks (some with young children), a space for knights, and a location for dragons. Robots made sure certain lines were not crossed. The faces of the robots gleamed in the sunlight.

Amelia wondered what would happen if a maiden got lost and ended up in the dragon area. She was tempted to try it but, for her sake as well as that of the dragons, she decided not to chance it. She didn't fully trust the robots not to harm maidens.

When it got dark, carols were sung on the beaches and in the streets by maidens, mavericks, and small children. Amelia was asked to join in but bowed out, saying quite truthfully, she didn't know the words to any of the songs. On television and radio, choirs could be heard, and there were stories about Mary and how wise she was to listen to the Great Goddess and obey her.

A week after Mary-mass, a tin box was unearthed. It was buried deep, only a few hundred yards from where Amelia had been found. Among its contents, there were a dozen cricket cards and a snow globe from New York, showing the Statue of Liberty in a wintery setting. There were also some clippings downloaded from the Internet.

The archaeologists who first found the box marvelled at the snow globe and what New York, especially the Statue of Liberty, used to look like. *Did these New Yorkers worship the Great Goddess after all?* an archaeologist wondered. The cricket cards informed Megan that Amelia was right when it came to the cricket ball found earlier.

One of the clippings told the story of Cecil Brooks, an Aborigine from Wellington, New South Wales who saved the city of Perth from being taken over by enemy Globalists. The commando raids he led delayed the aggressors long enough for the regular army to be brought up to deal with the threat. Megan wondered if Amelia had ever met Cecil. She got her answer at the very next meeting they had over coffee at what had become Amelia's favourite coffee shop.

"No," said Amelia. She shook her head and smiled sheepishly. "I didn't know Cecil Brooks personally, but my dad did. I was told he was half Koori, half Chinese, and all guts. He was the bravest man my dad ever knew, and it was a wonder he lived so long. He did love Australia and didn't want her to fall into the wrong hands."

"How would Australia have been in the wrong hands?" Megan adjusted her glasses.

"They were still having too many children," said Amelia, looking sternly at Megan. "Long ago, we had stopped being so foolish, but they continued. They would have made life impossible even for themselves with overcrowding and lack of food and water. You can't justify such stupidity."

"But you had been just as foolish?" Megan cleaned her glasses with a tissue before putting them back on. She didn't want to look into Amelia's eyes. She hoped what she had said wasn't too much of an attack upon Amelia's people.

"Oh, yes! We had been foolish. And it was a long time ago, centuries ago, in fact." Amelia sighed deeply before continuing. "The people we were up against, those in black were not all bad, but they had to be treated that way because it was war, you know. We were fighting for our very existence."

"I think I understand." Megan said the words slowly as if to convince herself they were true. "There's an article here about an attack upon an enemy battleship."

"Oh, yes, I remember. We got wind that the enemy, the Globalists, planned on shelling East Timor, one of our allies in the South Pacific." Amelia went into a trance-like state, reliving events. "I flew over that battleship and strafed it good while one of our subs launched a couple of torpedos to sink it. I don't recall seeing survivors in the water. If there were, they would have been in for a long swim."

"There's something here about keeping the beaches free?" Megan's voice was contemplative. She put her hands on her chin, awaiting the answer.

"Some people in our community had gotten it into their heads that women should dress more modestly everywhere. I, for one, disagreed." Amelia smiled broadly. "We were fighting for our freedom as much as anything else. I wasn't about to give some of mine up to some Christian preacher. We told him to mind his own damned business, and it got on the internet."

"What about this piece on food shortages?" Megan asked, taking her hands from her chin.

"That happens with continual hostilities. If you are in the service, you are assured of three good meals a day." Amelia held up three fingers. "If you are a civilian, you make do with what you can get. Here, in Australia, we were better off than elsewhere in the world."

"Yes, I see." Megan frowned, trying to visualize being a civilian in those days.

"It was the people trying to take that 'better off' away from us through overpopulation we had to fight," said Amelia with conviction in her voice.

CHAPTER TWENTY-FIVE

By the beginning of January, Liverpool-based archaeologists had gotten through the rubble, reinforced steel, and concrete to the bomb shelter that lay under Number Ten Downing Street, London. They found more than just the occasional dead fly.

Apart from World War Two memorabilia, there were boxes filled with more contemporary files and a laptop from the time just before London's destruction.

A week later, a computer expert found a replacement battery for the laptop that could power up the machine without overloading it and thus destroying it in the process. On it was information on the Mars dome and ecosystem that British as well as American and Australian scientists had envisioned. Copies of the notes and schematics of the Mars project were then sent by flyer first to Houston and then to Wollongong.

Dean Renate gave Jens access to the material Wollongong University received. Jens realized, upon looking it over, that it was now probable rather than just possible life existed on the red planet.

In order to break all the data down to where it could more easily be understood by Dean Renate and the university board, Jens got out her recorder.

"The Martian soil is good if nothing else," Jens told the recorder as she sifted through the information. "Apparently, that was discovered by unmanned probes a long time ago. Whether there is still human life there is another question."

Jens recalled how a five-year gap in the wars on British, American, and Australian soil had been a boon time of high optimism and this spurred on the desire to once more reach out to the stars. Over those years, NASA and a dozen other space agencies pooled their resources and managed to first build a space station capable of manufacturing the dome then get on with doing so.

To avoid having to gather materials from Earth, space junk that had been floating in Earth orbit and creating a hazard for space travel was taken in tow and used as much as possible. Both the Americans and the Europeans also mined the moon's surface. *All that cooperation*, thought Jens, *all those nations coming together must have been something.*

The dome had to be light but durable. It had to be able to stand up against punishing high winds that would, at times, carry sharp rocks and other debris. One small tear and the people inside would die, for the atmosphere on Mars was lethal.

What's more, the artificial ecosystem had to imitate Earth normal as close to perfect as possible. Also, there had to be a system where underground Martian water, if it existed, could have the oxygen removed from samples whenever there was a need to bolster the oxygen level within the dome. The right animals, birds, fish, and plants for the journey had to be selected.

"Some Earth soil was sent with those people going to Mars," noted Jens into a recorder, "but they hoped that the Martian soil was everything the earlier unmanned probes had indicated and that it would be just as useful in yielding necessary crops."

Jens rubbed her nose then continued, "The seeds chosen were the best. Back then, there was the possibility the dome could eventually be expanded by the colonists and vehicles sent from the space station used to explore the surface of Mars more thoroughly."

They did have high hopes back then, thought Jens. *Too bad they couldn't last.*

"Ah, this is interesting," Jens said into the recorder. "Before Earth lost contact with the Mars colony, dozens of old, artificial satellites that were of no further use to anybody were sent into the Martian atmosphere to crash. The idea was they could be taken apart and made use of in the future by whoever's on Mars."

Then the wars resumed in earnest, and Mars was all but forgotten until now, thought Jens.

"Those on Mars were supposed to be sent back to Earth after they had been there six months and replaced with new recruits," said Jens into the recorder, "and this business of humans on Mars was only meant to last two years. After that, robots were to replace humans. That didn't happen."

Jens paused a moment to think about the original plan then continued with the recording. "There were two rotations back to Earth and replacements sent and then nothing. No more rotations. Those there were stuck there." She paused again. "Good news came from the colony just before being cut off for good from Earth. The discovery of caves led to fresh drinking water. An underground river flowed for miles. Whether it contained ancient Martian life of any sort was not at that time known. It was felt that exploration of this river might have kept the people stranded there not only alive but also sane. Who knows? Human life might still exist on Mars. Unless we send a team back there, we'll never know."

CHAPTER TWENTY-SIX

During the last two weeks Dreadnought was in the hospital in Rome, he finished the novel given to him by Amelia. He turned once more to the bird books she had also given him. He requested colourful paper from the hospital staff, and they provided him with all the sheets he wanted. Then he made forty-six dragons.

On the day before Amelia took him out of the hospital and onto the flyer headed back to Wollongong, he was photographed in bed with his paper dragons.

He was interviewed by a maverick journalist who asked, "Why only forty-six dragons?"

"For now, there are only forty-six dragons," Dreadnought replied. "I can count."

The paper creations were the storybook style European dragon and not the reality. Even so, Dreadnought beside them in bed was a sensation, and it played well in press services throughout the world. If his fame and popularity had shrunk at all in the months since his last fight, it was now on the rise again.

Amelia had travelled with Megan and Malcolm to Rome. In Honolulu, they had time for a swim in the clear, warm waters there. At St. Louis airport, Malcolm got into an argument with a fellow maverick over whether Dreadnought should still be allowed to compete for the golden fifty.

"Dreadnought must not become a maverick," said the argumentative maverick in the yellow striped shirt and black pants.

"He has every right to try for the golden fifty." Malcolm thought he was being reasonable but could see the other fellow was getting red-faced mad.

"And you want him as a maverick? You must be mad!" Hands were fluttering.

"I don't care," said Malcolm.

"Well you should! We all should damn well care!" More hand fluttering.

"Look! It's not up to us, "Malcolm said, trying to calm the other.

"And you have travelled with him, haven't you?" accused the other maverick. "You have taken him to where he has competed?"

"What if I have?" Malcolm had a bad feeling where this was going.

"You're a traitor! A traitor!"

Amelia thought faces might get slapped and that would be amusing. Instead a robot airport security officer intervened.

"I detect raised voices," said the robot in monotone. "I register the growing possibility of violence. I am authorized to make arrests to prevent violence."

"No violence here," said Malcolm, shaking his head and looking sheepish. "It was just a healthy discussion."

"And your friend is now leaving. He appears be neither happy nor unhappy, but he is leaving, so all is well." The robot backed away and Malcolm got closer to Megan. He was white-faced and visibly shaken.

"What a suicidal lunatic!" Malcolm shuddered. "What that stupid maverick might have done to both of us is terrible."

"Yes," agreed Megan. "It wouldn't have mattered who struck the first blow, if a blow was struck, and it might not have mattered if there was no retaliation."

"I would have lost my maverick status." Malcolm sighed. "It's as simple as that."

"That is harsh," said Amelia. *I never thought I would feel sorry for a maverick.*

"It is the law," Malcolm told her, "and that idiot almost broke it for both of us."

"He must have known what the consequences would be," said Amelia.

"He's a purist, a fanatic," Malcolm replied. "Mavericks are mavericks and knights are knights, and there should never be any way one can become the other. But I don't agree with that, so I am the perfect maverick to make an example of, even if it costs the weasel his life too into the bargain."

The touchdown at Rome was smooth, and they were greeted by officials keen to make them feel welcome.

"We are sad to lose Dreadnought," a Rome maverick said as a hovercar riding on an air pocket with them inside drove away from the airport toward the hospital.

"He hasn't been too much trouble?" asked Malcolm.

"Not at all," said another Rome maverick. "He has been as close to a gentleman as possible for a knight."

It was a short ride to the hospital where they were mobbed by reporters and other interested parties. No one in the crowd, however, turned out to be a threat.

Amelia was open-mouthed surprised to see how pale Dreadnought had become. After the initial shock she endeavoured not to show it. "Are they treating you well?" she asked him.

"Yes," replied Dreadnought. "They treat me very well."

"I am glad to see you again," said Amelia and meant it. "I have been spending too much time of late with mavericks. Even well-meaning ones can drive you crazy. But you'll be all right?"

"Yes. I will be all right."

Dreadnought didn't have much to take back with him, just some clothes, and pills given to him by hospital staff. There was also a fistful of books and a box stuffed with paper dragons.

"I have missed you," he told Amelia. "And I appreciated the letters, books, and food."

At St. Louis airport, Malcolm again met up with the troublesome maverick that had almost cost him his way of life.

"Oh no! Not again!" Malcolm shook his head.

"He has a knife!" cried Amelia.

"Die you bastard, die!" yelled the belligerent maverick, waving the knife about.

"He's going for Dreadnought!" Malcolm couldn't believe how dumb this fellow maverick had turned out to be.

Dreadnought saw the danger and punched before his would-be assailant could stab. The fanatical maverick then went soaring into a robot officer who immediately arrested him for intended assault.

"We'll never allow you to ever become a maverick!" cried the would-be assassin as he was taken away.

"He won't last long come May," Dreadnought told his companions.

"I think he knows that," said Megan.

In Honolulu, they stopped by the statue of King Kamehameha. He was still stretching his hand out to the future. Some photographers photographed them with the statue, and one maiden reporter wanted to know about the statue's significance.

"Ask the people of Hawaii," Dreadnought's answer came. "They built it."

Wollongong held a dinner party in Dreadnought's honour. Strangely enough, he was the only guest there who happened to be a knight. The rich food on offer, on this occasion, did not agree with Dreadnought nor did most of the company. Only Amelia, Megan, and Malcolm were the exceptions.

Dreadnought got a tummy ache and had to endure what he considered to be silly talk. A maiden wanted to discuss clothes that would better suit him if he ever did become a maverick.

"I don't care about clothes," he told her.

"But you will, you will." She fluttered about with her fan.

"Oh yes that is so true," put in a maverick wearing a pink suit with black zigzags.

"Excuse me," said Dreadnought. "I must speak to Malcolm." He would have preferred Amelia or Megan but he couldn't see where they were in this crowd.

"Well if you must." With the wave of her fan, the clothes conscious maiden let him go.

"Having a good time?" asked Malcolm. He smiled weakly, realizing this was not the case.

"Just talk sensible please," said Dreadnought.

"I'll do my best," replied Malcolm.

I don't know why I give a damn about this particular maverick, thought Dreadnought. *Maybe he just isn't as stupid as some of the others.*

****

Three weeks later, Dreadnought started jogging one morning with Amelia, Megan, and Malcolm to get back into shape. A dozen knights followed them.

"Why are they following us?" asked Malcolm, looking back on the knights, feeling a little intimidated.

"They are following me," said Dreadnought. "If you are with me, they will protect you too."

"Do you need their protection?" asked Malcolm.

"It is enough they believe I do."

Dreadnought was calm as he kept pace with the others. What was going on in his head he kept to himself. The forty-six dragons were not far from his thoughts on these jogs nor were the remaining four. He wondered if the twinges of pain would cease in his shoulder so that he would be right for May. Painkillers helped but he knew he would have to be off them by May if he was to do any good.

On one of the jogs, Amelia asked Dreadnought about The Spear and Shield and whether he had ever been inside the place.

"I used to drink," Dreadnought replied, "but I gave it up when I realized the fifty was possible. Alcohol can be a comfort, but it can also slow you down, your reflexes I mean, when you need your speed. It can also cloud your mind. I haven't frequented The Spear and Shield for some time. Why do you ask?"

"I was just wondering," said Amelia.

"Do you ever think you might frequent The Great Grape?" asked Malcolm.

"That place mavericks and maidens go to for whatever reason?" questioned Dreadnought.

"That's the place," said Malcolm.

Dreadnaught shook his head. "Amelia couldn't get me in kicking and screaming."

"I wouldn't even try," said Amelia.

"No." Malcolm nodded in agreement. "It's not for everyone."

"I took some dragons to Hobart once," said Amelia. "They were young, bright..."

"Stop!" Dreadnought raised his hand. "I don't want to know. I cannot know." Dreadnought was adamant.

"Why not?" asked Amelia, concern in her voice.

"Please stop. I cannot deal with them if I have any sympathy for them." Dreadnought bowed his head.

"I understand." Amelia's voice was soft. She waved her hand in understanding. She remembered a time when she feared making the enemy so human she couldn't have carried out her duties as an RAAF pilot.

****

It was in early February that a news report took Amelia by surprise. Two young black-scaled dragons, which had had their first taste of combat in Hobart, somehow slipped out of their pain collars and were on the run. They had picked up spears out of their barracks before making a dash for freedom. *The chess players*, thought Amelia, and she was right.

They had robbed a supermarket and a sporting goods store at spear point before heading toward the nearest bushland with knapsacks and bags full of stolen items. Much was made out of how frightened shopkeeper maidens and shop assistant mavericks were by what the dragons had done. *They didn't get over Hobart*, Amelia concluded. *They had made up their minds never to kill for someone else's pleasure ever again or be butchered for the same reason.*

Amelia got the notion that they wanted to hide away in dense shrub and forest for the rest of their lives, living off of whatever food they might find. Naturally, the spearing of fish and other wild game was not out of the question. The food taken from the supermarket would tide them over until they figured out how to live in the wild.

A week later, thanks to aerial reconnaissance, they were tracked down and robots sent into where they were camped to deal with them. Spears were ineffectual against steel bodies, but bullets easily ripped past black scales. The news reported the dragons dead. On one hand, Amelia was sorry it happened. On the other hand, she was glad it wasn't Dreadnought who had put an end to their lives.

The next day, Amelia received a chess set in the mail. She returned it, via mail delivery, to the dragon friends of the deceased chess players who had sent it. She had to wonder why it had been sent to her in the first place. Maybe those two wanted to be remembered in some way by people other than their fellow dragons and knew that their bid for freedom would most likely fail. Regardless, she felt she didn't have the right to keep it. After all, she still didn't know their real names and felt she remained better off not knowing.

CHAPTER TWENTY-SEVEN

By mid-February, Jens put Megan in charge of exploring the underground floors of the Mitchell Library in Sydney. The check for radiation led to it being considered safe to do so. Geiger counters were at first used to make the determination; then researchers wore tags that lit up when a certain level of radiation was present.

One day, a university student assigned to work at the dig baulked at the need for a tag, and Megan said with some annoyance, "If we get winds blowing in from elsewhere in Sydney and they are deadly, you'll be glad you're wearing a warning tag."

A metal ladder was put into place, allowing Megan to get safely to the first underground floor. For the rest of the floors, there were stairs in good order. No one cared to try the ancient lift. "It's a cage lift, and it creaks just by looking at it," Megan said to her associates and students, "so best leave it alone."

The first floor dealt with pre-19th century history and art. There were early paintings of wildlife that were quaint but lacked accuracy.

"It's as if those who did the paintings long ago were homesick for England," Megan said to a student as she mused over a picture of a kangaroo that was half-greyhound but with a pouch and a thick tail.

There were portraits of famous people and early maps of the South Pacific.

"Here we have a painting of Captain Cook, famous explorer." One of Megan's aides pointed this out. "He was a fine maverick."

"Yes," agreed Megan. "He was a fine maverick."

Megan's team found all sorts of puzzling items on the second and third floors.

"What's this?" asked a student, picking up a whistle.

"Blow into it," said Megan. The student did so and jumped at the noise.

There were memorabilia from the First and Second World Wars, including photographs, records, gramophones, poetry, and novels. Silent movie films had been stored in their original format and also on more durable discs. What interested Megan the most were the works on early flight.

"It's amazing humans managed to get off the ground," said Megan to a student, "let alone go into outer space."

The fourth and fifth floors had statues and models of people, planes, and ships. Some were miniatures of the Oberon and Collins class submarines and the ANZAC class frigates. Also, there were old military uniforms stored in airtight containers to prevent damage from the elements. Some of them confirmed the fact that Amelia wasn't the only woman to wear a uniform in her earlier time.

Going down to the sixth floor, Megan discovered magazines, periodicals, and newspapers dating back to the 19th century. Some of them were on microfiche with a microfiche machine handy. Others were on slides or movie film. Not much was on paper, and what there was had deteriorated to where it was almost illegible.

On the seventh floor, Megan found models of space vehicles and lots of boxes filled with printouts on aviation and space travel. One corner was dedicated to the first landing on Mars and Australia's contribution in setting up a colony on that planet.

"It will take years to go through that lot," Megan told Jens over coffee at their favourite Wollongong coffee shop. "For the moment, I am concentrating on floor seven."

"Good," said Jens. "We need to know more about space travel in the past and of the Mars project."

"I leafed through one document you might find of interest." Megan paused for effect. "It was about a French experiment in the development of a super cress which is highly nutritious, easily grown, and doesn't take up much room."

"Did the colonists take it with them?" Jens wondered if such a super cress could keep human colonists on hostile planets alive for decades, even centuries.

"I would say the Mars colonists did take it with them." Megan couldn't see why they didn't and made this clear to Jens. "The French were keen on doing their bit for the program and getting it right. From what I have read so far, this super herb could sustain the settlers until other types of food became available. We know they had chickens and ducks for eggs from another unearthed document."

"Perhaps something might be found in the ruins of Paris." Jens smiled warmly at Megan.

"Perhaps." Megan waved her glasses about in thought. "When it comes to Paris, we just don't know where to start digging. Our best bet, for now, is to keep exploring the seventh floor of this library in Sydney. I'm sure we'll find plenty that will be helpful to Houston."

****

Days later, Amelia flew five boxes of files and other material from floor seven to Houston. After getting permission, she took Dreadnought along with her.

They flew from Wollongong to Midway, where a flock of seagulls hampered their efforts to land. They had to circle three times before they could come in. Dreadnought watched as Amelia dodged the birds with precision flying. Even so, a seagull did smack into their windscreen. Fortunately, the bird shrugged off the collision and joined the rest of his mates in the air.

Halfway to mainland USA from Midway, they encountered something Amelia had never seen before. Two sharks came out of the water, climbed, and began circling the flyer. They had the usual row upon row of ragged teeth plus leathery black wings. They had grey heads and tails plus shiny white bodies.

"They're just as comfortable in the air as they are in the ocean," said Dreadnought.

"Anything else you want to tell me about them?" Amelia sounded anxious. Then one hit the flyer, causing it to rock. She wanted to scream, but her air force training kicked in. She could do that later when she and Dreadnought are safe.

"They want to crack our craft open," said Dreadnought soberly, "so they can get to the meat."

"The meat meaning us," said Amelia, her breathing getting more and more rapid, but screaming was out. It would not happen while she could think.

"Yes," replied Dreadnought, his eyes fixing on those rows upon rows of sharp teeth.

More circling followed; then the second shark struck the flyer, causing it to vibrate. Amelia had the flyer climb and then level off. "I hope the rarer atmosphere here will get the ocean life to back off," she said with a touch of anger in her voice. Unfortunately, the sharks followed them upwards and, levelling off, resumed the circling pattern. "This is ridiculous!" cried Amelia. "Sharks aren't meant to do that! I mean they do circle, but not up here!" Dreadnought saw no need to argue with Amelia on those points.

Amelia watched the sharks intently, and Dreadnought became afraid for her. He feared she had become hypnotised by the movement of the beasts and was now useless to both of them. He drew his sword, ready for a fight he knew he most probably couldn't win. More hits and more shocks to the craft. Dreadnought had never felt more helpless, wondering whether he should simply put his sword back in its scabbard and accept his fate.

"Do something!" Dreadnought cried. "Don't let fear consume you!"

"Shhhh!" was Amelia's only reply as she continued her observance of the sharks. Suddenly, she pushed the controls of the flyer forward, smashing her craft, with some speed attached, into a shark, hurling it into its companion. Both spiralled down into the waters below.

"You were timing their movements," Dreadnought said, putting his sword back in its sheath and feeling a little sheepish in having it out in the first place. "You were working out where they would be so you could act. I was wrong."

"It was our only chance," Amelia told him. "We couldn't have stood up to much more buffeting."

"You were not afraid," said Dreadnought. He smiled warmly at her, the face scar crinkling.

"I was so afraid." Amelia grinned and shook her head. "But sometimes you have to put that aside." She no longer felt like screaming.

"Yes," Dreadnought said gently. "I agree."

"It's hard to believe sharks have evolved so much." Amelia could still see in her mind's eye those rows upon rows of teeth coming for her, and she shuddered with the fear she couldn't very well express earlier.

"The flying ones are more than likely a product of radiation," reasoned Dreadnought, "though the design is superb. It's a grey nurse with black wings."

"I suppose it is a great design," Amelia agreed, "if you like killers."

"Yes," said Dreadnought in a soft voice, "if you like killers like me."

At Houston, the damage to the flyer was examined, and minor repairs made. Doctors there, though, insisted on giving both Amelia and Dreadnought full examinations. Amelia thought this odd.

Meanwhile, the scientists were happy to receive the boxes and were eager to find out all they could about super cress.

"Is this substance all that Jens and Megan say it is in their communiqué?" asked one them.

"I suppose so," said Amelia "I don't know for sure, but I do trust Megan."

Two young people had been picked out at last for the flight to Mars from all the candidates on hand. One was a maverick named Scott Simon from St. Louis and the other Mai Tan from Hong Kong.

"Why do you want to go?" asked Amelia of the adventurous couple.

"We want to do what hasn't been done for a very long time," Mai Tan replied. "The Chinese were getting together an impressive space program when war and then plague put an end to it. I am so glad I was chosen."

"I always wanted to be the best of the best." Scott Simon smiled. "Now I am."

'We accepted the dangers involved," said Mei. "We're not naive."

The trip back to Wollongong for Amelia and Dreadnought was uneventful and the touchdown without any difficulties. A hover car, floating on a cushion of air, was waiting for them, manned by a knight.

****

While Amelia and Dreadnought were in Houston, Jens and the High Priestess of Wollongong had a special meeting behind closed doors.

"What I am about to divulge to you must remain a secret," said the High Priestess.

"I won't say a word to anyone," replied Jens, wondering what it could be.

"It is common knowledge that only male dragons are ever born." The High Priestess spoke calmly, but there was an edge to her voice Jens took to be a warning. "Have you ever wondered whether that can be true with what you know about DNA and genetics?"

"No," Jens replied.

"Well, it is wrong." The High Priestess looked sharply at Jens before continuing. "The truth is one in every ten dragons is, in fact, female."

"Really? I find that hard to believe." Jens was open and honest.

"We wanted it to be hard for you and others to believe." The High Priestess smiled a wicked smile. "Nevertheless, it is true. We make sure they meet their Goddess not long after they come into this world." The High Priestess paused a moment so that this would sink in. "We do this via lethal injection. We know it is the kindest way. They are then recorded as stillborn. Only the doctors and nurses are ever to know what really happened. The mother, of course, is dead from having the dragon claw her way out of her."

"But why tell me? I can understand something being horrible but necessary, but where do I fit in?" Jens felt the ground at her feet shifting with this new information. "I am neither a scientist nor a doctor. I am a university administrator."

"Patience!" the High Priestess cried. "I am getting to that."

"Yes." Jens nodded, looking pale. "I will be patient, your highness."

"A long time ago, I made a mistake," said the High Priestess. "The scientist in me wanted to know how many days a female dragon could live, so there was one who wasn't put down."

"She lived?" Jens was open-mouthed incredulous.

"She still lives."

"She's alive somewhere?" Jens wondered what she would be like.

"She was of the black-scaled type. When she was young, it was possible to fob her off as a male dragon. We could dress her for that role. Then she developed breasts, and it became more difficult. We knew she would be eventually exposed, and the notion that only male dragons are ever born would end. People then might start to ask awkward questions about how dragons eventuate, and we couldn't have that. The fact we inject certain pregnant women with dragon DNA must never get out."

"Our economy is based on knights being knights and dragons being dragons," Jens said. She knew this to be true.

"That's quite right!" the High Priestess agreed. "Of course, we still had the option of lethal injection, but I didn't have the heart to do it or command anyone else to do it."

"What did you do then?" Jens wondered if she should ask such a question, but she was now in deep with knowledge she knew might someday get her killed.

"We hid her in a cottage on nearby Mount Keira. She liked it there, but we knew she couldn't stay in that locale forever. Sooner or later, someone not in the know would find her, and she'd be a curiosity for a while. Then she'd be put into combat, and that would be the end of her. I didn't want that."

"It sounds like you grew fond of her." Jens wondered if that could be true.

"I did," agreed the High Priestess. She shook her head and smiled. "That female dragon was bright. She loved books and bushwalks. Despite the scales and tail, I couldn't have asked for a better daughter. But for both our sakes, she had to go."

"Couldn't you have had the scales and tail removed?" Jens wondered if that was even possible.

"No. That kind of surgery has been tried on male dragons; the dragon dies soon after from shock and blood loss. The only exception was Dreadnought, who for some reason lost everything about him that pointed to dragon soon after he was born. We knew the scales on Elanora, my female dragon, ran too deep and so did her tail. Surgery was out of the question."

"So what did become of her?" asked Jens.

"She's on a small island off the coast of New Zealand. We airdrop her supplies every month. She does survey work of the heavens for us, plus wildlife research; but only a handful of people know it is being done by a female dragon. The greater establishment believes the surveyor to be a maiden who prefers the contemplative life."

"Why bring this up?" Jens had to know since this knowledge was dangerous.

"Don't you see?" The High Priestess waved her hands about as if trying to bring Jens into the fold of that exclusive part of her world. Her face, for the most part, remained calm, but her eyes were actively searching Jens for acknowledgement. "We have tossed this isolation idea around as a possible solution for Dreadnought. I don't mean the same island. It would be a different one. What do you think?"

"I'm sorry, but it won't work." Jens shook her head. "From an administrative point of view, it would be a bad move."

"Why?" The question from the High One was delivered sharply.

"You kept the dragon, as she grew up, away from the public eye. That was her saving grace. For most of our citizens, she hadn't earned any recognition in any meaningful way. Hence her disappearance, if that is what it was, and her reappearance as this mysterious maiden who resides in a hard spot to get to could happen."

"Yes." The High Priestess sighed. "I begin to see what you mean."

"If you try to do the same to Dreadnought before or after he has won the golden fifty, there will be an outcry among too many knights worldwide. They would say he is dead and the golden fifty a fraud. The result would be mass rebellions by knights everywhere, and the balance you priestesses talk about disturbed for a very long time."

"What if we were to show Dreadnought on his island all

nice and cosy?" reasoned the High Priestess.

"Some mavericks would be outraged by the sight while certain knights would demand that you return Dreadnought to society to fulfil his role as a maverick. If he did, there would be uprisings of mavericks against him, and counter uprisings of knights in support of him. Our robots would struggle to keep order."

"Yes," the High Priestess agreed. "It is a problem, and there is only one obvious solution."

"And that would be death in combat?" Jens had known this for some time.

"Yes, I am afraid so," the High Priestess spoke softly.

"And the uncertainty of it bothers you?" Jens felt she was out of line but had to ask.

"Dreadnought has survived so many encounters." The High Priestess sighed.

"There's no way you can make sure he doesn't survive the next one?" Jens couldn't see any other way out.

"We'll have to think about that," The High Priestess said in a calm monotone, "and thank you for your advice."

CHAPTER TWENTY-EIGHT

In the first week of May, Dreadnought and nine other knights were sent by the High Priestess of Wollongong to Japan to compete in the games there. They went in two flyers. Amelia flew one, and Malcolm piloted the other. Megan talked her way onto Malcolm's craft.

Their only short stopover was Luzon in the Philippines, where they had no problem getting into or out of the airport.

Halfway to Tokyo, two flying sharks came out of the water, observed the two flyers, and chose not to go on the attack. They simply returned to where they had come from.

"Those sharks could have been trouble," said Amelia over the radio.

"I'm glad they decided not to take us on," Malcolm replied.

Tokyo was lit up for their arrival and that of other expected guests. Like every other major city that had survived, its population had shrunk due to war, famine, and plague. What had bounced back from all of that was lively and noisy. Coloured posters of famous singers and television stars were everywhere along with billboards for everything from headache powders to maiden hair spray. Cars that hovered before running on a motorized cushion of air met them and took Amelia, Malcolm, and Megan to one of the better hotels. The knights were driven to a locker room in the sports stadium where they were to fight. All were provided with translators so they wouldn't have trouble understanding and being understood.

Amelia, Malcolm, and Megan were shown their rooms, and then, as a common courtesy given to special visitors, taken to the big robot factory on the edge of the city by a guide assigned to them. It was a large complex, and what went on there was rather startling for Amelia.

In the time Amelia was born into, the robots had been rudimentary. Here, all but the faces of the mechanical men being produced smacked of a sophistication that was not evident in the home computer Jens had given her.

"Why are the faces so ill-formed?" Amelia asked their guide.

"It is a preferred style," answered the young maiden guide. "Why? Does it disturb you?"

"Yes," said Amelia.

"I think that is the intention." The guide's voice was matter-of-fact as if this was generally understood. "Here we have the hands being constructed, over there the arms and legs. We are free to show you the body coming together, but not the brain." Here the guide sounded apologetic. "The finished products are given uniforms of various kinds to wear and are then shipped to the major cities."

"Has there ever been any trouble with them?" asked Amelia. She still didn't like the idea of robots being armed with lethal weapons.

"Good Goddess, no!" The guide threw up her arms in surprise at such an outlandish question. "There happen to be safety devices built in so they are unable to harm either maidens or mavericks. They are, however, capable of arresting anyone if that is part of their function in society."

"How lucrative is the market for them?" asked Malcolm. He felt someone should ask that question just to be polite, and he was genuinely interested in how well they did as a commercial item.

"The demand is growing, especially since your Dreadnought has almost gained fifty dragon kills," the guide replied.

Amelia, Malcolm, and Megan had drinks in the hotel wine bar before retiring. A young maiden journalist found them there.

"Our dragons are special," said the maiden journalist. "Do you think your knights have much of a chance?"

"Your dragons have dark blue scales." Megan shrugged. "I suppose that is special. I'm sure our knights can cope with that. They are not colour blind."

"So you are beaming with confidence?" questioned the journalist.

"Yes," said Malcolm, "why not?"

"Are your dragons very skilful?" asked Amelia.

"Oh, yes!" The journalist beamed with pride." Our dragons are highly skilled as you will find out tomorrow."

Just before he was due to join his fellow knights in open-air combat with more than half the world watching, Dreadnought fashioned four dark blue dragons out of paper. It took the shakes away, calming him down. He knew he was being optimistic, but he saw no sense in being otherwise.

My shoulder still plays up on me on occasion, he thought to himself, *but I'm sure I can hold it together with the help of the other knights. I'm glad the maverick who tried to stab me is not in my company as a knight. He's going to make a poor effort somewhere, and I prefer to be with knights who know what they're doing.*

All but Dreadnought had the spiked maces, the morning stars, which had just been cleared for use by the Highest of High Priestesses.

At his barracks, a maverick representative in a bright yellow and orange suit urged Dreadnought to use one of them in the up and coming battle. The maverick made it clear he was representing Brian Tiller, a maverick industrial giant of Wollongong. Dreadnought refused to do so. The maverick representative said there would be disciplinary action taken against him if he didn't comply, Brian Tiller being a power in Wollongong, but Dreadnought brushed the representative aside with a motion of his hand.

"Unless your boss, Brian Tiller, plans to have me killed for not using his mace, I am safer with my sword," Dreadnought said bluntly to the maverick representative. The representative, seeing menace in Dreadnought's eyes, felt he had to back off, leaving Dreadnought alone with his thoughts. In the end, no disciplinary charges were laid against Dreadnought for not complying.

"I don't care that some Wollongong arms manufacturer isn't pleased with me," he later told Amelia. "I keep my short sword. I do not like the balance of the morning stars. The weight distribution feels wrong to me."

"There's something to be said for retaining a weapon you are familiar with and that had already served you well." Amelia remembered being particularly fond of a fighter plane because it had managed, time and time again, to safely get her home.

All the knights, including Dreadnought, had breastplates and shields.

Amelia watched, from the comfortable seat given to her, the knights as they came onto the field. The spikes on the maces glittered in the sun. Malcolm and Amelia were beside her. Only Amelia felt anxious, rubbing her hands together. It was quite a crowd looking on from the stands, and cameras were there so the action could be televised to at least fifty cities and numerous townships. Screens placed in strategic positions assured those watching live wouldn't miss a thing.

The dragons came on last. They were wearing loose black clothing and had samurai swords in their belts as well as daggers. Whatever else they had was hidden by folds of material. They peered out at the stadium through a slit in the face cloth they wore. By the slit, hands, and feet, it was apparent they had the dark blue scales they were known to have.

"Dragon ninjas!" cried Amelia.

"What?" Megan cried.

"Never mind," Amelia said. "I just hope Dreadnought knows what he is in for."

"You know?" asked Malcolm.

"Not precisely," said Amelia. "I just have this feeling they'll be tricky and hard to beat."

The dragons lined up in an odd fashion. It was a small dragon followed by a large dragon followed by a small dragon. It was a pattern that didn't make much sense to Amelia. Dreadnought and his knights formed their usual circle and waited for the dragons to attack.

The big dragons moved to within fifty feet of the knights and stopped. The smaller ones came on at a slower pace and stopped within sixty feet of the knights. Suddenly, the smaller dragons ran, leapt onto the shoulders of their larger comrades, and from there, flew into the midst of the knights. Dreadnought yelled, "Shields up!" But the call came too late for two of his knights who had their throats cut. As quickly as these dragons came, they bounced off of the shields of the knights and made it to safety. It happened so fast it took Dreadnought a moment to discover blood spurting from two of his fighters. They did not take long to die.

With speed one would not expect to see in such large adversaries, the big dragons charged. A knight dispatched one with his mace, tearing off his face cloth and half his face. The others were only successful at keeping the big dragons at bay. Meanwhile, the smaller dragons, now on the other side of the knights, brought star knives into play. Most of them thumped harmlessly off shields, but two got a knight in the neck, bringing him down squirting blood. A small dragon tried to separate a knight from his shield using a line and a grappling hook, but Dreadnought saw what was happening and managed to cut the line in time.

The large dragons retreated as three of the smaller ones cart-wheeled into action. Their swords moved as fast as they did, and before the knights knew it, three of them were shield-less, and then cut to pieces in buzz saw fashion.

Dreadnought moved forward with the remainder of his men. He had them separate so as not to get in each other's way, and then swing their maces in wide arcs as they got closer and closer to the larger dragons. Two of the smaller ones came at Dreadnought, and after furious swordplay, he cut them down. One of his knights tossed his mace and was able to brain a large dragon. Before he could be set upon, however, he picked up a samurai sword and gutted a smaller dragon with it.

A large dragon threw down a smoke bomb to confuse the knights, but Dreadnought had his warriors continue swinging though virtually blind until dragon skulls met spiked maces. The smoke that should have been to the dragon's advantage was instead of a help to the knights.

The remaining dragons charged. One knight was sliced in half, but all the dragons that hadn't been killed were clubbed to death.

There were bloody bits and pieces of knights and dragons everywhere. Everyone applauded the surviving knights, especially Dreadnought. Back in the locker room, Dreadnought crumpled up two of the paper dragons he had made and threw them in the bin.

Dreadnought was glum on the way back to Wollongong; his mouth drooped. He knew there would have to be one more battle. Amelia noticed the arm associated with the shoulder he had hurt shaking. She didn't say anything, and it stopped after a while.

"Japan was a close one," he told Amelia. "If not for those spiked maces the other knights had, I would have died. How much luck do I have left? How long can I hold my nerve? Once that has gone, I've had it."

"You've done well," assured Amelia. "There are only two more to go. You can do it. I know you can."

"Yes," agreed Dreadnought. "Only two more and I can stop. I can rest."

****

The following day at The Great Grape, Megan came across a petition to do with Dreadnought. Some well-placed mavericks wanted to stop him fighting altogether and to be executed by the robot constabulary instead. No way did they want a bloodstained knight in their midst posing as one of them. They had standards. Megan took a copy of it to Jens, who tore it up. "It won't happen," she told Megan.

****

Meanwhile, at The Spear and Shield, there was great rejoicing. "Dreadnought will do two easily," said a happy knight. A knightly reporter took notes of the joyous atmosphere found among his fellows. He just hoped the last two wouldn't be too much for the knight everyone he knew was depending on.

Two days later, it rained heavily. The weather did not improve Dreadnought's mood. Amelia visited him and took him out for a meal.

"I'm tempted to go into The Spear and Shield and get drunk," he told her.

"Don't!" Amelia was adamant.

"Why not?" asked Dreadnought.

"I think you know why." Amelia hoped this was the case. "Instead, let's have lamb stew together at your favourite restaurant."

"I'm only flesh and blood," he told Amelia over tea. "Yet so much is riding on me."

"I know," said Amelia in a soothing voice, "but you can do it. You have to for the sake of your fellow knights. Even perhaps for the sake of the dragons. If by becoming a maverick, you can pull down this rotten business of murder for entertainment, you'd be doing a lot of people some good."

"Is that even possible?" asked Dreadnought. "Would my becoming a maverick end all the bloodshed? That's hard to believe."

"I don't know," mused Amelia. "First the golden fifty, then we'll see. Have you given any thought to maverick Brian Tiller?" Amelia paused for a moment to gather her thoughts. "I know he's a slime-ball Wollongong arms manufacturer, but you'll need money for your new life. He once told me that if you were to back what he makes and sells, that in terms of money, you'll be set. If he wants you to help him push his products on television, radio, and in magazines to a wider audience, maybe you should. I know that is an awful thing to have to do, but you might not have many options."

"I can say the spiked maces Tiller now manufactures played a crucial role in Tokyo. I didn't use them, but other knights did." Amelia knew Dreadnought was being truthful because she had been there. Even if he wasn't, his words had the ring of honesty about them. "I can also tell a television audience they were made in Wollongong by Brian Tiller's factory."

"Good. It's almost over." Amelia sighed, happy to change the subject. "How's your shoulder?"

"Fine." Dreadnought did not shrug his shoulders, indicating he was anything but fine.

"I know it still bothers you." Amelia could see the truth in his eyes. "Have you been to a doctor recently about it?"

"Yes. Last night I went to a well-known maiden physician. She told me not to aggravate it with too much activity since it was still in the process of healing." Dreadnought stroked his hurt shoulder. "When May is done, I'll take her advice, but not before." He then shook his head sadly. "I used to be able to get into the heads of dragons, but I couldn't do that with the Japanese. Maybe they moved too fast, or perhaps I'm losing my touch. It could be what has kept me alive so long is now fading away."

****

In the second week of May, Megan was tidying up the seventh underground floor of the Mitchell Library when she came upon a diary. The last pages were written just before Sydney's ruination. A combination of Malaysian and Indonesian task force of jet fighters had decided to teach the Australians a lesson. There was strafing of civilians and the loosing of non-nuclear missiles.

Bullets and explosions ripped apart anyone caught out on the streets. Windows shattered, sending shards of glass down, cutting men, women, and children in two. There was nothing neat and orderly about it as in the movies. This the diarist made clear. He was fearful of what was to follow. He suspected the nukes would soon follow in a few days, and he was right.

RAAF fighter planes had shot down some of these enemy jets before they could take too many lives or do too much damage, but what had been done was still horrific. One of the pilots who had done the shooting was Amelia Warren's cousin Frank, a relative of Megan's friend from the past.

Megan learned, from a book written by a University of Technology scholar, that for a century, Australians had financially supported the Indonesians and, apart from the gratitude of the Balinese, had gotten little for it. Too many poor and disadvantaged Indonesians believed that Australia belonged to them and so should be taken by them. This notion mounted as tensions increased between the two countries.

Money stopped flowing from Canberra to Jakarta, and this resulted in the collapse of the Indonesian economy. Only the Balinese, with their goodwill continuing, remained all right financially. Megan remembered Amelia telling her she was keen on bombing Jakarta but not Bali. Even so, she did admit not everyone living in Jakarta was guilty of anything, but war tended to lump people together as the enemy.

It seemed to Megan, from what a computer printout found on the seventh floor revealed, that those Western powers with nukes limited their use to avoid a nuclear winter. The others, being poorer due to overpopulation, didn't have much of a supply anyway, so they had to use what they had sparingly.

In a small metal box, Megan found black opals from Lightning Ridge still worth a fortune. There was fire in them. Megan suspected they were meant to be on a different floor.

Nearby was a box containing a space helmet prototype marked as such she thought Houston might be interested in plus gloves specially designed for use in zero gravity. *There's still plenty of finds to be made here*, thought Megan, *let alone the other six floors.*

****

While Megan was examining the seventh floor in more detail, Amelia was sent to Calgary, Canada to deliver Emile Tarn, a maverick scientist, to a forum on continued human population control and wildlife diversity.

Emile was fat, old, and talkative. He was in a red and white suit. He had a wife and two children, and so felt no need to be too flowery around Amelia. This she found to be a relief.

"Back in the early twenty-first century," Emile told Amelia on the way to their first stopover in Hawaii, "a crazed leader brought into Canada over a million of the haters of freedom and the lovers of overpopulation."

"My grandfather told me about it," said Amelia. "It had something to do with orders from the United Nations."

"In the latter half of that century," Emile continued, "Toronto had to be bombed out of existence to stop the contamination spreading. It was such a tragedy. Toronto was a beautiful city gone forever, though it was already dying. I feel for them having to do that, having to make such a terrible decision, such a horrid sacrifice."

"Yes," Amelia agreed. She shrugged her shoulders. "I remember. Luckily the Nationalists were able to sort out Montreal and Winnipeg without going that far."

"They vowed it should never happen again," Emile said proudly, "and it won't."

"Are you from Canada?" asked Amelia.

"Winnipeg," Emile replied. "But I have lived the last ten years in Wollongong. They sent me to this forum to represent your city because I love Wollongong and I know how Canadians think."

"How clever of them," Amelia replied.

In Honolulu, they were mobbed by maiden and maverick reporters asking questions about Dreadnought. One even wanted to know what he had for breakfast. After hearing that particular question with its implications, Amelia decided not to answer any more questions. Emile was ignored. Apparently, no one wanted to know about his mission to Calgary.

Over two pineapple punches at a bar, Emile had to ask what all the excitement was over Dreadnought.

"I have been out of touch, studying up for the forum, immersed in statistics," Emile confessed. Amelia gave him a rundown, and he sat back in amazement.

"This will come up in Calgary for sure," he told Amelia. There was excitement in his piggy, little eyes. "This could change everything."

"For better or worse?" asked Amelia, unsure what Emile was driving at.

"I don't know," Emile told her, pulling at his left ear. "I think for the worse."

Amelia had to admit the pineapple punches in Honolulu were good. They were almost as delicious as the ones made along the Queensland Gold Coast.

After she gave Emile the news about Dreadnought, he didn't seem to enjoy his drink as much as she did her own. She finished hers and thought of getting another. He didn't finish his, and she suspected he had no thoughts toward getting another.

"The news concerning Dreadnought almost reaching fifty will no doubt send ripples through the financial world." Emile took out a red handkerchief and wiped sweat from his brow. "If he does get to fifty, it will be disastrous everywhere."

"How so?" asked Amelia.

"Banks may close and never open again." Emile continued to wipe his face.

On the way to Calgary from Honolulu, Emile talked about what a disaster it would be if armies of knights became mavericks.

"There would be fewer workers with picks and shovels. Trade would be down everywhere." Emile was driving himself into a panic over what might happen, his eyes bulging and that handkerchief ever present to mop up his tears and sweat. "The games in May and November would cease for fear of producing ever more mavericks out of the knights. What's more, no one would know what to do with the dragons. Wars might even resume."

"You must have known this would happen someday," said Amelia philosophically.

"No, we didn't," replied Emile, wiping the back of his neck with his handkerchief. "Fifty is impossible. Dreadnought, therefore, is impossible!"

"He's a one-off," agreed Amelia, trying not to smile. "He may not reach fifty, and even if he did, it is not likely to happen again."

At Calgary airport, Emile was the celebrity and not Amelia. This was fine with her. There were conferences taking place, and she wasn't invited to any of them. She was, however, given a nice hotel room and plenty of time in which to explore Calgary. It had the flavour of a frontier town grown up. The air was crisp with a dash of cold, and there were nature walks available to check out the local wildlife.

A bookseller gave her the lowdown on what the forum was all about. Every year it was decided here just how many knights and dragons would be required and how many were surplus and could be sacrificed to the games. Amelia found the whole business appalling, but it did fit in with everything else she had discovered about this society that had developed while she was in her deep freeze.

Here, the coffee was cheaper than in Wollongong, and the hotel cook knew how to serve up a thick, juicy steak. She came across a few knights working in a field, but no dragons.

When Emile had finished with his meetings and conferences, and the forum was over for another year, they headed back to Wollongong. On the way to Honolulu, a giant albatross shadowed them. Emile wanted her to ram it, but she refused.

"It's just a damned nuisance," he reasoned. "Why not have some sport with it?"

"It's a bird," Amelia told him coldly. "And I'm not risking this flyer." She also didn't want to go about hurting and killing something that didn't need hurting and killing.

The albatross lost interest in them over Honolulu and flew away. Emile would have liked to have spent more time in this paradise, but as soon as the flyer was refuelled, they were off again. Amelia had decided she wanted to spend as little time with Emile as she possibly could.

On the way back, he talked about new measures in keeping the population down, including the latest approved weapons for the knights to use on the dragons. He claimed that bringing the morning stars, the spiked maces, back into the games was his idea from last year. What's more, he was happy to be able to find a local Wollongong arms manufacturer capable of making them. Amelia listened but didn't say much.

At Wollongong airport, she was greeted by Malcolm, who had just flown in from Hobart. Emile went on his way, and Amelia had drinks with Malcolm at The Great Grape.

"I managed to get some nice apples from the Hobart fresh fruit market," Malcolm told her. "Also, I scored some fresh strawberries. I look forward to going back there soon."

"I haven't had fresh strawberries in a while." Amelia sighed. "Wollongong doesn't seem to be famous for them, though we do all right with fresh blackberries."

"How was your trip to Calgary?" asked Malcolm over glasses of white wine.

"Did you know they play with millions of lives there?" Amelia grimaced at the thought.

"You mean knight and dragon lives?" Malcolm knew about Calgary but wasn't prepared to get overly excited about the place.

"That's right." Amelia frowned deeply and crossed her arms. "They weigh up who is needed and who is expendable. And it all has to do with numbers. It's done with statistics. Can you believe it?"

"Yes. It's what they do." Malcolm said this in a matter-of-fact tone set to annoy Amelia. "Without them, we couldn't live the good life."

"Are you so sure?" Amelia stared daggers at Malcolm.

"I don't doubt it," Malcolm assured her, wondering why she was getting upset. "From what Megan has told me, what we have here now is much better than the world you left behind when you went for your long sleep."

CHAPTER TWENTY-NINE

The High Priestess of Wollongong would have liked nothing better than to stop Dreadnought from being entered into any future games. Questions were already being asked by the Highest One as to how Dreadnought could be as good a knight as he has turned out to be, and for the High One, those questions were dangerous. They might lead to answers that could only end in Wollongong's High Priestess losing her much favoured position.

If Dreadnought did not compete, he couldn't gain those troublesome two kills he needed to make fifty. Unfortunately, even delaying giving him a second chance that month would cause too much unrest among the knight population who would cry foul. The robots could and would put down armed rebellions by knights, but the result would be an imbalance for which the Highest of High Priestesses would blame her. She was, however, able to keep him out of the annual Wollongong One Hundred Knights Versus One Hundred Dragons event.

At the beginning of the third week of May, Dreadnought received what he knew, one way or the other, would be his last engagement as a knight. He was to go with nine of his fellows to Edinburgh, Scotland, to battle with Scottish dragons. Amelia and Malcolm would take them there, and Megan would tag along with Malcolm.

Dreadnought's eyes watered when he received the news. Amelia wondered what she could do to improve his mood and his chances of getting through it alive. A pep talk wasn't going to help much. Then it came to her.

Amelia got permission from the High Priestess of Wollongong to arrive in Scotland five days before they were due. She asked if she could take her five knights with her, including Dreadnought, and do some sightseeing beforehand. The High Priestess asked Dean Renate if giving the nod for this was indeed a sensible thing to do, and the dean said yes. The dean further stated she couldn't see it making any difference to the outcome of the battle that would occur.

"Why are we going early?" asked Dreadnought of Amelia before he got in the flyer.

"You'll find out," said Amelia. "It's nothing bad. It may even be something good."

"I don't like surprises." This wasn't anything against Amelia. For Dreadnought, the unexpected usually meant a new way to die. He looked twice at Amelia to try to fathom her purpose. He didn't think she wanted to see him dead. Then he looked at his knights to see if they might have a clue. No such luck. With a deep sigh and the shaking of his head, he boarded Amelia's flyer. The four other knights followed him. The slowness of the four getting onboard reflected Dreadnought's mood. It could have been better.

"You'll like this surprise," Amelia said, smiling with confidence. This took Dreadnought further by surprise. What could she possibly have in mind? What did she know about him that he would like enough to be happy about going to Scotland early?

Their first and only stopover was New Delhi in India. It was a dusty, dirty place where the people had suffered from radiation sickness and then plague by being too close to Pakistan during the wars. The plague was an offshoot of the famine that came when the wind blew in the wrong direction and ruined otherwise perfectly healthy crops and killed livestock. Those that bombed Pakistan had no intention of hurting anyone in India, but it happened anyway. Amelia remembered reading about it. Three of the great western powers had gotten together. They decided on three aircraft and two runs to get rid of the Pakistan navy and air force for good, along with a great portion of the people, the good and the bad. It would also stop leaders in that country from giving support to religious uprisings in countries as far afield as the USA, Canada, and Australia or so military leaders believed at the time.

Before lift-off in her flyer, Amelia was warned by New Deli Airport staff about the terrible winds that still came out of the towns and cities of Pakistan and that landing anywhere in that particular country would mean certain death. Even now, the levels of radiation were way too high for humans to take, even in small doses.

Regardless, Amelia and her passengers braved the winds. It was the quickest route to Scotland and also potentially the most dangerous. *Surely by now, those winds would have eased*, thought Amelia, *and the danger much less than in my earlier time.* In this, she was wrong. If anything, they were more manic.

"Is this what you wanted me to experience?" asked Dreadnought of Amelia as the craft they were in was buffeted about. Something came out of the shadows, a large, bat-like creature that shrieked and then flew into a cloud that crackled with energy.

The other knights onboard remained silent. They looked stone-faced as if it didn't matter if they lived or died. More pitching of the flyer and two of them began to pray to the Great Goddess for salvation. Perishing in combat was one thing; it assured them a place in paradise, but this was something else.

"We'll make it through." Amelia tried to sound self-assured. She chewed her lip and held tight to the controls. She had to make it through for everyone's sake, especially Dreadnought. She didn't want him to hate her as they all were sparking and burning in the hell below.

Swirling colours shot up before her as if to bedazzle. She could imagine being enticed by them to surrender and allow her flyer to fall. She had no intention of doing so. The bat-like creature appeared once more, screaming. How it could survive at all in that satanic mixture of sulphur, carbon monoxide, oxygen, and unrelenting atomic energy was a mystery. Perhaps it had wandered too far into this wild place and was dying.

"How can this be?" cried Dreadnought, waving his arms.

"Madness from another time," said Amelia softly, wondering if he had heard her.

Then the swirling ended, the rocking stopped, and the sky cleared. The danger from radiation had concluded. Pakistan could now be a dreadful memory. She was thankful they had made it through without any damage to themselves or the flyer. If the flyer had been compromised, or so Amelia reasoned, leakage would have resulted in coughing fits and other possible respiratory ailments.

It was fortunate their machine had some radiation protection built into it. Even so, Amelia promised herself never to go that way to Europe or Britain ever again. She thought by now Pakistan wouldn't be a problem. She should have asked Malcolm about prevailing conditions over that part of the world before leaving Wollongong.

Instead of landing at the airport in Edinburgh, Amelia put down on a small nearby but useable strip on the Isle of May situated in the mouth of the Firth of Forth, south of the Fife coast and north of the Lothian coast.

"Puffins!" cried Dreadnought, his eyes watering again but for a different reason. He had just arrived with the others when he saw a couple of those clown-like birds flying overhead. Their colourful beaks, chubby bodies, and strangely comical eyes revived his sense of wellbeing, bringing a great big smile to his face.

"Early spring here," said Amelia. "It's still a bit chilly. Shall we have a look around?"

"Yes," Dreadnought agreed. "Is this my surprise?"

"Of course!" cried Amelia. "Please enjoy. We have a few days we can spend here before Edinburgh needs us. Let's make the most of it."

"I am a boy again!" Dreadnought trotted off with a pair of binoculars Amelia had given him. The others went after him. He was headed for the cliffs to get a better look at the nests.

"But they're just birds," reasoned one of the other knights, looking rather puzzled. He smiled, frowned, and covered his mouth with his hand. He knew he was missing something, but what?

"Yeah," agreed another knight, "they're just birds. Does this have anything to do with origami?"

"I shouldn't think so," yet another knight said. "All the birds here are kicking up a racket."

"Yes!" Dreadnought's eyes twinkled. "Birds I have only ever seen on television and in my dreams. I have always been fascinated by flight."

"Look!" Amelia cried. "There's one with two little fish in its beak. No. I'm wrong. There are three!"

"There's plenty of fish for them here." Dreadnought beamed. "Nothing seems to change for them."

"Nothing," Amelia agreed. "It is nesting time, and they are feeding their young."

Amelia had arranged for the old visitor centre to put them up for two nights with lamb's stew for supper, hot porridge for breakfast, and bread and jam in between. Hot black tea was provided as a warm me up. The meals and the lodging were much appreciated, though two of the knights decided to stay with the flyer at night just in case of a sabotage attempt.

The days spent on May Island, Amelia knew, were well worth coming early to Scotland to encounter. She had never seen Dreadnought happier.

Even so, those days came to an end, and the knights had to prepare for the upcoming ordeal. It took fifteen minutes in the flyer to travel from the island where they were to Edinburgh. In that short period, the mood aboard changed. Amelia thought of it as coming back from a short holiday to the demands of the death-dealing trenches of the Great War. None of the other four knightly warriors, despite themselves, could say they hadn't enjoyed May Island. Now Dreadnought looked determined to win, no more the hangdog look, the eyes that said, *finish me off; I'm ready for the scrap heap.* This suited Amelia just fine.

Officials greeted their arrival at Edinburgh airport. There they caught up with Malcolm, Megan, and the other five Wollongong knights. Amelia, Malcolm, and Megan were taken to comfortable rooms in a nearby castle, and the knights, with all their combat gear, were placed in the castle's dungeon by robots assigned to them.

Amelia was informed the next morning by a maverick steward, a pompous fellow in a blue outfit with green stripes, that the fighting would take place in the castle grounds. Already, cameras had been set up so that the action could be seen live in numerous cities and towns. On the top floor of the castle and the battlements, seats had been placed for guests so they could look down on the proceedings. While this was going on, Dreadnought fashioned two silvery paper dragons to hopefully go with the rest of his origami collection. He got the paper earlier on from Amelia, who understood the importance of fashioning these objects to Dreadnought's state of mind.

At midday, guests sat together with the local gentry, and there was a display of bagpipe music before first the knights, and then the dragons came out, escorted by robots that smartly left them. The dragons had been kept in a different section of the dungeon. A great cheer went up for the silvery, Scottish dragons rather than for the Wollongong knights.

The knights had a mix of short swords and spiked maces along with their breastplates and shields. The dragons, dressed in kilts and blue shirts, had claymores with a longer reach than the short sword plus small round shields with spikes on top for added protection. No pain collars in sight. A horn blast told all that the fighting was about to commence.

"Ten knights, ten dragons," said an announcer over a speaker system. "Who will triumph?"

The knights formed their usual circle and waited. Then the dragons charged.

The claymores clanged against the shields of the dragons as they came on, causing an awful din. A blade came down hard, and a knight found himself bereft of his shield. The blade went down a second time, cutting deep into the knight's neck and shoulder. The knight next to the dying one then crashed down on the attacking dragon's head with his mace, adding bits of dragon brain and blood to the awful mess.

Elsewhere at the same time, a dragon ripped a shield away from a knight using his tail as a third hand and then cut the knight's head clean off his shoulders with his claymore. Blood rose where a head should have been, and Dreadnought's face was splashed by it. He only just cleared his eyes with his hand in time to avoid two claymore strokes and to deliver a fatal stabbing to his foe.

The dragons retreated, and the knights let them. Both sides assessed for a moment their losses and gains. One knight became mesmerized by the severed head on the ground at his feet. Dreadnought kicked the fellow in the leg to get his attention and said, "That will be you if you don't concentrate on the living."

Ten minutes later, the dragons charged once more, their claymores banging against their shields. Two of the knights looked like they were about to bolt but held their ground. They drew strength from Dreadnought's calmness in the face of danger.

A dragon used the spikes on his shield to cut a knight's hand, causing him to drop his shield. The knight thus became vulnerable to a downward claymore strike. The knight fell to the ground, twitching before he died. In the furore, a knight bashed aside a dragon's shield and laid into him with his spiked mace. Two knights went down, carved up by the relentless slashing actions of the dragons with their Scottish blades. Then the remaining dragons retreated.

"They'll form up and charge again," said Dreadnought. "Let's fool them by breaking the circle and charging when they do."

Dreadnought's hand shook as he moved with speed toward the dragons. It shook so bad he dropped his shield, giving a dragon a tempting target. The dragon in question tried to punch him in the head with the rolled-up end of his tail while bringing up his claymore for the death stroke. Dreadnought stopped quivering long enough to grab the tail coming at him like a fist and slice into it with his sword. The dragon's howl was cut short by Dreadnought stabbing him in the neck and tossing him at another oncoming dragon. The surprised dragon looked into Dreadnought's eyes long enough to hesitate before striking and thus was quickly dispatched by Dreadnought's blade.

Then Dreadnought's hand resumed shaking. He was about to have his head removed by a dragon because of this when another knight saved him with a couple of hammer-like blows with his mace. Dreadnought recovered in time to help his saviour slay the dragon with a mace to the face and a short sword to the stomach.

Meanwhile, three knights surprised three dragons with their speed. Spiked maces hammered their way past shields, scoring head busting blows. The last dragon hacked at his opponent's arms with the spikes on his shield while looking for the opportunity to cut into heads and shoulders. He received a gut wound from a short sword followed by a knee to the face.

"You have your fifty," said the knight who had saved Dreadnought's life. They and three other warriors stood upon the blood-soaked field, some of the bodies still moving but beyond repair. The losses were tremendous, but the knights had won. A great cheer went up from the crowd as they exited back to the dungeon.

"I wash this off me for the last time." Dreadnought splashed water from a basin all over himself then went under a shower. He watched as the red life essence of a dragon or two, not to mention a knight, left his body and went down the drain.

"You're lucky," said one of the knights.

"Yes," agreed Dreadnought, "I am fortunate."

"I will take up bird watching," said another knight. "If it worked for you, it might work for me too."

"Find your own way," advised Dreadnought.

"Yes, maverick," answered the knight.

Dreadnought was taken aback by the title then realized it was appropriate.

After they cleaned up, the knights met Amelia, Malcolm, and Megan for their ride home. Amelia decided to take Dreadnought plus one other knight back in her flyer, and Malcolm would take the rest.

As they were flying away from Scotland toward St. Louis, they received a message from Dean Renate to refuel there, at St. Louis, then to proceed with all haste to Houston where they were urgently needed.

"What's that all about?" asked Malcolm of Amelia over the radio.

"I have no idea," answered Amelia.

As they approached the coast of the USA, a jet fighter of the same vintage Amelia used to fly appeared out of a cloud bank and began strafing both flyers. Both Amelia and Malcolm peeled off, out of the way of the bullet spread, but figured it was only a matter of time before they were goners. They had nothing to fight back with, not even speed. Yet they had to do the best they could with what little they had.

Amelia was pumped up with too much adrenalin to be as frightened as she should have been. She was dodging a superior enemy, so having her wits about her was far more important.

"Scatter!" cried Amelia to Malcolm over the radio. "We bunch up, we're dead!" He didn't reply but did as she commanded. *Some of my training as a fighter pilot may buy us a few seconds,* thought Amelia.

On the second run by the jet fighter, bullets punched her left wing and just missed her fuel tank. She swerved her craft then made it climb up and over until it was facing the enemy. This shook up both herself and her passengers.

Normally, this would have been a stupid thing to do, but the enemy bought it. Thinking she must have something to attack with, her adversary cut away to avoid a volley of machine gun fire that couldn't possibly happen. It was a mistake Amelia knew the enemy was not likely to make a second time. She knew, from the vibrations she felt, that the damaged wing was only just holding together. More fancy manoeuvring and she understood it would most certainly fly apart. The flyer wasn't built for combat. *At least, my death and that of my crew might save Malcolm,* she thought.

Then out of another cloud bank came a second fighter. *This is it,* thought Amelia. To her surprise, instead of targeting her or Malcolm's craft, the second fighter sprayed death at the first one, finishing it off with a missile strike. A great mid-air explosion lit up the sky and knocked the two flyers about. When the air around them settled down, the remaining fighter waggled its wings as a friendly gesture to them then flew off at top speed.

If the first jet fighter had missiles, Amelia knew, the game would have been over much sooner and to her disadvantage. What's more, she had to be grateful that the first fighter had been so obviously inexperienced. They would never have become an RAAF pilot without a lot of time in a simulator before seeing action.

There were knights with bruises in embarrassing places, but no one with any broken bones.

"I must have sweated a gallon in the last five minutes," confessed Malcolm wryly over the radio.

"No shit!" replied Amelia, who has also sweated a great deal in a short space of time.

"My Goddess!" cried Malcolm. "You've got to know what that was all about!"

"I have no idea," replied Amelia. "I have a feeling we'll find out in Houston."

"Yes, of course," said Malcolm, "in Houston."

CHAPTER THIRTY

The two flyers touched down in St. Louis. Their planes got top priority in refuelling. A few streets away, however, something exploded, followed by screams and another explosion. Gunfire ripped through the air.

"What's going on?" asked Malcolm of the airport staff.

"We just got it over the radio," answered the young maverick refueler. "A couple of our robots have been reprogrammed by a maidenly fanatic to kill knights, mavericks, and maidens on sight. The world's gone mad since Dreadnought became a maverick!"

"This isn't Dreadnought's fault," said Amelia.

"Has the maiden been arrested?" asked Megan.

"She was the first victim of her robots," the refueler told her. "She left a note, so we know it was her. Over the radio, they stated she was paid to look after them for years, and she was good at it, too. Not a problem. Now she does this!"

"We just need enough fuel to get us to Houston," said Malcolm. "How long will it take?"

"Another ten minutes," reasoned the refueler, "but there are five aircraft coming in, so it will be half an hour before you can take off."

"Do we have half an hour?" asked Megan.

"I don't know," replied the refueler.

"If we don't have that half an hour, we need to do something or we're dead," said Amelia.

The rapid-fire gunshots were getting louder, punching the air a shorter and shorter distance away. Dreadnought spotted the robots. They were about two hundred yards from them, cutting down with bullets two mavericks unable to get out of their way in time.

"We need a plan," Malcolm said. "Do you have any ideas, Amelia?"

"Stop the refuelling!" she ordered, and it was halted for both planes. "Hurry, everyone! Get on board. They're almost on us!"

"We can't hide from them inside our flyers," reasoned Malcolm.

"We won't be hiding," said Amelia. "Hurry now! No time to argue. Everyone, do as I say, and Malcolm, do as I do."

They piled back into the two aircraft, the refueler joining them. Amelia revved up her engines and speared her flyer toward the first of the robots. A couple of bullets hit the windscreen, splaying spider web cracks across the glass. A crunch followed as wheels first knocked down the robot and then pummelled it. The gun went flying out of a mechanical hand. Amelia ran over the robot a few times with her flyer just to be sure enough damage had been done. Not far away, Malcolm did something similar.

Dreadnought cried out, "Don't do it!" Unfortunately, Malcolm couldn't hear the warning. He was already out of his craft and approaching Amelia to congratulate her. A shot rang out, and Malcolm fell. The robot he'd crushed had retained its firearm and the ability to use it long enough to fire once before its electronic brain collapsed, rendering it harmless.

"No!" Megan screamed as she rushed to Malcolm. Amelia and Dreadnought left their craft to see what they could do for the injured pilot. Amelia took the flyer's first aid kit with her. They discovered Malcolm still breathing. He was face down, so Dreadnought turned him over to make breathing easier and to examine where he had been shot.

"The bullet has torn through his left hand and has made a hole in his left leg," Dreadnought told the others in a matter-of-fact voice.

"He's bleeding out." Amelia looked about for some way to stop the blood flow. "We need a tourniquet on the leg. The hand's bad but the least of his worries for now. There's an industrial-strength rubber band here in the kit we can use. Get me a blanket. Hurry Meagan, move!"

Meagan was like a statue. She wouldn't, couldn't move. It was Dreadnought who got the blanket out of the flyer and found a pillow for Malcolm's head.

"I'll radio for an ambulance," said Amelia. "Keep him warm and talk to him until I get back."

"I don't know what to say," said Dreadnought. "Megan! Think! Snap out of it for Malcolm's sake." He shook her until he heard her sigh like a balloon losing its air.

"What should I say?" asked Megan, who was now in tears. Amelia was already in the flyer.

"Anything you like," replied Dreadnought. "Just keep his mind active. He mustn't go to sleep."

Dreadnought found some sulphur powder in the kit and put that on Malcolm's wounds.

"What will that do?" Megan wiped tears away from her face and glasses.

"It will help prevent infection," said Dreadnought. "I've used it on my wounds and that of others over the years."

Before long, a hospital hover van on air cushions and anti-gravity units rather than wheels arrived and took Malcolm away. Megan went with him.

"Now, what do we do?" Dreadnought asked.

"We go to Houston," said Amelia.

The smashed robots were taken away by other less volatile robots. The windscreen of both flyers had to be replaced. After that was done and the refuelling completed, Amelia could take her craft to where she was expected. Malcolm's flyer, however, would have to remain in a St. Louis hangar until he was able to resume his pilot duties.

The four knights plus the new maverick joined Amelia in leaving St. Louis for a short hop to Houston. There, they were greeted by knights and mavericks anxious to get them away from the landing field and to where the spacecraft to Mars was being stored.

"We have mavericks that don't want Dreadnought to be a maverick," a maverick technician told them on their way to a large structure with a roof that could fold away. "Me? I don't care. We also have maidens who don't like the idea of any maiden being free to marry him. The priestesses have mixed feelings, too! It's a real mess out there!"

"Out where?" asked Amelia.

"In every major town and city," answered the technician. "We also have knights and some maidens and mavericks ready to riot if anything bad happens to Dreadnought. A lot of it is tied up with religion and interpretations of scripture and so forth, so I don't understand much of it. There's the book of the Great Goddess. It is rather lengthy. What I can tell you is this: feelings are running high."

Jens and Dean Renate greeted Amelia and the rest near a set of lifts. They went up to the eleventh-floor observation deck with them where a dozen priestesses, maidens, and mavericks were already seated around a conference table headed by the High Priestess of Wollongong. Amelia looked out at the enormous spaceship ready for launch before taking her seat with the other important newcomers. The knights were made to stand. Dreadnought thought he would have to stand with them, but someone offered him a chair next to Amelia.

Coffee and biscuits were served to all except the knights by knightly servants. Dreadnought felt he couldn't refuse what was offered to him. This was his new position, and the knights were all happy for him. Once the servants had left, the High Priestess of Wollongong called the meeting to order. "We need to carry out the plan we have discussed in detail," she said. "And we have to do it in such a way as to cause minimal damage to our social structure."

"After the incident at St. Louis," said a visibly shaken young maverick in a white jacket with gold trim, "the robots in Sparta were deactivated and put into storage. Do you know what happened after that? Well! I'll tell you! The Greek knights went crazy. They rounded up all the mavericks and maidens and forced them to fight against the local dragons. It was a blood-bath."

"I heard the maidens did better than the mavericks." A young maiden smugly put this in, making the young maver-ick feel even worse about what had occurred.

"Be that as it may," said the young maverick, getting his composure back, "all were still slaughtered. Then the dragons were killed off. The knights used guns on them stolen off the dysfunctional robots, so the dragons didn't stand a chance. You'd think the knights would have needed lessons on the use of firearms, but they knew how to pull a trigger and what end the bullets come out of, and that was enough. It took knights and robots from Athens to restore order."

"How did they do that?" Amelia asked candidly.

"The knights and robots from Athens slaughtered the renegade knights. It is unlawful for any knight to slay a dragon outside the May and November games except in self-defence," said the young maverick coolly, now sounding officious. "It is also unlawful for a knight to detain a maiden or a maverick, let alone put them in danger. Knights who use firearms are subject to the death penalty, and that applies everywhere. So, the knights with the firearms had to be put down and the others as well. It's that simple. No mercy. I don't know what those rene-gades thought they were doing, but as soon as any of them

picked up a gun and did what they did with it, they were finished."

"The fighter jet that was taken out of a museum and re-
armed by a self-sacrificing maverick aeronautical expert would
not have solved anything," an older maverick wearing a grey
suit with crimson dots put forward in a smooth voice. "Luckily,
we had an inkling of what he was up to and were able to rearm a
similar fighter to protect Dreadnought and Amelia. It shows,
however, to what lengths some mavericks and maidens will go
to start up the civil wars we all fear."

"We are not here to discuss current events," said the High
Priestess, using her hand dismissively. "The Highest of High
Priestesses expects us to find solutions. So let's get on with it. We
cannot allow Dreadnought as a maverick to remain, and yet he
simply cannot be removed. These are the facts."

"We know what we can do." A priestess with a keen eye
leaned forward conspiratorially. "It must, however, be with the
cooperation of Dreadnought and Amelia, or it will fail."

"Yes," the High Priestess agreed. "Bring in the astronauts."

The priestess with the keen eye left the room and returned with astronauts Scott Simon from St. Louis and Mai Tan
from Hong Kong.

"Have you told them yet?" asked Mai.

"Not yet," said the High Priestess. "Why don't you tell
them?"

"Very well," Mai agreed. "The mission to Mars was never
intended to be a two-person venture. The maidens and mavericks who designed our craft always expected it to hold four, not
two."

"The offer could not be put to you until Dreadnought
made his golden fifty," said Scott. "Now that he has, please think
about going with us to Mars."

"You mean me?" Dreadnought almost choked on his
words; he was that astounded.

"Yes," said Mai in a matter-of-face voice, "you and Amelia."

"Why?" asked Amelia. It was a word that left her mouth while all sorts of other questions were manifesting.

"We cannot have Dreadnought here as a maverick," said the High Priestess coolly. "Already, his presence as a maverick is causing disruptions, unnecessary deaths, and imbalances."

"So ship him off to Mars." Amelia was getting angry but had to hold her temper in check.

"But he has to want to go." The High Priestess smiled a cunning smile. "You have to want to go."

"Why?" asked Amelia. It slipped out, and she was glad it did.

"If it were obvious you were forced to go," said the High Priestess calmly, "it would not go down well with many knights and some maidens and mavericks. It would be just as bad as having you and Dreadnought executed here and now."

"So what do you want from us?" asked Dreadnought in monotone.

"We need you on camera talking positively about being new members of the Mars expedition," a priestess informed them. "We need your enthusiasm for the project to get out there."

"Make fifty and go to Mars," Dreadnought mused. He knew he couldn't easily fit into maverick society but didn't believe he'd be thrown this option.

"Something like that," a priestess replied.

"We need more," said Mei, with energy behind her words. "We cannot have passengers. We cannot have a maverick and a maiden sitting on their hands the whole trip."

"We'll train you," said Scott. "The controls of the spacecraft are not that much different from the flyer you, Amelia, use now. Then there are emergency procedures, and if you are to venture outside the craft for any reason, how to handle zero gravity."

"We have a month to get you up to speed," said Mei.

"A month is required for the publicity campaign." The High Priestess smiled knowingly. "It has to get out your willingness to go, or when you do leave, your departure won't make a difference."

"Do we have a choice?" asked Amelia in a small voice.

"Not really." The High Priestess waved away the possibility of Dreadnought and Amelia remaining on Earth with a hand gesture. "But your cooperation would be valuable."

"We could fudge something together based on old film footage of you and Dreadnought, but it would be messy," said a technical maverick.

"Another thing." The High Priestess leaned forward and smiled a devilish smile. "We want you and Dreadnought to marry."

"What?" Dreadnought cried. He looked at Amelia and then put a hand on his facial scar. *Marriage is not possible*, he thought. *I am too damaged.*

"Mei and Scott are married," reasoned the High Priestess.

"Let me think about all this." Amelia needed time to do so.

"You have until tomorrow to give us your decision." The High Priestess crossed her arms.

As the meeting broke up, Jens, who had remained silent in the room up until now, said to Amelia, "Decide quickly. We need you to get moving on this."

"You know what has to be done," added Dean Renate, who also hadn't contributed anything to the actual meeting.

CHAPTER THIRTY-ONE

On their second day at the Houston space complex, Amelia and Dreadnought met Doctor Ester Grant, the maiden in charge of the technical side of the Mars mission. She was a short, fat woman in her forties with red hair and sharp blue eyes. "I thought it was about time I paid you a visit," she told them as she interrupted their canteen meal. "The spacecraft is my design. Some of the items rescued recently from old Sydney confirm I have been heading in the right direction."

"That's good," Amelia said, wanting to have confidence in the final product.

"Once the fifty could be achieved," she told Amelia and Dreadnought, "you had to be part of the plan. We allowed for this in our calculations. Do you have any questions?"

"What are our chances of getting there?" asked Amelia.

"Good," said Doctor Grant.

"What are our chances of surviving on Mars?" asked Dreadnought.

"Not so good." Doctor Grant looked down at her feet before continuing. "We don't have enough data to be sure of current conditions there. We hope the dome is still sound, but you won't know until you get there."

"Why weren't you at the meeting?" Amelia looked deep into the Doctor's eyes. Dreadnought leaned forward menacingly.

"Oh, you mean the one with your High Priestess?" Doctor Grant brushed them aside with her pudgy, little hands. "I'm too busy assuring you of a safe ride. I leave politics and religion to others. You can leave the technical side of your trip to me, Mei, and Scott. I don't expect to see you again, so good luck."

"That's it?" asked Amelia, incredulous.

"That's it," confirmed Doctor Grant.

Amelia and Dreadnought watched the doctor waddle off, wondering just how safe the spacecraft could be with that maiden in charge.

"What do you think of Doctor Grant?" asked Amelia.

"I'd rather not say," replied Dreadnought. "I don't know any rocket designers, so I am not aware of what they are supposed to be like."

Mei came over and said, "Doctor Grant knows her stuff, but she's no diplomat. She has the best brains from over a dozen countries working under her. I bet she left that out. So relax. She'll get us there."

Getting ready for space included plenty of mornings in an Olympic pool, running, push-ups, and other forms of exercise. Much of it was nothing new to either Amelia or Dreadnought. It became apparent, though, that Dreadnought's shoulder and thus affected arm had to be kept out of some of it.

"You're coming along nicely," a maidenly medical doctor committed to the space program told him, "but such injuries cannot heal overnight. Your last battle, the one in Scotland, was a shock to your system, but you're getting over it. You'll be fit by the time we launch you into space."

"When will that be?" asked Dreadnought.

"A month," said the medical doctor, "minus the three days you've already been here."

Dreadnought donated his fifty paper dragons to his old barracks in Wollongong, hoping they would do the knights living there some good. Thanks to him, origami and bird watching had now become a craze among knights throughout the world.

A report came through to Amelia from Megan that Malcolm would live. He'd need a new robot hand and a replacement leg, but he'd be fine. What's more, Megan and Malcolm planned to get married once he was better and able to resume flying.

While Malcolm was in hospital recovering from one of his operations, a couple of journalists interviewed him to get what they could on Amelia and Dreadnought that hadn't already been published. He had nothing to say other than he regarded Amelia as a good pilot.

He could have mentioned being dragged into a knight's pub by Amelia but chose not to do so. He found he had some scruples after all. Besides, she had saved his life. He did, however, tell Megan about the pub incident. She burst out laughing.

"I could have been killed!" he cried in his defence.

"With Amelia around, no way!" threw in Megan.

"We've been on some ride with those two, haven't we?" said Malcolm.

"With Amelia and Dreadnought, you mean? I suppose you're right."

"I don't know whether to be sad or relieved adventures with them have come to an end."

"Me too!"

In talking to the press, Amelia did most of it. Dreadnought was reluctant to open his mouth but spoke on occasion when either Mei or Scott prompted him to do so.

"Are you two getting married?" asked a cheeky correspondent maverick.

"Why, yes," said Amelia.

"Is that true, Dreadnought?" pushed the correspondent.

"If Amelia wants it to be true, it is true," answered Dreadnought.

"How fascinating." The correspondent smiled and leaned forward with his recording device, anxious to capture every word uttered.

"Is it true, you will marry me?" asked Dreadnought, his voice broken up with emotion.

"Only if you ask nicely," Amelia said, her eyes twinkling.

"May I interrupt?" The correspondent was insistent. "It is the maiden who should propose, not the maverick."

"I believe it is the custom," said Dreadnought, looking away from Amelia.

"I have to ask?" Amelia was taken aback by this.

"That's right," confirmed the correspondent.

"You may not want me as a maverick." Dreadnought looked down and shuffled his feet.

"Will you marry me?" asked Amelia to the joy of the correspondent.

"Only if you wish it so," said Dreadnought, still looking down.

"I want to marry you!" Amelia lifted his chin and kissed him on the mouth. This shocked both Dreadnought and the correspondent.

"Such signs of affection are rare," the correspondent said.

"Such a shame," replied Amelia. Dreadnought was red-faced but happy. Amelia detected a crinkly grin.

Dreadnought pulled Amelia aside, away from the correspondent for more serious talk.

"I was never handsome, and I have scars all over my body from various encounters with dragons." Dreadnought felt he should be honest with Amelia. "The scar running down my face is particularly hideous."

"Oh, I've gotten over that ages ago," said Amelia.

Dreadnought couldn't help thinking she could do better, though he couldn't imagine too many mavericks suiting her rugged nature.

"I have no idea what romance is like and couldn't say how well I could perform the tasks of a husband." This was more honesty from Dreadnought. "I know the rudiments of sex, but how to transform that into making love is something I'd have to figure out."

"Relax," Amelia told Dreadnought. "On our wedding day, I promise I'll be gentle."

"Be serious," he said sternly.

"I am," she retorted.

The High Priestess of Wollongong performed the wedding ceremony, which was televised. It outraged some maidens and mavericks while causing others to snigger. In wine bars, maverick and maidenly faces were hidden behind handkerchiefs and fans. There was a lot of whispering. A maverick in such a bar in New Orleans fainted and had to be carried home by two burly knights. He was heard to whimper, "It's the end of the world!" The next day, of course, the world was still there.

The wedding brought tears to the eyes of knights everywhere. For once, they were not afraid to show emotion, and so, even the barkeeps at the knightly pubs, cried openly and long. One of them, at last, had made it. Fifty dragons and a maiden! Handkerchiefs of a rougher kind than those owned by mavericks came out, and noses were blown.

At The Spear and Shield, a fistfight broke out when a knight called Amelia a maiden he wouldn't care to spend any time with.

"She's a strange one," said the fellow, "Too weird for me."

He got a fist in his face over that, and then a bottle smashed over his head.

"She cares for Dreadnought," cried the barkeep. "She helped get him his fifty dragons. I'd kill for a maiden like that!"

A hefty looking knight then picked the bad talker off the floor and threw him against a table.

"Get him outta here!" cried the barkeep. The swinging doors were opened wide, and the hefty knight threw the unfortunate out onto the street.

"If he ever returns, make sure he gets the same treatment," said the barkeep. "We do have our standards."

The next day, the knight in question reviewed his cuts and bruises, realising he was lucky only to get beaten up and thrown out.

In The Great Grape, a young maiden, who had only recently returned to Wollongong from Rome, dumped a glass of wine onto a maverick's head for telling sick jokes about Amelia and Dreadnought. "You should get better, more polite customers," she told the barkeep before storming out of the place.

The barkeep, a balding maverick, handed the wet, younger maverick a towel so he could get dry. Even this small act did not suit other maidens and mavericks who also walked out of the bar in solidarity with the maiden who did the spilling.

In Scotland, knights made pilgrimages to May Island, the locale that had inspired Dreadnought to go on to win the fifty and get the maiden.

There was a dragon rebellion in Lyon, twenty in all, but they were swiftly put down by two dozen armed robots. According to witnesses, a maiden had unlocked their pain collars and told them they were doomed, thanks to Dreadnought's success. Five local knights were surprised and murdered with sword and axe before the robots could act.

Later the robots arrested the maiden responsible. She told authorities that she had acted in the name of the Goddess and in view of the sanctity of marriage.

"How have you acted in the name of the Goddess?" asked a priestess magistrate. "How could letting those dragons loose put an end to Amelia's marriage?"

"What I did was still Amelia's fault," declared the maiden, unrepentant. "All her fault."

"Madness!" cried the priestess magistrate and fined the maiden two hundred dollars. She would have loved to have given her jail time, but maidens were never jailed, just fined.

The High Priestess of Lyon made it clear in a speech on television that there should be tolerance toward the dragons in her city. Those who had not engaged in criminal activity must not be executed by Lyon's robots or lynched by Lyon's knights. If they are to die, then it should be in the games and nowhere else. This was said in the name of Mary and also in the name of the Goddess.

Unfortunately, the High Priestess of Liverpool, in recognition of the problems that had occurred in Lyon, France, banned participation of both French knights and dragons in games held in her city for a year. This caused outrage among French knights, maidens, and mavericks. To add further insult, the High Priestess of Liverpool said that French knights are not up to taking on Liverpool dragons like the knights of Wollongong anyway. "The knights of Wollongong are marvellous," praised the High Priestess of Liverpool. "A pity Dreadnought is no longer one of them." The High Priestess of Oxford, the High Priestess of Honolulu and also that of Salzburg also agreed with the ban placed on Lyon.

French dragons, watching this announcement on television, no doubt hoped they would be spared participation in the games for a year. This reprieve for the dragons was not likely to happen, however, since the High Priestess of the city of New Orleans stated she was more than happy to have, in November, French knights and dragons in her domain.

It was because of this outrage that restrictions on trade between France and England were tightened. This resulted in an economic dive for both countries. It was, however, a boon for Wollongong and Hobart because both the English and the French wanted to open up more trade agreements with the Australians to get their economy back on track.

Malcolm, on his hospital bed in St. Louis, heard about all of this and wanted to be a part of it. *Even if most goods will go by ship and, from there, by whatever remains of the ancient railway system rather than by flyer*, he reasoned, *there will still be plenty of action for a good pilot, and yet I have to miss out.*

In Honolulu, knights remembered the interest both Amelia and Dreadnought had shown toward the statue of King Kamehameha. They wanted to know all there was to know about this Hawaiian ruler and what connection he could have with Dreadnought. "Could the mighty knight, now a maverick, be a descendant of that powerful monarch?" asked one Hawaiian newspaper publisher of his staff. The answer was no. Magazine articles and books came out about the king. No one, however, could find the link to Dreadnought the public wanted them to find.

Jens and Dean Renate, upon their return to Wollongong, turned their attention toward the work still being done on the seventh underground floor of the Mitchell Library in Sydney. Dean Renate appointed Jens to personally supervise the onsite activities until Megan went back to doing so. She was expected to stay in St. Louis for at least another month.

In Rome, the Highest of High Priestesses blessed Amelia and Dreadnought on camera, wishing them all the best on their historic journey. She also blessed Mei and Scott.

All throughout the holy city, there was talk of the Highest of High Priestesses getting old and soft in her thinking. She was supposed to be celibate like all good priestesses, but rumours persisted that she had a maverick husband somewhere. Of course, this was not true. She viewed the imminent departure of Amelia and Dreadnought as being good for her reign and her world. "We cannot kill Dreadnought without causing unrest everywhere," she told one of her closest advisors. "If he is alive but gone, then we can get back to the way things should be. He may now be a maverick, but he is no longer our concern." She wondered if she should demote the High Priestess of Wollongong for, months ago, failing to keep a closer eye on Amelia and Dreadnought. That she realized could wait until everything got back to normal everywhere, and threats of civil unrest came to a close. She also had plans for those priestesses she knew were after her position that would not make them happy. She also had rewards in the making for those priestesses that were standing by her.

A priestess living in a small village in the French Alps decided to jump off a cliff in protest of Amelia and Dreadnought's union. She left a note stating her contempt for a marriage between knight and maiden. She had refused to recognize Dreadnought's status as a maverick.

The four knights that had accompanied Amelia and Dreadnought were sent back to Wollongong, where they praised both Dreadnought and Amelia's bravery. When pressed at The Spear and Shield about May Island and the puffins, one of them said there was something magical about the funny looking bird that "gets to you after a while."

At Demons, the dragons debated whether or not Dreadnought's golden fifty was good for them. A couple of dragons felt it might lead to the end of the pain collars and the killings but were not sure how that could come about.

In temples everywhere, priestesses said great things about the union of Amelia and Dreadnought. They countered any argument that it was blasphemy. Dreadnought's success was held up as the indisputable will of the Goddess. All praised the Goddess in her infinite wisdom. Dreadnought surely would have failed, like so many others had, without her help. Now he was needed on Mars.

CHAPTER THIRTY-TWO

A special elevator system allowed Amelia, Dreadnought, Mei, and Scott to enter the spacecraft. The ride up in it, especially in clumsy spacesuits, was not for anyone scared of heights. It was a metal cage system that creaked as they ascended. At the top, there was a great thump as the elevator stopped. They were expected to climb out into a metal tunnel they had to walk along to get to the ship. The tunnel was like a spider's web in steel. It was possible, during the walk, to look down and see how far up the elevator had taken them.

The suits were not comfortable but necessary against expected G-forces on takeoff.

"Well, this is it," said Amelia to the others, taking her seat.

"Yes," agreed Mei. "There is a certain sense of finality. Now we strap ourselves in and pray to the Great Goddess for success."

Over the intercom, a maverick technician asked, "Everything okay in there?"

"We're fine," said Mei.

"Countdown is at minus one hundred and counting." The technician sounded calm. "Final checks from our end are commencing. All systems are looking good. We will be able to retain contact with you until you pass the moon. Then you're on your own."

"Understood," said Scott, trying to sound just as calm.

Amelia looked nervously at Dreadnought, wondering what she'd gotten herself into. Dreadnought looked back, wondering the same thing. Amelia reached for Dreadnought's gloved hand and held onto it with her own gloved hand.

The numbers came down to zero a lot faster than Amelia thought they would. The roof above them opened to reveal stars. The spacecraft vibrated as it prepared to push away from the Earth. *This is it*, thought Amelia as she felt herself being shoved back into her seat; *if something is to go wrong, it will happen now*. She figured a massive explosion would be a quick death. She tightened her grip on Dreadnought's gloved hand.

For some, the blowing up of the spacecraft, due to a supposedly unforeseen fault, would be fine. It might even be put down to the Goddess' will. Certain mavericks, maidens, and dragons would be in favour of it. Knights throughout the world, however, needed Amelia and Dreadnought to leave safely so they could envision a brighter future for themselves.

A cloud came across their view screen as their spacecraft climbed. After a short while, the vibrations that were troubling them stopped, and the cloud disappeared. A great cheer went up over the airwaves when open space replaced the atmosphere outside their vehicle, and they knew they were leaving the Earth behind.

"You have successful separation of the booster rocket," a technician in monotone told them over the speaker system," and the ion drive has kicked in. You're looking good. Congratulations."

In that instant, Dreadnought was caught up in all he was leaving behind and in how his life had gone so far. He dropped Amelia's gloved hand and looked at the stars. Then he picked up her gloved hand and looked into Amelia's eyes. Suddenly, he didn't know what he wanted or could want from a future with this maiden. Fifty dragons meant he had been broken and sewn up so many times he was numb in places. His belief in the sanctity of life had been tested so many times he wasn't sure he had any of it left from his childhood. He had such dreams before he was made into a knight. He sighed deeply. There were the birds, always the birds. As a child, he wanted very much to study them. Perhaps there were some on Mars or at least lizards. He might like to acquaint himself with those. *I will become the explorer I always wanted to be,* thought Dreadnought. He looked at Amelia, who was smiling at him and added, *with her at my side, anything is possible.*

"I was a good boy," he said to Amelia. "I could have done anything, given half the chance."

"Well, you have your chance now," replied Amelia tenderly, meaningfully. "Just don't go weird on me."

"I hope not to do so," said Dreadnought with a touch of humour in his utterance. "What do you think these Martians will be like?"

"The descendants of the explorers from Earth?" asked Amelia, shrugging her shoulders. "Who can say? In my time, there was talk of someday being able to terraform hostile worlds. Maybe they cracked that one. Maybe Mars is now not so barren."

A blip appeared on the control screen near Mai. It was moving rapidly in their direction. "We have a visitor," she told the others.

"Is it on an intercept course?" asked Dreadnought. "Would they dare?"

"If they did, they could be looking at a total breakdown in society," said Mei. "We're still too close to the Earth. Too many people are tracking our movements and that of this object."

Amelia looked out and saw a green flash of light that receded as they continued on their way.

"A well-wisher," concluded Scott. He breathed a sigh of relief.

"More than that," said Mai coolly. "They just sent across to us the latest information on our destination. Some new data on Mars has been unearthed where Number Ten Downing Street, London used to be. It isn't much to add to what we already know, but it will help in working out the coordinates for landing. It ended with the word success."

"A spaceship like ours?" asked Dreadnought.

"No," said Mei coolly. "It has a much shorter range and is unmanned. The information was sent by an automatic signal that was pre-programmed. I think it came from some part of England, probably Liverpool."

"Yes," said Dreadnought. "I remember Liverpool."

****

At the successful launch of the spaceship, Jens and Dean Renate shared a bottle of champagne. They drank a toast in the dean's office in Wollongong to the last year and a bit and all it had brought them.

Attendance at Wollongong University was up. The connection the institution had in the hearts and minds of academia to Amelia had helped rather than hindered.

"I'm glad I let your experiment with the maiden from the past play out," said the dean warmly.

"It was a rocky road to begin with, full of hazards." Jens smiled at her recollection of Amelia making her first statement to the press. "But it was well worth it."

"We managed to impress the prestigious Liverpool University, thanks to Amelia and Megan." The dean beamed with pride. "The faculty members who were against Amelia, not to mention certain outraged benefactors to our university, have long since backed down."

"It could have gone so wrong with Dreadnought." With a sigh, Jens recalled how Amelia chose him to be her knight despite there being younger knights to choose from. "Dreadnought was a publicity nightmare waiting to happen, but it didn't work out that way."

"Megan did well." The dean looked meaningfully at Jens.

"Yes. She did well." Jens beamed with pride, not only for herself but also for Megan.

****

Just before reaching the moon, the crew of the spacecraft

received one last message from Houston. A maverick technician said, "All is well here. Just in case you don't know, the High Priestess of High Priestesses in Rome has sent you her blessings for a safe trip over every television in the world. Right now, we're monitoring you. A disc in the centre of New South Wales is helping with our tracking. You're looking good, the best of luck to you all. End transmission."

"Thank you, Houston," replied Mei calmly, "and thank the Highest of High Priestesses for her blessing and the best of luck to all of you back on Earth. End transmission."

The moon loomed up at them, all shiny and pockmarked. They could see where there had once been human activity.

"Great Goddess, this is quite a sight!" Scott cried.

"It hasn't always been so," said Amelia.

"What do you mean?" asked Scott.

"The heads of the Catholic Church once believed there couldn't be any craters down there. They wanted the moon to be round and white like a pearl. Then men with telescopes began to record the truth. In the end, the heads of the Catholic Church had to change their minds."

"That must have been a long time ago," said Scott.

"Yes," agreed Amelia in a gentle voice. "It was centuries ago."

"What was the Catholic Church?" asked Mei.

"Something that existed before everything went wrong. It had its good moments and its bad. Maybe in the end, it was too human for humanity. It had a male head called the pope. Some popes were brilliant and others not so. In the end, a not so brilliant pope tried to make peace with would-be conquerors. It was a bad move."

"The would-be conquerors were not Goddess enough in their thinking," reasoned Mei in her unruffled voice.

"I suppose you could say that," replied Amelia, knowing from her history studies and her time as a fighter pilot that the Catholics had always believed in a God rather than a Goddess.

Past the moon, they got out of their seats and removed their spacesuits. Underneath, they had on a white jumpsuit with an interior cooling unit and also a heating unit to maintain body temperature. They floated for a while until Scott flipped on the artificial gravity.

"I would have liked to have floated more," said Amelia dreamily.

"So would I," added Dreadnought who, for a few moments, imagined blissfully he was a bird in flight.

"Not practical," concluded Mei in a matter-of-fact voice.

There was a space behind the seats for standing. A storage area ran for a couple of hundred yards from there. They had a table and comfortable chairs plus bunks for sleeping. They had water, but it was to be used sparingly. Showers were not an option. Instead, they had roll-on deodorant tubes and shampoo packs that would hopefully last until they got to Mars.

They would be able to drink seven glasses of water a day only. Before they reached their destination, it was expected to be recycled a few times through a system designed for that purpose. There was also a gallon of water they were told not to touch and a dozen large cylinders filled with air and a dozen more with pure oxygen. They were to be a gift to whoever was alive on the planet they were going to, along with data on Earth. They also brought along a selection of seeds and cuttings plus super cress that has to be kept cool and damp.

There were five lightweight shovels Dreadnought didn't think would be of much use. He had shovelled dirt for a living, so he knew a good shovel when he saw one. "Whoever was in charge of these things," said Dreadnought, pointing at those implements, "should have consulted me or someone like me on the matter."

"Why is that?" asked Mei coolly.

"With a little pressure put on them, they bend." Dreadnought demonstrated. "With more pressure, they'll break. We don't need shovels that bend and break."

"Yes," agreed Mei in monotone. "I agree with you. If we could jettison them, we would, but that is not possible."

"So we're stuck with a mistake," said Amelia.

"Yes," agreed Scott calmly. "At least it's not a serious one."

They had packaged food to eat and none of it either Amelia or Dreadnought found particularly appetising. They grimaced as they ate. Some of it was to be kept for the Martians. Mei and Scott were more used to the taste of it. There were limited supplies of toothpaste and mouthwash to keep their teeth in reasonably good shape.

Each member of the crew had brought a book with them they could add to whatever library the Martians had managed to keep together. Scott had brought along a guide on gardening and Mei a cookbook. Amelia's was a first aid manual, and Dreadnought had *1984* by George Orwell, a prized possession given to him by Amelia. She didn't have the heart to tell him where she had originally gotten it.

The Highest of High Priestesses donated religious books Amelia would have been happy to have jettisoned. She didn't think it a good idea to have anything religious onboard, though she didn't express this to either Mei or Scott. She pointed them out to Dreadnought and shrugged her shoulders. Dreadnought, his shoulder now in better shape, shrugged back.

The weeks passed slowly on their voyage. Instruments were checked daily to make sure they were on course. Once, they had to avoid a meteor. Doing so, however, hadn't taken them too far off, and within a few hours, they were back to heading in the right direction. Cosmic rays were a menace in outer space, being so far from the protection of Earth's atmosphere, but they kept an eye out for the deadlier amounts. At one stage, they had to put their spacesuits back on for a day to avoid being harmed by a dangerous though invisible wave.

To pass the time, they told stories about their life back on Earth. Mei and Scott had lived rather sheltered lives and so were fascinated by what Amelia and Dreadnought told them. They were shocked at the very idea of mass slaughter from the air.

"Did you really do that?" asked Scott of Amelia. "Did you drop bombs on people?"

"Not my proudest moments, but yes," replied Amelia. "They were the enemy, and it was my duty."

"How barbaric," Scott said with passion in his voice.

"Yes," agreed Amelia. "I suppose that is a fair comment."

"Thank the Goddess we no longer have wars." Scott shook his head and smiled.

Neither Mei nor Scott was taken aback by Dreadnought's killings.

"It's still hard to believe you're a maverick," mused Mei, "let alone married."

"I find it hard to believe, too," said Dreadnought.

"Where we're going, all that will seem like nonsense." Amelia smiled at the very idea. "The difference between knight and maverick, I mean."

"You really think so?" asked Scott.

"I know so," said Amelia.

"And all the dragon blood washed away." Dreadnought spoke dreamily.

"Yes," agreed Amelia. "No more dragon blood."

Eventually, the red planet loomed up, and they had to handle its gravitational pull with care. They wanted to enter the foreign atmosphere gently and not burn up in it.

They circled the planet once, throwing out radio signals. No reply from the surface. They circled a second time, trying to get a radio response. No luck. The third time was the charm. A crackling sound greeted them, and what sounded like the word welcome. A bright, green light then shone out from a beacon on the surface and, on closer examination; there was a dome that looked very much intact beside it.

"Our new home," said Mei as she launched an information capsule back to Earth. It contained a log of their journey so far, including the discovery that life probably did still exist where they were headed.

"Don't get your hopes up," said Scott. "It could have been a fully automated message, and the light might have also been set the same way."

"The two passes in which we didn't receive a reply makes me believe that whoever is down there had to get to where they could give the message and turn on the light," said Mei hopefully.

"It could still be something as simple as faulty wiring after all these years." Scott knew he was being pessimistic.

"We'll soon find out," said Dreadnought.

"Prepare for landing." Mei had sharp ice in her voice. "Stay alert! We have to make this a good one. No second chances."

They got back into their spacesuits and steeled themselves for descent. Instruments were looked over for problems, but none were found. All knew there was no walking away from a crash. Once one breathed the air of Mars, one wouldn't survive for long.

Sweat accumulated on Mei's forehead as she continued to make adjustments to the landing. The winds of the red planet began to kick up. She wanted to avoid the spaceship being knocked over. Scott read out the speed of the wind, and Amelia applied the retrorockets to slow decent when called upon to do so. Dreadnought could only watch the others and hope all would go well.

The landing was rough for Amelia and Dreadnought, the shaking, bouncing, and roaring of the dying engine unexpected, but not so for Mei and Scott, who had had longer space training.

When the smoke and dust cleared, Mei threw a switch that sent metal bolts into the soil to prevent the spacecraft from tipping.

They then looked out upon a new world with its surprises. It was ancient and dead, but they hoped there was still life. Both Amelia and Dreadnought felt young again, smiling broadly at each other and holding gloved hands, the past with all its sins falling away from their bodies like an ill-fitting suit, their future looking as green and as bedazzling as the beacon they could see not far away.

"Make sure the seals on your spacesuit are all working before you leave our spaceship," said Mei in monotone. "It is only a short walk to the dome, but it is the most dangerous walk you are ever likely to take. When the wind dies down, we go."

"We need to employ the buddy system," put in Scott. "I check over Mei's suit to make sure everything is okay, and she checks over mine. Amelia and Dreadnought, you are to do the same. You cannot afford a mistake."

"Please take into account the great length of time anyone from Earth has been here," said Mei. "They may be milky white or have translucent skin. Do not be overly shocked if you can see their internal organs."

"There may be radiation in the soil here and especially underground we are not familiar with," added Scott, "so their appearance may be alien to us. Their skin may be of a different hue than what we expect."

"Got it!" cried Amelia. "Don't judge them by the colour of their skin."

"Precisely!" snapped Mei.

The seal checks done, they put the gifts they were taking to the Martians onto an anti-gravity sled for easy transport and then waited for the wind to die away before exiting their spacecraft. One by one, they began the trek across five hundred yards of red and brown dust and sand. The anti-gravity sled, operated by Mei by a remote-control device she could fit in her pocket, trailed behind them.

At the dome, they found a panel to press for entry. It immediately sealed itself once they and the anti-gravity sled were in. The Martian air was then jettisoned out of the space they were occupying before they were permitted entry into the heart of the complex. This took twenty minutes.

Once inside, they made their way to the observation deck up some winding stairs and looked out at the unearthly landscape.

"I observe that the dome has been extended into the nearby caves via a funnel," said Mei with hope in her voice. "The extension may not be new, but it isn't part of the specs I have viewed, so it was done some time ago by the colonists. "

"A person could walk from the caves to the dome via that funnel," observed Scott with wonder in his utterances.

There was a clanking sound as someone or something was making his, her or its way from the cave to where they were.

"Greetings!" cried the newcomer as he approached them, his yellow eyes blinking. He was in shadow as he climbed up to them, so they were still not sure what to expect. They all switched on the translator in their helmets so they could best understand him. "Greetings!" they replied.

Then, when the newcomer came fully into the light, Mei was aghast by what she saw and Scott revolted.

"No! This cannot be!" cried Scott. Mei was unsteady on her feet. She had to be braced by Scott. Amelia was amused, and Dreadnought taken aback.

"Well, we don't know the colour of his skin," said Amelia. "We'd have to get past the flashing tail and grey scales to find out."

"The name is Boz Allen," said the newcomer and held out his claw. To his credit, it was Dreadnought who "shook hands" with Boz.

"We come in peace," said Amelia. Mei was supposed to say those words but couldn't bring herself to do so. She was hiding behind Scott, her confidence gone.

"We are three hundred strong," said Boz. "You are welcome to join our ranks."

"Thank you." Amelia smiled. "You're too kind."

"Come!" cried Boz. "Do not fear the funnel. It was made of the tough material of the spaceship that landed my ancestors here long ago and has since been reinforced against leakage by clay and rock."

Boz led them down the stairs and into the funnel. At the end of the funnel at the mouth of the cave were a dozen grey humanoids like Boz, some male like him and others decidedly female.

"Gray dragons," Dreadnought whispered to Amelia.

"Yes," agreed Amelia, "Gray dragons."

ABOUT THE CONTRIBUTORS

Author Rod Marsden was born in Sydney, Australia. He has three degrees, all related to writing and history. He spent nine and a half years as a civilian clerk with the Royal Australian Navy. His proudest moments there were in the publications area.

He enjoys wildlife photography and in recent years, joined Illawarra Birders. He went on a birding expedition to the main north island of New Zealand, where he came upon wildlife unique to that country. He shares his fascination with nature with his entire family, including his niece Jasmine Perala. Her pet, Kiki, is a young, female eclectus parrot and, soggy from a recent shower, is featured on Rod Marsden's shoulder on the back cover of this book.

His stories have been published in Australia, England, Russia, the USA, and Canada. He has work in the Australian anthology *Small Suburban Crimes*, the American anthology *Cats Do it Better*, the American steam punk anthology *Break Time*, the Canadian anthology *Morbid Metamorphosis,* and also in the Canadian anthology *Grey Matter Monsters – Takers of Souls*.

Many of his short stories, including "The Antarctic Pineapple," have been published in *Night to Dawn* magazine. *Undead Reb Down Under and Other Vampire Stories* is a collection of his early short fiction on vampirism. *Disco Evil* is his first venture into the vampire novel. *Ghost Dance* is his first undertaking into dark fantasy involving a quest plus secret agents out to prevent demonic takeover. It has been reprinted with a new cover. *Desk Job* is his salute to Lewis Carroll.

His short plays, *Zombie Vision, Hyde and Seek,* and *Smarty* were well received at Cronulla Arts Theatre, south coast, New South Wales, Australia. Both his plays *Smarty* and *Hyde and Seek* made it into Sydney's Short and Sweet contest.

He has a short story in *The Twofer Compendium* edited by Ruth Littner and Ann Stolinsky (2020) in which he mentions the Berry Celtic Festival, which took place every May in a farming community on the south coast of New South Wales, Australia. It is a festival that, unfortunately, had to be cancelled this year because of the coronavirus but will hopefully resume in May 2021.

Illustrator Sandy DeLuca sold her first drawing in 1979 when her work was exhibited in a friend's beauty salon. Her art has been exhibited throughout New England and in New York's Hudson Valley. Her small collages have been exhibited and sold in France, Asia, Italy, Spain, Canada, and throughout the United States.

She was awarded a solo art show while still a student at CCRI in 1986. She also won an award for Most Original Use of Mixed Media. Two of her paintings were chosen to hang in the reception area of the college's president in 1987. Since then, her artwork has been featured as cover art and interior art for various publications, including notable books such as the Bram Stoker © winner, *Vampires, Zombies and Wanton Souls* for Marge Simon's poetry.

Sandy has written and published numerous novels, several poetry and fiction collections, an art chapbook, and several novellas, including the critically acclaimed novel *Descent* and *Messages from the Dead* (winning the Gothic Readers' Choice Award). As an author, she is known for dark and surreal prose, often visceral and shocking. She is best known for her work in the horror genre. However, she has written noir fiction, fantasy, urban fantasy, and mainstream fiction as well. Also, in the 1980s, she was a photographer and writer for a string of sports magazines.

She was a finalist for the BRAM STOKER © for poetry award in 2001, with *Burial Plot in Sagittarius*; accompanied by her cover art and interior illustrations. A copy is maintained in the Harris Collection of American Poetry and Plays (Brown University) Poetry, 1976-2000. She was also nominated once more in 2014, with Marge Simon, for *Dangerous Dreams*.

She has owned and operated several publishing companies; in the 1990s, GODDESS OF THE BAY produced several monthly fanzines; and she went on to produce novels, novellas, and collections from dark literature's finest authors (including Brain Keene, Mary SanGiovanni, and Greg F. Gifune).

She retired from her day job several years ago and now spends her days making art and writing. At present, she is focusing on completing two novels in progress.

She lives in New England with three feisty tortoiseshell cats and an elderly tabby cat. She is an avid book collector, spending her time reading, researching family genealogy, and studying the metaphysical.

www.ingramcontent.com/pod-product-compliance
Lightning Source LLC
Chambersburg PA
CBHW021514240626
47154CB00002B/627